Ghastly and Ghoulish
Tales from the ER

A saga in sixteen parts

by Mitch Goldman

Copyright © 2024 Mitch Goldman MD

All rights reserved. No part of this book may be reproduced or transmitted in any form or by any means, electronic or mechanical, including photocopying, recording or by any information storage and retrieval system without permission in writing from the publisher.

Madlong Publication— Pinckney, MI
Paperback ISBN: 979-8-218-49819-1
eBook ISBN: 979-8-330-39390-9
Library of Congress Control Number: 2024918485
Title: *Ghastly and Ghoulish: Tales from the ER*
Author: Mitch Goldman
Digital distribution | 2024
Paperback | 2024

This is a work of fiction. The characters, names, incidents, places, and dialogue are products of the author's imagination, and are not to be construed as real.

Published in the United States by New Book Authors Publishing

Dedication

To all those I've laughed, mourned, yawned and triumphed with down in the trenches, heroes all.

And to Laura, the girlfriend I was lucky enough to marry.

Author's Note

These stories are based on true events. They are very real, just modified in a "few" ways. It's different with the characters - they sound real but are all fictional. Actually, I brought a few of them back from an earlier novel, *Apocalypse Blue*. I missed them.

When you begin your life in the ER you quickly get used to saying, "you can't make this shit up," because you'll utter it many times to yourself, your colleagues and to outsiders; and you'll also encounter all those "yeah, right…" looks from the outsiders. Get familiar with both these phrases – you'll be saying them soon, between laughs and gasps, but please know that the more unbelievable stories here are the ones you may want to trust the most.

Please read the tales from the first to the last – they're in chronological and spiritual order. With collections of "short stories," it's always tempting to peruse the table of contents as if were a menu, looking for an interesting title or just the right amount of pages. Not so with Ghostly Tales – it's *not* a random collection of short stories.

In fact, I personally don't consider them to be short stories. Actually, I (presumptuously) consider the book a saga, defined as a long story of heroic achievements.

There's a glossary at the end. Use it, please! It will teach you ER speak/slang, and navigate you through our mysterious, insular universe, with its unique customs, values, and mindset. Using "civilian" words rarely uttered in the ER except during inspections and interviews, or slowing the stories' flow with awkward explanations, would ruin the gritty rhythm and feel of our world – remember, you've been promised real. So, refer to the glossary PRN…pro re nata, Latin for 'as needed.' Besides being quite educational, it's a fun read.

Welcome. Though political correctness, corporate mentality and the rise of technology have all caused some erosion, the emergency room remains the medical world's Wild West.

ps.1 This book may seem raw and over the top, abounding with locker room talk, gallows humor and very odd stories. Yeah, it is. In truth, I had to tone down every tale you're going to read (and the rowdiest of them are the truest).

ps.2 Part Five, entitled The Trainwreck from Hell, is particularly intense - anyone on the fence might want to skip it – it won't affect the overall read. I re-wrote it several times to cool it off, with limited success. I put my heart and soul into that one – it's one of the truer ones, by the way – and I couldn't yank it. Worst case scenario, you'll read it and realize why the ER is not for the faint of heart.

(I briefly considered writing comments, advisories and cautionaries of sorts for every one of the tales, as they all push the proverbial envelope. How much do they push it? To paraphrase a favorite song of mine, 'you'll find out when you get there.')

ps.3 As for the sex talk, cynicism and outrageous behavior – well, there's an old saying- pack a room with highly trained professionals, dress them in glorified pajamas, work 'em and stress 'em to the max, and guess what happens: ninth grade breaks out. No one really said that, but they could have. And after 35 full-time years in the game, I can attest that the women curse, joke and talk sex as much as, if not more than, the men. It's a lot of fun working in an ER, by the way.

Ps.4 Most, but not all, of the main characters are male. I find it difficult writing from a female perspective, if that's even possible for a man, and didn't want to start fixing it on these pages. It's on me.

Ps.5 Enjoy. Thanks for taking a look, and sorry about those ps-es.

Table of Contents

Author's Note v

Introduction ix

Part One: The Little Voice 2

Part Two: Stonehenge 20

Part Three: Going to the Chapel 32

Part Four: My Big Beautiful Car 42

Part Five: The Train Wreck from Hell 49

Part Six: I Know Something You Don't Know 75

Part Seven: La Noche De Amor 87

Part Eight: Harry Loses His Virginity 109

Part Nine: Space Pearl 120

Part Ten: The Protein Mission 129

Part Eleven: The Radiology Bash 133

Part Twelve: Night's End 152

Part Thirteen: The Comeback Kid 160

Part Fourteen: The Magic Bathroom 173

Part Fifteen: The Barbarians of Maryland 179

Part Sixteen: Applause 203

Glossary of Terms: 207

About the Author: 224

Introduction
Let's Take a Trip

Place yourself in a squarish-shaped room, about one hundred forty by one hundred forty feet give or take, built forty to fifty years ago. It's well-lit and seems roomy enough, but between the pasty walls, darkish floors (so as not to show stains), low ceilings and the clutter that blocks almost every line of vision, the place exudes an almost terminal dinginess. Welcome to a big city ER.

Carve into this human warehouse fifty rooms – lots of eight-by-tens, three doubles – the Code/Trauma Bays – and one quadruple – the Big Room, reserved for invasions from Hell. Most are for the 150 or so guests who check in daily, but throughout are sites for triage, meds, supplies, linen storage, dirty stuff and sharps. There's also space for Security, Admitting, patient registration… and the much-used grief room.

Most health care consumers - there, we got those words out of the way; from here on in they are what they are, patients – come here voluntarily, but not all. Some arrive alive and kicking, some are DOA; most, though, are somewhere in the middle, often pushed to the limits of their existence. It's our job to move their needle in the right direction. A handful will take their last breath here, others their first - by the way, immaculate conceptions are alive and well in emergency medicine. Police, corrections officers and state troopers seem to be here 24/7, along with their criminal justice consumers, who arrive dressed to the hilt in bracelets and ankle chains. Lots of stuff goes down here, and a common joke is that most people work here just for the good stories. (Actually, almost always, the worse a shift is, the more fun it will eventually seem.)

In the midst of this alternate universe is the ER's heart, a square within a square if you will, with desks and cabinets for walls, computers, monitors and radios everywhere, and maybe a touch of drywall in a few places to lend an illusion of security. Stationed within this improbably high-tech fortress are the elite troops of modern medicine, up to twenty people at any given moment – docs, nurses, nurse practitioners and/or physicians' assistants (referred to as mid-levels by just about everyone and in this book, from here on in), techs of all stripes, mental health and social workers, students, and more.

These professionals foray into the patient rooms, deeply immersing themselves in the lives of people they are meeting for the first and last time. It's their life, their calling; few outsiders could understand. They wake up each working day, put on their clothes and get in the face of violence, sickness, suffering and death. Many have been shoved, kicked or punched at least once in recent memory, and all have been cursed or physically threatened. It comes with the job. They are also among the most brilliant and dedicated medical people on the planet.

Just as it's a mistake to judge a surgeon by the good or bad scar left on your belly, it's even worse to pre-judge the scruffy doc in the scrubs standing next to your stretcher, studying your EKG. If you were stuck on that desert island and had to pick just one doctor to take along, you know who you would choose.

These hopelessly cynical/idealistic veterans work so tightly together they often seem as one. They're a team, playing on a field with no middle ground - you either love it here and stay for a full life's chapter, or you hate it and quickly get the fuck out of Dodge.

Relationships down here can become deeply intertwined and intense, sometimes very much so. The work is often brutal, exhilarating, grotesque and comical, often all in the same hour. One minute you're high fiving each other triumphantly, roaring with laughter; and the next minute you are repulsed, infuriated and overwhelmed. Sometimes these givers of emergency care just can't help but cry; others sometimes wish they knew how…and then, it's time for lunch.

Welcome to the life. And if you ever want to call an ER person a hero, go ahead - they've been called worse.

welcome to the tales…

Part One
The Little Voice
(How It Began)

There was a crash, followed by screams.

Aaron Freeman PA, who was talking on a nearby wall phone, instantly flinched. The slightly built man nervously looked up and around, searching for the source. When he saw several of the staff plus Security rush into a patient's room – Bed Five, for the record – he grunted softly, put an index finger in his open ear and returned to the call. Two minutes later he hung up, slumped with resignation, and weaved his way – in this cluttered ER even the soberest man in the universe couldn't walk a straight line – towards the doctors' area in the department's center. He was searching for someone.

The sounds of fifty-plus voices, rattling equipment, ringing telephones and beeping monitors all melded into an ocean-esque hum, enveloping him. He loved working here. Days down here were in a way like snowflakes, so very similar yet each completely unique – you could make a movie about every one of them. Even the craziness here was soothingly predictable – you expect chaos, and you get chaos, thus you're never shocked or surprised. (Have you heard the joke that you know your life's gone crazy when you pick up an extra shift in the ER just to relax?)

Every patient room in the large ER was occupied, with some people waiting to be seen, others waiting to go home, but by far and away most were somewhere in the middle of their visit, with ailments ranging from boo boos to full blown agony. In other words, it was a typical day.

Freeman walked up to the Doctors' Station and began scanning the small crowd before him, looking this way and…there he was. An athletic looking man with short red hair and wire-rimmed glasses, wearing a white lab coat, was entering orders into a computer. He seemed to radiate intensity and seemed oblivious to everything and everyone around him.

Freeman approached and cleared his throat. The doctor paused.

"Doc, can I sign something out to you?" the mid-level tentatively asked. "There's a problem at school and I need to pick my daughter up, like right now. I just can't wait for the results on this last case. Everything else is cleaned up. Please."

Lars Anderson reluctantly looked up at Aaron. It was busy in the ER, and the doctor was already juggling nine patients, just at the edge of his comfort level – and had already signed up for a facial lac. Bob Finkel and Peg Ferguson, the other docs working today, were probably running even more. Yeah, it was a bad time to pick up a stray. But Freeman was a good guy and wouldn't leave early unless there was a good reason. He looks awfully nervous, Lars admitted to himself; he's been pre-occupied all day.

After a moment's contemplation he realized this was legit. ER people watch out for each other, everyone has each other's back, that's the code. And yeah, everyone signs cases out (or 'hands off,' a replacement term coming into vogue), himself included. But that was almost always when your shift ended, and patients needed either further testing or observation, or if pending results were ages away. You keep that stuff to a minimum – it's gospel that the road to lawsuit hell is paved with signed-out charts. But when you gotta do it, you gotta do it.

"Yeah, sure, Aaron, what's one more. Is everything okay?"

"My sixteen-year-old, she's getting suspended. Fighting again… of course. What can I say, she's reached yet another fork in the road and, once again, went down the wrong path."

"The new boyfriend didn't make things better? I remember your stories about the last creep."

"Nah, he's just as bad. My girl likes fishing in the same swamp, so they're all gonna be like that until she gets her life back on track."

"Sorry. So, what you got?"

"Easy case in Fourteen. Fifteen-year-old girl, name's Cara, sore throat. It began this morning after a screaming match with her mom at home. She's afebrile, vitals are solid, throat's a bit pink, and her heart and lungs are clear. Oh, and there are really adorable cut marks on her forearms. In fact, the only real findings are that she's hoarse and has a bad case of nerves. I gave her a Xanax just to keep her from jumping off the stretcher.

"Anyway, her throat is swabbed, and I ordered some basic labs and a mono test - over an hour ago. Get this, the lab *just* drew 'em - I swear she's gonna die of old age before the stuff comes back. I'm sorry I even ordered them. I also ordered a soft tissue neck, and they haven't even wheeled her down to x-ray yet. Now she's just giving everybody the silent treatment. The parents are getting edgy, and they're a piece of work themselves.

"She's all written up. Just drop the chart off in the rack when everything comes back. If you think she needs a script, feel free…but you and I both know the real diagnosis: 'Fifteen-Year-Old Girl.' Thanks, Lars, I owe you…and I pray this stuff never happens to you and yours. Teenagers can be living hell."

"Don't worry about it, go take care of your daughter. I'll check things out."

Freeman walked a few steps away and turned around.

"It gets so unreal, sometimes," he said haltingly. "You know, when I was her age, I practically still believed in Santa Claus."

Then he slowly exited.

Sounds like he needed that Xanax more than the fifteen-year-old, Lars thought, opening up his new chart. I sure hope when my kids get older, I won't be asking for favors like this. He looked around until he saw the girl's nurse.

"Anthony, how's that fifteen-year-old doing? The one in Fourteen."

"You got the case now? Yeah, she looks pretty good. Quiet, no problems."

hmmm…

Lars started at the sound. His eyes darted from side to side.

"You okay, doc?"

"Yeah, thought I heard something."

Tony looked around, then shrugged.

"I'll let you know when the labs come back," he said.

"You got it. I'll be stitching in Eight."

The ER doc looked up at the tracking board on the wall. Good, no new patients, he contentedly thought. Maybe I'll make a dent in this mess after all.

Anderson was walking to his patient's room, himself surfing around various people, carts and double-parked wheelchairs, idly daydreaming about what suture size he'd use; the hot shots bragged about how they *only* used 6-nylon for faces, but he rarely had luck (except bad) with them. Too fragile. Nah, I'll stick with good old-fashioned 4s and 5s on a small needle, he concluded. I'll pass on the glory…

fourteen…

What?

He stopped and looked at Earnest, the person nearest him.

"Did you say something?"

"'Say something'?" the security guard asked. "I didn't say anything."

"I heard…or thought I…never mind."

Anderson frowned and continued on his way. He approached Eight and put his hand on the door handle.

fourteen…

Anderson spun around – this section of the hall was actually empty.

fourteen, now…

Am I going crazy here, he thought, more than a little frazzled. He started turning the handle, paused, shook his head, and turned back.

He headed to Fourteen.

Seconds later, he was standing alongside his teenage patient. Cara looked good enough, except…well, maybe she looked *too* good. She was sitting quietly…*too quietly?*… leaning forward, her outstretched arms in front of her, propping her up on the mattress…

tripoding… denial can be a terrible thing……

Her eyes looked at him wearily. Was it the Xanax, or…

Freeman should have passed on this case, Lars thought, feeling just a trickle of anxiety. There's no way he could have not been biased …

"I'm Doctor Anderson," he said quickly, introducing himself to her and her parents. "I'm going to do a quick re-check."

"Oh, she's going home," the mother said. "We're just waiting for the x-ray."

"Please, please," he told her, holding up his hand, and he turned to the girl.

"Hi, what's your name?"

"Cara," she whispered.

"Cara, tell me, how do you feel?"

"Throat hurts…"

"Mom, tell me something, is that her regular voice?"

"God, no, she's been like this for a few hours. The other doctor said it might be from all that yelling."

"And maybe it is. Cara, let me take a look at you."

Lars started to reach into his coat's breast pocket for a wooden tongue blade, instantly thought better of it and stopped.

"Cara, just open your mouth, stick out your tongue and say 'ahhh' the best you can."

He was impressed how well she complied, but disappointed at not seeing beefy red tonsils with lots of pus. That would have been way too easy. Even kissing tonsils would have been a mild relief. All he saw was a little redness.

"Cara, take some nice breaths."

The girl breathed quietly, her nostrils all the while moving a bit oddly.

goodness, that's pretty decent flaring...

The doctor went through the perfunctory motion of listening to the girl's back for about two seconds, hoping against hope he'd find something benign...but he knew where the money was, and that he was stalling to avoid facing the truth.

"Okay, almost done, just one more quick listen."

Anderson gently, gently, gently, put his stethoscope on the girl's neck – and then winced as if in pain. Sounds from Hell assaulted his ears - in medicalese it was called stridor; in plain English he was hearing her breath squeaking through a lethally narrowed airway. This girl was slowly suffocating.

"Vaccines – has she gotten her vaccines?" the doctor asked nervously, looking at the parents intently, stethoscope still resting gently on her neck.

"She got a few, but not too many, the mother replied, looking at her husband, who nodded. "They kill way more people than they help, so we got a waiver."

quickly now...

"Listen, we need to perform a very important test, to make sure it's safe to discharge her. We need to check the voice box and her neck," he said affably but firmly. "We'll put her into a bigger room, start an IV, and get a CAT scan. We'll make it stat, which means right away. It's important, and if it's normal you all go home, and everything is good. I'll check on her again in a few minutes."

The parents started to protest, but Lars stared at them fiercely and shook his head, fighting off the urge to shake them. His eyes screamed 'you do not say no, you do not play around with your child!' They backed off at once and nodded their consent.

"I'm going to make some phone calls now. Excuse me."

Thirty minutes later Cara was in the OR, sent straight from CT, getting an emergency airway. The radiologist had called and actually prefaced her remarks by asking if this patient was still alive, saying that this was the worst case of epiglottitis she'd ever seen. That girl's breathing through a fucking swizzle stick, she had said.

"Man, we dodged a bullet that time," Tony said, after Recovery called to inform them that the patient was stable and doing well. "How'd you do it, Doc?"

"I don't know, a little voice spoke to me."

"Yeah, yeah, okay. Hey, next time you speak with that voice, check on my Microsoft."

"I'll do that. In the meantime, I'll be writing Eight up for discharge."

*

(A few weeks later)

"So, you're cool with the sign-out?" Dean Miller asked Anderson cautiously. The night had been a long one, and he seemed to be in a slight rush to head back to the hotel. (Many docs commute a bit to work, which affords them some level of anonymity, and most stay at local hotels during shift runs. And there's another bonus – when you're back home you won't get your pizza from the same person you knowingly treated for an STI the night before – wayward pepperonis are indeed found everywhere, but it's the "knowingly" part that gets to you. Thus, while you can fearlessly dine in blithe denial in your hometown, when staying at the hotel, well, you just hope for the best when ordering takeout.)

"Yeah, looks pretty good," Lars said, looking at his sheet of paper. "You just want me to check five thousand CAT scans…"

"It ain't that bad…"

"Joking, joking, my friend," Anderson said with a smile. "Get out of here and have a splendid feast. Hey, anyone joining you?"

"I'm gonna plead the sixty-ninth on that one."

"Ahh, the best kind of feast. Lucky you."

They both laughed. With a wave Miller departed, chuckling as he walked away. He passed Karlita, a night nurse, and they exchanged an imperceptible nod.

Anderson took out his stethoscope, puzzle book and code gum and laid them on the table. He watched X-Ray wheel a patient back from CT scan into Room Four, which was across the hall pretty much in front of him. And that would be Mr. Garcia, the COPDer with hemoptysis, he surmised, perusing his sign-out list. Dean told me he was stable, and to send him home if the scan was negative…hmm, maybe this is a good time to grab some coffee.

He walked into the nurses' area, a few feet away.

"I'll be in the doctor's lounge. Anyone want something?"

"I'd like a banana," Karlita answered casually, not looking up from her computer screen, trying to wrap her shift up asap.

"Don't listen to her, Lars," Skye, a new grad, said mysteriously. "Karli's getting all the banana she wants, like, really soon."

Those in the know giggled a bit.

four…

Anderson paused and listened. After a few seconds he turned to the two or three staffers who were studying him quizzically.

"Last call for coffee or junk food…going once, going twice… okay, I'll be back in a few minutes."

He approached the hallway door.

four…

Anderson stopped in his tracks and stood motionless. A few people looked at him.

"What's up, doc, you forget something?" someone called out.

"How's Bed Four doing?" he asked nervously, checking his sign-out list.

"Yeah, he's pretty stable," Ronda, the day charge, said calmly. "He coughed up some blood last night and just got back from CT. I'll re-check him in a minute, he's next on my list. Why, what's going on?"

"I'm not sure. He's okay, right?"

"Yeah, he's great. Dean just wanted to rule out a PE."

"All right…"

Go into Four. Now.

Rather than go through the electronic doors leading to the lounge, Lars about-faced and bolted into Mr. Garcia's room.

"Doc, the scan's not read yet," Karlita called out from her seat. "We'll call you…"

The door swung back open with a crash and Lars emerged, his eyes bulging.

"Call a code!" he shouted.

Katrina, the unit secretary, nervously picked up the phone.

Skye and Karlita ran into the room, and they gasped. Mr. Garcia lay unresponsive on the stretcher, his skin an eerie shade of pale arctic blue.

Within seconds the hospital overhead was booming out the words, 'CODE BLUE, EMERGENCY ROOM,' repeatedly.

"Can you believe it? The tech just dropped him off and didn't re-attach the wall oxygen!" Karli hissed, racing to the bed. She grabbed an ambu bag and placed it over the patient's face, connected its tube to a green wall port, turned a small black wall knob, and started breathing him, all in a matter of seconds. Skye performed a single precordial thump, then pinched his nipples. A tech slipped a hard board under the patient's back and began compressions. CPR now began in earnest.

"Wake up, honey, come on," Karli pleaded. Looking at her colleagues, she shook her head angrily. "Those fuckers. See? You use agency, you get agency!"

"And that is why oxygen-dependent people are dependent on their oxygen," Lars murmured back, looking around the small room. "I guess we tube him here."

A Respiratory tech entered. He took over breathing for the patient, who's skin was starting to pink up a bit.

"What you want, boss?"

"Give me a Mac and a size eight…"

At that moment Mr. Garcia coughed. He slowly opened his eyes and looked around. His death pall melted away as if by magic. Everyone in the room sighed deeply, looked at each other and smiled. Mr. Garcia smiled back – he seemed a bit dazed but overall, pretty decent for someone just pulled back from the other side. Karli checked his vitals and smiled tightly. That was a close one, she thought.

"What happened, did something happen?" the patient genially asked, looking at Skye. "You know, I swear I had a dream about you…"

"Welcome back, Mr. Garcia," Lars said jovially, listening to the man's heart and lungs. "Very good, just a touch of a wheeze. Let's give him an albuterol, get an EKG, draw some tropes and put him in the code room. Considering the CPR he had, I'm glad he wasn't put on heparin, at least not yet. Sir, how do you feel?"

"My nipples hurt, what do you make of that?"

"Don't worry about it, hon', we'll get you some Tylenol," Karli replied, giving Skye a quick frown before turning to Lars. "Great work, Doc...what are you, haunted or something?"

"I don't know. A little voice inside of me told me to check the room."

"Doctor Anderson, we sent someone to the lounge for you," Katrina called out. Lars grunted his thanks, and he stayed by the patient's side for a few minutes. After a final re-check, he left to go chart these latest developments, shaking his head all the way.

The nurses were furious. This was not their first run-in tonight with Radiology.

"You want to speak with the nursing supervisor, or should I?" Karli asked her fellow nurses. "Those lazy fucks!"

"No, you go, I'll make the call," Skye said. "Get out of here. Your shift is officially over. Get some rest, you know, lay in bed, put your feet up, and take it easy. Oh, and, uh, enjoy your breakfast, darling."

Karlita visibly softened. She'd worked on a thousand codes, and this one had been a piece of cake. She smiled broadly and winked at her friend.

"My little voice is telling me to do my best or go down trying."

**

(Yesterday)

Almost six pm. Nearly sixty minutes to go. It's the time when an ER doctor's fantasies turn from sex, food and football to choreographing his exit out. Thus, you subtly begin looking for the quickies: strep throat, twisted ankles, even a dislocation, fun stuff. In and out stuff.

Not today, it wasn't meant to be.

Lars was headed to Fifteen – a roofer had slid down a ladder with an exposed nail, which had sliced his thigh wide open. Per EMS, the gash was long and ugly. As always, he reviewed his choice of sutures - he'd need 3s and 4s galore, with some absorbables for selective areas that needed that extra layer of closure. So much for getting out on time.

put the chart back now and go into Eleven…

Lars stopped. Who the hell are you, he demanded. And what's your deal!

By this time, Lars sensed (feared?) that something was happening – again - to him, but what? Knowing now that it was useless to fight, he quickly walked over to the chart rack. The idea that his colleagues would think he was cherry picking burned through his mind - this rose to the level of a dump. Tradition held that in the final hour of a shift it was reasonable to bypass the ugly stuff and go for the easy cases. The rationale here was that incoming docs much prefer starting cases from scratch rather than taking over someone's end-of-shift sloppiness, which often entails slogging through a swamp of unnecessary, what-the-hell-was-he-thinking tests. But it was just a little too early…

Eleven, now…

He placed Fifteen's chart back and picked up chart Eleven.

"Tell Finkel the roofer needs to be seen next. My advice is to have the surgical residents admit him, or at the very least, have them close the wound down here - it's a dream case for an intern. I've got to see this guy."

He could feel the baffled looks headed his way as he walked off in the other direction. Someone whispered, 'there he goes again.' He didn't care. He just did what he had to do.

Moments later the doctor was face to face with Maximo Murphy. The man's wife rested her hand on his left shoulder, standing guard. Wow, this is one big puppy, Lars thought, staring at the huge man. He's bigger than Tony.

His chart read 'belly pain.'

Anderson introduced himself, and in less than a minute got right down to business. He was not in the mood for pleasantries.

"What can I do for you, sir?"

"Doc, I just don't feel right. I got this weakness; you know what I mean?"

Lars Anderson involuntarily frowned. Weakness could be anything. He much preferred pinpoint symptoms, like chest pain, breathing stuff, or a broken leg, for that matter. Hell, in a way he'd even prefer a knife or gunshot wound - admittedly not so good for the patient but, still, at least you'd know where to start looking.

He glumly looked the massive 79-year-old up and down. He did seem to be uncomfortable, but nothing jumped out. The monitor showed controlled a-fib (not a big deal), his BP and oxygen sat were okay, his color was decent, his skin was dry, and he wasn't in obvious pain (ER people can almost always detect genuine pain). And yet, there was something going on...some *thing*. The doctor could just tell. He just couldn't tell what that thing was.

"Anything else?" Lars asked, trying not to seem gruff – he wanted to wrap this shift up, and sensed this was becoming a lot easier said than done. "Can you be a little more specific? Please?"

"Don't look at me. She brought me here."

With his thumb Maximo pointed to his wife. She stared at him impassively.

He was massive, exuding an aura of once enormous life force now eroding with each passing second. Yeah, there could be something brewing in this guy, Lars thought.

For starters, the man was old. It wasn't so much his numerical age as the sense that Mr. Murphy was no longer on life's "endless" middle plateau. And once you're old the warranty's expired, all bets are off – and when it comes to any serious illness, you've forever become the underdog. Something told Anderson that Max was in the badlands.

Yeah, there was something...and the little voice in his brain whispered, *do it, go to code yellow*.

"Sir, I need you to talk to me," Anderson implored. "If you want me to help, you must tell me why you're here."

"Damn stomach," the man said finally, rubbing his mid abdomen. "It's killing me."

sit down...

"Okay, that's a good start," Anderson said hopefully, sitting down on a stool, which he reserved for the more serious cases – it forced him to focus on the situation at hand, and often put the patients at ease. "Tell me some more."

pay attention, listen...

"Mother, tell him how I feel," Maximo said to his wife.

Anderson sighed, turned his head and looked at the woman. She had a pretty face and was as small as her husband was large. Back in the day they must have been quite the couple.

"Mrs. Murphy, apparently it's up to you," he said wearily.

"Well, he seemed fine last night. This morning he just woke up suddenly screaming, and he started grabbing his belly. It seems a little better now."

"Any vomiting or diarrhea?" the doctor hopefully asked the patient, who shook his head. "Where is this pain, and does it travel anywhere?"

sudden onset...

"She'll tell you."

Anderson helplessly looked again at the woman.

"Mrs. Murphy?"

She looked at her husband and shook her head.

"He pointed to the middle," she said. "And he grabbed his back a little."

"Blood in the urine, pain when he pees?"

"I don't think so."

"Who knows, maybe it was the pizza last night," Mr. Murphy grumbled.

"Max, does moving or changing position make it better or worse?"

"No…and you know, doc, I'm getting tired of all these questions. Just give me something for pain and we'll be out of your hair."

The doctor thought of his seven other patients. Most were somewhat stable, but two probably needed LPs – and there is a longstanding rule that if you even seriously consider whether to tap or not to tap, you damn well better do it – rationalization is a leading cause of death in the ER. And, you don't sign spinal taps out. So while part of Lars wanted to let this infuriating man sign his butt out AMA, all his other parts knew he would never allow it.

"Show me where this pain is," he said with a hint of brusqueness. "Lift up your gown and let me see what's going on."

Grudgingly, the large man lifted his gown, exposing a massive belly. Anderson took one look, blinked hard and then stared. The man's abdominal wall was a veritable roadmap of scars going in every which direction. In the center though, dominating the landscape was a dark red superhighway running north and south, from stem to stern. This one's fresh, Anderson realized, and I bet that's where the money is.

His little voice gave the command, and he went into code orange.

"What is this?" he sternly asked Mr. Murphy, feeling exasperated. "It's not mentioned in your ER chart. What is all this?"

"I don't know, they took something out," the patient replied glumly. "Can I go now?"

The doctor frowned and looked at the woman, his eyes pleading. He pointed to the newest scar.

"Last year in Florida there was a bubble on a blood vessel," she explained. "They said they caught it in time…"

"Where else do you feel this pain," Anderson demanded, now on high alert. "And sir - you, yes you, will answer!"

"In my back," Max finally said.

The doctor scanned through the chart, shaking his head.

about time for code red, wouldn't you say?

"You're meds aren't even listed," he murmured. "Are you on blood thinners?"

"Go ask my wife."

Anderson looked helplessly at the man's stomach, trying to think of some cause that wasn't fatal…

come on, you know what it is.

He gently touched the large man's belly. No pulsatile mass – well, you couldn't really feel anything under all that fat. No tenderness or guarding – normally that's good but not now; their absence in the setting of pain often bespoke volumes.

(The condition he was dreading caused pain but not tenderness – there's a monster difference, by the way.)

In about three seconds he had the diagnosis – no tests really needed – a leaking abdominal aortic aneurysm (aka AAA, aka Big Red). The odds were that Maximo Murphy had maybe a few hours to live.

The doctor decided to forego his little show of doing some sort of "deluxe" exam, such as looking in the man's throat, shining a light in his eyes, and checking reflexes, and instead listened to the man's heart and lungs and felt his groin and legs. The whole thing took one minute. He straightened up and put his cards on the table.

"This condition looks serious. We need to start IV's and then get a CAT scan to make sure your aorta is okay, and that the bubble didn't come back," he told them, not mincing words. "It may need the OR. In the meantime, we'll run some tests, and we'll carefully give you something for pain. Mrs. Murphy, is your husband on any blood thinners?"

The woman looked at him blankly.

"I'll have to call our daughter. But doctor, they told us they fixed it."

"Well, things happen…"

"Doc, I don't give a damn about bubbles, just give me something for the pain!" Mr. Murphy snapped angrily. "We've been waiting here for over an hour."

"We'll take good care of you, sir."

"I don't give a shit what you do. Do you hear me - I'm going home."

Even after all these years, Anderson was both mildly hurt and surprised. *This guy came to me, voluntarily, to be helped. What the hell…*

be nice…

At that moment the pulse on the monitor quickened to 100. *Maybe it's because he's upset,* Anderson nervously thought, imagining that his own pulse had quickened as well.

"Sir, you may have a serious problem here."

"Aww, that's too bad. Mother, get my clothes…"

"No, you can't do that," Anderson interrupted. "Let me be clear. There is a chance, possibly a good one, that you have something going on with your aorta. Maybe it's related to the last problem you had with it; maybe it's new. Either way, Mr. Murphy, this could be life threatening. I'll order some tests."

The large man waved him off.

"You and your tests – you don't have a fucking clue, do you…see, now you're making me feel worse."

The monitor showed the heart rate slowly inching up. Anderson looked at it, then beseechingly at Mother and spoke very softly to her.

"Is he, you know, competent to make these decisions? Are you power of attorney? We really must go fast on this."

She held up both hands.

"He's a grown man, he makes his own decisions."

pulse now 110.

Anderson suddenly reached out and touched Mother's forearm. He led her out of the room.

"Give me one minute with him."

"I don't think it will get you anywhere. That man is so stubborn. Can't you just send him home with a pill?"

"One minute, okay?"

The doctor entered the room alone and closed the door. Mr. Murphy glared defiantly at him; his large arms folded across his chest.

"Back so soon?" he asked sarcastically, glaring at him.

"I am asking you nicely," Anderson pleaded. "Please, let us take care of you. I'm begging you, Max."

"Fuck off, I'm leaving. You just want to cover your ass and run the bill up. I know what you guys do."

Pulse, 116.

The doctor leaned forward. Now he was glaring. Their faces were inches apart.

"Back off or I'll hit you!" Murphy hissed, raising a large fist in the air. "I swear it!"

"Then hit me! Let me tell you something. If you want to be stupid, be stupid and go home! And you will fucking die! You hear what I'm saying? You really want to die? Then go ahead, sign yourself out and get out of here. Eat a steak, have a beer, make some phone calls and go to bed. Just know you will never wake up. You'll be gone. Guaranteed. Dead! Or you let us fix you up, and then you go home and live your life. Your call, my friend."

There was a pause, the room quiet but for their loud breathing and the steady beep of the monitor alarm.

"I want to speak to my wife."

Panting a bit from his own anxiety, Anderson opened the door and beckoned for Mrs. Murphy to enter. She walked up to her husband, who was trembling.

Suddenly the giant of a man started to cry.

"Mother, he says I'm going to die!"

She looked at the doctor, her face a mask of concern.

"If he goes home, ma'am, he probably will. Please let us…"

"Do whatever you have to do," she firmly said, as she cradled her sobbing husband in her arms. "Max, stop arguing or I'll kill you myself."

"Thank you," Lars said gratefully. "We're going to move him into one our big rooms. Again, thank you for helping. And, uh, Max, I'm sorry for some of the things I said."

He turned to leave – gotta order those tests, he thought, listing them in his mind. Maximo continued to cry.

lift up the sheets again…

I did that already. Listen, whoever you are, I gotta…

look at his legs again…

Anderson raised the sheets again, took a look, and became dizzy. The man's legs, in a matter of seconds, had turned a pale blue, up to his lower thighs. The heart monitor indicated a jump in the pulse as well – it now read 122. His systolic had dipped to 100. He raced out of the room.

code red!

As he speed-walked to the nursing station, he approached Ronda, and literally grabbed her. He spoke rapidly. She nodded her understanding and signaled two nearby nurses to join her. They entered Eleven and took hold of the stretcher. Quickly, shouting "make way!" they sped the clearly weakening patient towards the Big Room. Wordlessly, in time-honored tradition, the seas parted before them.

"I need Respiratory and Anesthesia stat," Lars shouted to the unit secretary. "And page Bozian stat on the overhead!"

"Lars, you mean vascular Bozian?" she asked.

"That's him. And call the nursing supervisor. My guy's gonna crash…we got minutes!"

"I just saw the doc in the cafeteria," Tina from the lab said, as she affixed labels onto test tubes full of blood.

"Keep paging him."

"Man, what the hell?" Bob Finkel, one of the other day doctors, asked. He was reading an EKG, standing nearby.

"Looks like a leaking triple-A or dissection, and the guy's starting to crash," Anderson replied. They watched Mr. Murphy, who appeared semi-conscious, being wheeled into the code room. A team of nurses and techs surrounded the stretcher, placing pacer pads, EKG stickers and oxygen on him. The radiology tech and his portable machine started rumbling down the hall in their direction.

Finkel looked up and shook his head.

"Glad he ain't mine. Does he always have purple feet?"

Anderson's eyes bulged. Max's legs were mottling up to his groin, splotches of blue and purple slowly ascending. Things were getting worse fast.

"Max, how do you feel?" he asked.

"Not so hot, doc," he whispered.

"His pressure's ninety, Lars," Ronda said. "We'll start another line."

At that moment Bob Bozian, the vascular surgeon, walked up. He was wiping some ketchup off his face.

"Well, gentlemen, what can I do for you?"

Bozian's eyes bored into the patient while Anderson synopsized the case in seconds.

"You wouldn't have a CT on him by any chance, would you?" he asked, not taking his eyes off Mr. Murphy.

"Didn't have time. You really want one?"

Momentary pause.

"Nah."

The surgeon picked up the phone and dialed the OR. Quick words were exchanged.

"Dr. A, his pressure's dropping!"

"Everybody, listen!" Bozian barked, walking over to a sink, where he began washing his hands. He turned to Ronda.

"I want sterile fields, lots of betadine and my trauma box. The one with the clamps! Bring two nurses and a Respiratory tech along with you. We're taking him to the OR. Let's go! Let's go! And run in those fluids."

"His pressure's seventy!"

"Come on, everyone, let's get him upstairs! NOW!"

There was a scramble as the team raced the stretcher containing Mr. Maximo Murphy toward the elevator. He'd become unresponsive. His wife shuffled twenty feet back – she seemed dazed. The nursing supervisor walked up, gently put her arm around her, and led her away.

Ronda calmly helped Bozian put on his gloves while the team hustled to the elevator. Security was holding the door open. They paused for a moment, as the surgeon gave them instructions. The team and their patient then entered.

The doors closed. The vascular surgeon nodded at the group, who nodded back and pulled up the patient's gown. A nurse poured betadine all over Maximo's mid-section and groin. The elevator slowly ascended. At that moment Bob Bozian placed a fifteen blade on the man's skin, and commenced slicing his abdominal wall open…

***

The ER seemed eerily silent. Everyone was digesting the last few moments in their own way.

Anderson, leaning heavily on the front counter, was the first to speak.

"Great work, everyone. Now I'll be in Five, doing the LP. Tony, want to help?"

"Yeah, sure, I'll get the consent and your tray."

Finkel stared at his friend, smiling.

"Well, I'm glad to see that the black cloud of Anderson still flies high."

"Hey, listen, I'll need to sign out the LP results."

"Do not worry, brother, we'll take care of it."

As Anderson walked away, headed for his spinal tap, a few people actually patted him on his back. Ronda and her little group returned, looking very serious.

****

The hotel room was quiet and dark. Anderson lay in bed propped up on two pillows, drifting in and out of sleep. The harsh ring of his cell phone positively startled him, spilling some of the vodka still in a glass he'd been holding. It was nearly midnight.

"Hello?"

"Lars, it's Dean from the ER. I'm sorry, did I wake you?"

"No, no. Dean, talk to me."

"Your patient, he did great. That was a four-hour surgery. Boze wanted you to know that you also did great. That goes for me as well. Oh, and you had two champagne taps. Way to go, my man. Now, get some sleep, we need you fresh in the morning. And, well…good going, Lars. Listen, Finkel told me you worked way past your shift. Give yourself an extra two hours. It's on me."

"Wow, thanks, Dean, see you soon."

Lars exhaled deeply. He reset his phone alarm, and soon felt sleep, formerly so elusive, now rushing up on him. Soon he realized that he could not remember his last thoughts. He also realized that he was smiling.

well, that was a day and a half, wasn't it?

It certainly was, he thought. Many thanks. Many thanks, whoever you are. So, uh – are you me, or are you, You?

shhh…sweet dreams.

*****

Part Two
Stonehenge

Seven a.m. found Dean Miller and Bob Finkel together again. It was changing of the guard time in the ER; Finkel was coming on, and Miller was hotel bound. It had been a reasonably decent night, not too crazy, not too boring, and it had eased into a beautifully soft landing, with only one sign-out. Miller was intensely poring over a journal, nodding with approval.

"What's up, big guy," Finkel asked, taking his equipment out of his bag, and finding a nice nesting place for his code gum. "See anything interesting last night?"

"If I did, I missed it," Miller answered, not looking up.

"Hey, are you *reading* something? Dean, this is not like you."

"I can't believe it either," Miller replied guiltily, sneaking the publication back in a drawer. "I actually saw an article I may like. It's intriguing, at least the intro and first paragraphs are, that's all I've read so far. Sort of got me going. You know, Bob, I just may read this whole puppy tonight when I come back."

"Wow, really?" Finkel asked, feigning shock and surprise. "A whole article?"

"Well, maybe not everything, but definitely the results and discussion parts. Plus, it's got nice graphs."

"That's more like it," Finkel responded, sitting next to Dean. "Okay, so what's this masterpiece about?"

He held out a bag of salt and vinegar chips. Miller gratefully accepted, crunched a few in his mouth, and nodded appreciatively. Fighting off several yawns, the last of which morphed into a belch, he looked up and revealed his newfound secret of life.

"Well, if you take enough steps in a day you live a lot longer. It's official, my friend, it's in a journal. We walk four to five miles per shift! Forget 'live longer.' We're gonna 'live *forever*!' I always thought ER people died young…you know, nights, stress, junk food, swapping all those bodily fluids - remember those, uh, dancers at the hotel last week? But I digress. Anyway, it turns out we've been doing it right all along. Shit, we're fucking immortal... what's up, brother?"

Finkel was wearing his sad face. Miller looked at him quizzically, crunching away.

"What's up, Bob, I just said you're gonna live to a million. Come on, man, you're still not upset about that head bleed Saturday, are you? That thrombolytic shit, man, it comes with the territory. I could have been, I *would* have been, the ordering doc if she came in one hour earlier. She stroked, she met the criteria, she got the med, she died. Bada bing, bada boom. You did exactly what any of us would have done. Remember the first rule of emergency medicine - BFL happens, and usually on your shift. Now granted, it was unfortunate she was the deputy mayor's wife, but at least it had sort of a happy ending. I hear he's marrying his secretary."

"It's worse than that, Dean. I am not going to live forever. Sorry."

"Well, this article says you are, and articles are always right. Anyway, forget this immortality crap – put it on hold. I need your opinion. You know how hard it is for me to make a decision after a night shift, right? I can wander around supermarkets for like thirty, forty minutes. So, I'm going straight to Tony Baloney's, and I'm down to two choices - they made me salivate the most when I looked at the menu. Option A is a large Italian sub with extra salami; or the meatball parmesan with extra cheese. Of course, I'll be including a large Caesar Salad with both, for lifegiving fiber. I may even get both and eat the runner up for dinner. So aside from lots of napkins, I need your wisdom. Choice A or B - what dost thou think?"

"That deli, man, I love their stuff," Finkel said approvingly. "This is a genuine dilemma. Let's approach it scientifically. What are you drinking?"

"Vodka, with carbonated orange mango mixer."

Finkel leaned back, pondering the situation. He seemed to appreciate the distraction and began pulling on an imaginary goatee. Finally, he nodded to himself, and began to speak. Dean leaned forward expectantly.

"I'd go with meatball parmesan, with plenty of sauce. Nothing's healthier or more wholesome than a hot breakfast. And forget the napkins – get a towel. Plus, at least two brownies for dessert. And save the sub for when you wake up."

Staff members crisscrossed the hall in front of them, paying them little mind (some no doubt thought they were discussing advanced therapeutic strategy). Dean considered his friend's recommendation, then broke into a wide grin.

"You have spoken with the wisdom of the Nile, my man. Crisis averted. So, my turn, what the fuck's going on? It's unsettling to see you serious about something."

"Well, now I need *your* opinion," Finkel said quickly, turning his head all the way to the left and right, sounding mildly concerned.

"This I gotta hear," Miller replied. He yawned slightly and reflexively looked in both directions himself. "Fire away."

"I don't know, man, I'm getting old."

There was a momentary pause. Miller waited for the next part; when none was forthcoming, he shrugged, mildly confused.

"You're getting 'old.' Isn't that sort of the norm these days, like, doesn't that sort of happen most of the time? That's why God made Viagra."

"Dean, let's face it – I am not immortal."

"Really. That's heavy, I think. Is there anything in particular that brought this revelation to the fore?"

"Well, maybe. Last week I was with, well, someone of the female persuasion," Finkel said quietly, looking around again. "You know, I'm doing my thing, I'm really getting into it, and she's going crazy. And then…and then, every time I move my tongue up and down, back and forth, I hear, I *feel,* this creaking sound in my neck. It didn't hurt, but that creaking shit was real. And loud. Freaky. What do you think?"

Dean scrunched his face, somewhat at a loss.

"You think she heard anything?"

"She didn't let on if she did. But damn it, I heard it. My fucking neck sounded like a coffin lid going up and down. This isn't supposed to happen to me. I'm a doctor, doesn't that count for anything?"

"I really don't know what to say, Bob. Maybe there's just a chance, a slight one, that you really are mortal."

"But I don't want to be."

"That my friend, is quite the conundrum. What's your plan of action? More olive oil?"

"I'm not sure yet," Finkel replied disconsolately. He paused a moment. "When I realized that I wasn't immortal, I started doing some thinking. Did you know that when you die, most people you've known are already dead? Family, friends, neighbors. It's a documented fact, look it up. So, when it's your turn to kick, hardly anyone is around who remembers you. That's why young people have the best attended funerals. Face it, we become old farts and turn into last week's egg salad. Know what I mean? You have a couple of glory days, you go rotten, you get flushed down some cosmic toilet, and it's over. I certainly don't want that – do you?"

There was a brief silence.

"These images are going to take a lot of booze to wash away," Miller finally managed to say, his mouth full of chips. "Thank you, Doctor Finkel, for giving me yet another reason to drink heavily. And, with a great deal of effort, one day I just may bring myself to eat egg salad again."

The ER was on the slow side. The incoming people looked around uneasily, first because they were wired to hit the ground running, at warp speed if need be; and second, because they knew that when the pendulum finally started swinging the other way, which was as sure as the sun rising in the morning, it would pop them right in the ass.

Dean turned to the computer screen.

"Damn, these labs are taking forever! No wonder our satisfaction scores suck!"

Finkel emptied his backpack and set up for the morning.

Miller paused, then decided it was time for his puppy dog routine – he was ready to make his move. He slowly, carefully, turned his head to look at his fellow doctor, trying hard to look mildly beat up without overdoing it and veering into pathos. He launched into his well-honed, oft-recited shtick.

"Bob, dearest Bob, mind if I get out a few minutes early? I just have this one sign-out in Room 20. Forty-year-old frequent flyer tried to kill himself by drinking water, like gallons of it. He's weak and dizzy, (of course), and acting even crazier than usual. At least he's not thirsty anymore. EKG looks decent, QT is good, vitals are good. Just check the labs – it took a while to get them. If they're decent he goes to psych, if they're bad he goes to the hospitalist. Slam dunk case. Could you do it? I gotta double back in twelve hours. Man, oh man, two more nights and the run's over. You know, Prufrock measured out his life with coffee spoons. Me – I measure mine with night shifts."

"I have no idea what you're talking about."

"Sorry, I was an English major."

"Whatever. What did the urine tox show?"

"It just got to the lab…"

"The fucker's been here two hours," Finkel protested. "What's he doing in there, knitting a sweater?"

"Actually, he drank the first two samples before we could grab them. I'm telling you, man, the dude likes to drink…"

"Why did I ask. Yeah sure, go get your health food," Finkel replied in a voice slightly tinged with bored resignation. He glanced at the cardiogram on the desk, picking pieces of chips out of his teeth with a splintered tongue depressor.

"Many thanks, amigo."

Miller logged out and reached beneath the desk to gather his things. Then he turned to his friend.

"And Bob, regarding your pronouncement about this mortality stuff, I will say two things: first, take comfort in knowing that when you do get the 'ole flusheroo, you'll wind up in the same heavenly septic tank as everyone else. That could be fun. But much more importantly, you really may feel a whole lot better if you can get laid, like, really soon. You know, sex is the documented treatment of choice for just about everything. Oh, my goodness, I should charge for this wisdom, or at least put it in fortune cookies."

"That's where we differ, Dean, I aim for high spirituality, and you, base reality," Finkel proclaimed, entering his passwords to enter the EMR system, never looking up. "I, the great Finkel will, somehow solve this curse of eternal anonymity. I'll fight it, I'll take it to the Supreme Court if I have to."

"You do that, Bob," Miller said, standing up, his knees crackling as he walked away. "And, as for your neck thing, I don't have a fucking clue. Maybe there's an article…"

"Dean, we have breaking news!" Finkel shouted to the departing night doc, who reluctantly turned around. "Listen up."

Finkel's eye were riveted to the screen, which was flashing a red critical light.

Miller stared at him impassively.

Finkel was studying Room 20's lab results with laser-sharp intensity. Numbers were magically starting to populate the screen. He suddenly leaned forward, squinting, his eyes growing wide.

"Hey Doc, we have a critical," the unit secretary simultaneously called out. "Low sodium."

"Dean, this guy has a sodium of ninety-six!" Finkel cried out. "Ninety fucking six. Katrina, tell lab to verify that, stat. So what do you have to say about that, Dean?"

The doc upturned his hands, almost as if in surrender.

"I do hope you're not waiting for applause," Miller replied, stealing glimpses at the ambulance bay door, where freedom lay beyond.

"Dean, this is from heaven. I've never seen a sodium that low in my life. It isn't considered compatible with life, but here this guy is, a regular guy (okay, maybe a touch crazy), drinking his own piss and half a swimming pool, and *living*. God has answered my prayers, and I've only been here twenty minutes. You do realize the implications of all this?"

"Can't say I do," Miller murmured. "But I have a hunch you'll tell me."

"This patient has the lowest serum sodium in the history of mankind. I'm going to write it up and become famous! What do you say to that?"

Dean rubbed his face.

"Well, there's your Nobel. In the meantime, reality beckons. You know, man, this five on, seven-off schedule is starting to kill me, no matter what the article says. It takes one or two days to recoup, and then you spend the day before the run morbidly depressed. But this sounds like a broken record, doesn't it? One day, mark my words, I'll have the balls to stop…hey, meatballs, get it? But now, off to the deli, then to the hotel to eat, drink, merrily clog some arteries and fall asleep. It's weird how the three things that consume my brain after a night shift are hunger, self-pity and exhaustion. Forget football…sex, well, that's plus or minus…hey, that the radio?"

"Yeah, you better vamoose before it's too late. And for the record, we will share this Nobel. Hey, remember that woman I signed out to you last night, a lady with fever, headache and chest pain? How'd she do?"

Miller thought for a moment, frowning.

"This really isn't a good time to ask. I don't even remember what I did an hour ago," he finally mumbled. "As far as I can tell, Fink, she either got better or she died."

"Thanks for the follow-up. Get some shuteye."

With that Miller nodded at his friend and slowly walked away. He then quick-stepped across the ER threshold into daylight, his escape now complete, his arms uplifted in triumph.

Morning had officially arrived, and the 7a-7p crew now ruled the land, the departing night people vanishing like mist on a lake. The fresh staff went into startup mode, checking supplies, equipment, confirming the call schedule, and the like. Finkel ignored them, mulling over a potential shot at immortality. A nurse walked up.

"Bobby, you want something for the sodium guy?" Ronda asked. She'd taken over the case. "He's starting to twitch."

"How uncool of him," Finkel said, mostly to himself. "Put him in the Big Room. Let's touch him with fifty ccs of 3% saline, but do it slow, please, we don't want to fry his brain. Let's also give him Ativan, two milligrams IV, and start saline, a liter Q2H, and we'll see what happens."

"I'll put him in the unit when the lab verifies. Hey, get another red top and send it to the lab to re-check that sodium again – who knows, maybe it's even lower. Or, uh, higher, way higher. That would be so much better for the patient."

"Sure. You in for breakfast? Linda's going out."

Finkel rubbed his abdomen.

"Nah, I'll eat later. Belly's been hurting."

"Awww, your poor little belly."

"Your compassion knows no limits. Hey Ronda, see you later?"

The nurse looked at him, pursing her lips. They looked at each other, oblivious to the dozen or so people milling around them.

"Yeah, later."

"Ronda, wait. I've been doing this ER thing a long time, right? I must have seen over ten million patients by now, and I swear, I don't think anyone remembers my name, let alone remembers *me*. I'm anonymous. Doctor Anonymous. It's freaky."

"I'll remember you, baby. Your tongue belongs in the Hall of Fame."

The doctor grunted at the words. The nurse, now preoccupied, noticed nothing.

"Patient-wise, I mean," he said.

"Well, for starters, have you ever introduced yourself? Have you ever started a conversation? Ever act like you cared?"

Finkel fidgeted a little.

"I guess sometimes I did," he said defensively. "I'm sure I did, at least a few times. You do know that bedside crap is hopelessly overrated."

"They don't call you the 'Doorway Doc' for nothing. You know it, you even think it's cool. In a way, so do I. Maybe that's why I like you, you're so deliciously caveman. Well, catch you later…in more ways than one, huh? And do not forget to write that sodium order."

With that she walked away. Finkel stared more than a bit at her swaying hips, and then returned to the computer screen, it's brightly red sodium numerals practically screaming the now-verified sodium level at him. He stared and he stared, and his face suddenly broke into a smile. He stood up, walked into the nurses' station, stared at everyone near him, and cleared his throat.

"Attention, everyone, I have an announcement. Listen up. Listen."

The staff paused briefly, looking curious. For a moment, just for a moment, he would have their complete attention.

"There is magic in the air. We have in this ER today a living patient with a serum sodium level of ninety-six, the lowest level ever recorded on planet Earth. I'm going to write this case up. You may not think this is sexy but it's all I got. I will be famous, and I'll see that all of you get a piece of this glory. And, of course, all this is done in the name of patient care."

Eileen, the head nurse, aka the CMFIC (chief motherfucker in charge), who was doubling as day charge for the shift looked at him, her face deadpan. The room was as silent as it could get.

"Really," she responded.

"Yes, really. Aren't you impressed?"

"It didn't make me wet, if that's what you mean."

"Ahh, you're such peasants. Don't you see, you all have the chance to…. wait, I have to research this. Do I have a few minutes? Gotta go big time on the computer."

The unit secretary looked at her screen.

"Yup, the coast is clear. Have fun, sweetie."

They looked at him and smiled. For them, Dr. Finkel was always a source of amusement and varying degrees of affection. A fixture in the department, he came with positive things, negative things, and well, Finkel things.

The doctor returned to his keyboard, clicking frantically, checking and rechecking stats and records. Five minutes later, he slumped forward, as if stabbed in the back with a digital knife. Ninety-five, ninety-five sodium, he said over and over to himself. I'm such a loser,

I missed immortality by a point. Why couldn't that fucker have drunk just one extra glass...maybe I'll sneak him one...

"Doctor Finkel?"

Startled, he looked up guiltily. The first-year resident was looking at him expectantly. The first-year family practice resident who was assigned to him. The resident who could spend fifty minutes on a five-minute case, then spend fifteen minutes presenting it, and still get it wrong. The same resident who last week took nearly an hour to pronounce a patient dead. He hated the first-year resident.

"I'm glad to see you, Marten."

The first-year resident visibly straightened and beamed.

"Sir, may I assume it's because you finally have developed confidence and respect for my knowledge and abilities?"

"No, it's because I gotta take a shit. Watch the place. If Room 20 starts to seize give him some Ativan and page me. I'll be back."

With that Finkel grabbed a beeper, went through one of the ER doors and walked down the hallway until he reached the Magic Bathroom, known only to the ER staff. To the rest of the hospital, it was just another mysterious door down a quiet, mysterious hallway. But it was a special place – clean, private, free of graffiti and it even had toilet paper. The doctor opened the door and locked it behind him.

While seated, he grumpily realized he couldn't breathe through one of his nostrils. A quick excavating mission with a fingernail nabbed the offender, a green glob shaped a bit like England. It lounged on his fingertip, seeming to mock (yes, mock) him, as if daring him to do something about it.

The doctor smiled back coldly. Here was the chance to both avenge his stuffed nose and to channel all his life's frustrations in one fell swoop. He considered his options. Well, he'd always been a big fan of scapegoats – life is so much easier and simpler when you have one. This just may be the perfect time, he mused. Finkel lost himself in deep thought, then nodded sagely.

Assuming the role of both judge and jury he began his pronouncement.

You dared to invade my life, he accused the hapless particle. I hold you responsible for both my creaking neck and the loss of my low sodium fame. *You* are guilty of destroying my immortality. You are thus hereby condemned to the Flick of Doom, and once it is carried out, no one will ever know that *you* ever existed either. *Ha!*

Trying to work up outrage and anger (easier said than done, considering the defendant), he flicked, but...it stuck to his fingertip. He flicked again, and again – and still, no luck. *This one's harder to get rid of than that migraine yesterday. Oh, so you think you're a big shot? Thou shalt not maketh a monkey out of me!*

He took a deep breath and began the final countdown. T minus two, one...he began to tense. Zero!! Every coiled fiber in his being sprang into action, (years later Finkel would claim he could hear choral music in the background, but this was at best dubiously received) and the veteran doctor gave it his ultimate best shot.

This time the gods smiled on him. The helpless glob hurtled through space like a meteor, finally splatting onto the far wall with a microscopic thud. Finkel stared at it, nodding with approval. His work here was done. He chuckled, forgot all about it, and went back to the ER.

*

Two days later, during a slow moment, he returned. Without thinking his eyes drifted to the impact site from the earlier shift --- and his handiwork (if you will) was still there. Not only did this amuse him, in a very odd way it gave him a sense of stability, as if some things really don't have to change. Finkel gave quiet thanks to Housekeeping. Wow, he thought, through their inefficiency, part of me has lived on, if just for a bit. I'll take that. A life's lesson has been taught in the Magic Bathroom.

Days, weeks, went by, and each and every time Finkel used this bathroom he would first check on the status of the now fossilized booger. It was always there, calming and peaceful, and slowly...and slowly it took on a special, almost spiritual status, a good luck object if ever there was one, a constant in a turbulent, unpredictable world. A testament to the truth and reality of permanence.

He began offering prayers during these pilgrimages for the continued ineptitude of Housekeeping, and gradually developed feelings of affection and pride in his creation, which he started to inwardly rank as a genuine, admittedly minor, accomplishment.

This is a gift from the heavens, he thought one day, *it's positively religious, like Mount Sinai or the pyramids. No, it's shaped like England – what we have here is the new Stonehenge! And this has become an eternal monument to my everlasting glory, my very own personal Stonehenge.*

His mind reeled at this sudden, miraculous revelation. Doctor Finkel was now...complete.

**

A few shifts later Finkel arrived at work, and he smelled something new, yet oddly familiar. He looked at his buddy Dean Miller, who was again wrapping up a night shift.

"What's that smell?"

"Paint, what did you think it was?"

"They're painting? This place, it's ancient. I was used to all the drab lime-ness."

"Well, get used to drab tan-ness. They paint once every century..."

"I gotta use the rest room," Finkel suddenly said nervously.

"Was it something I said?" Miller asked, staring at the computer screen, double checking his patients.

Finkel looked around with a twinge of panic. The ER was medium busy, but no one was in the Trauma or Code rooms. He held up an index finger and stood up.

"Be right back. Can you stick around for just one more minute?"

"A real emergency, huh?" Dean asked.

"Got to check on an old friend."

"I'd rather not go there, if it's okay. Yeah, go."

With that Finkel strode out of the ER. No one paid him any mind.

Seconds later he was in the Magic Bathroom. There was a nearly overwhelming scent of fresh paint. Half holding his breath Finkel looked, and....there it was!

Before him, in plain view, was Stonehenge (ne'e Glob), proud and noble, encased in a brand new teeny tan sarcophagus, now forever immune to Housekeeping. Finkel's eyes grew wide, his pathway to eternity now officially brushed and rolled into its final resting place.

They paint once in a century, he calculated. And that's with proper funding. One more budget cut and part of me will be here *until the end of time.* In near trance-like reverence, he stared at his creation, oblivious to the occasional cautious testing of the door handle from outside. At last, my dream has come true, he thought. *Until the end of time!*

Elated, Finkel practically skipped to the ER. Not much had changed during his brief sojourn – except for him. Miller was standing in the hallway waiting, hunched over, his coat on, his gym bag bulging with snacks, puzzles, equipment, and a change of clothes.

"That was a long minute."

"I upgraded to a full dump."

"Okay then, yet another visual to wash away. Let me give you a verbal sign-out, it's really nothing."

Three minutes later Miller was shuffling out the door.

"See you on the flipside," were his last words.

Finkel walked up to Eileen, who was standing against a counter, charting. He tapped her shoulder and smiled broadly when she turned around.

"And to what do I owe this pleasure?" she asked drily.

"I just wanted you to be the first to know. I am immortal."

"You are immortal."

"Yes, I am immortal," he replied.

"And how many 'immortals' did you have before coming to work?"

"You do realize that only a peasant would say that."

"You do realize that you're crazy...by the way, m'lord, would you mind seeing the asthmatic in Four?"

"But of course, peasant."

"Take your meds next time," she called out after him. Then she returned to her charting.

Walking towards the room Finkel would look at every one he passed and tell them, I am immortal, you hear me, I am immortal. He seemed delighted with himself, and when he finally entered Room Four everyone looked at each other and smiled. Unbeknownst to the good doctor, for them Dr. Finkel was already a living legend.

**

Part Three
Goin' to the Chapel

The door to the director's office was closed. The two men faced off across a large desk. It was stone quiet.

Doctor Rob Keller leaned back in his chair, hands clasped as if praying, index fingers against his lips, mulling over the proposal he had just received. Finally, he cleared his throat and spoke.

"Let me get this straight, you want me to be your spy. This is out of a movie."

John Carr, Mainland Medical's ER director, smiled at him.

"Rob, spying implies dishonesty. That would be wrong and unacceptable. This is on the up and up. I'm just asking you to be our silent representative, our eyes and ears. I'm sure you're aware Southside's our number one rival. It's not like I can just walk into their ER and look around myself. I need to know why my place is leaking like a sieve. In three months, I've lost four docs to those guys. They pay the same as us. Our patient demos are the same. Something's going on."

"And what did any of your docs have to say?"

"I spoke with two of 'em. They gave me some non-specific bullshit like, 'personal dynamics,' 'spiritual growth' and they'd get off the phone," Carr replied. He was casually handling a new intubation blade a sales rep had dropped off for his review. He put it down and looked at Keller intensely.

"This is a little off the bell curve, you must admit," Keller said. "I'm an ER doc, not a commando."

"That's the beauty of it – you're a North Central hired gun, and we love you guys - you, Miller, Finkel. No one would suspect a thing. You know, I used to moonlight just like you. I started at a fucking zoo and I made shit, just like you guys make shit. They expect you guys to moonlight, they love it – they get quality docs and don't have to give them any benefits.

"I know where you're coming from, my man. I spent eight years at Charter, and we could match you guys train wreck for train wreck.

Sometimes we made your place look like a daycare center. I've been there, my friend. But I saw the light.

"Let's be honest, Rob, we work at the zoos for three reasons," Carr continued, his voice low. "First, for all that Wild West craziness, which eventually gets old; second, to become top notch docs who can handle anything and everything – we both know that if anyone from the foo foo shops worked at your place, or at my old place, they'd be wearing diapers within a half hour. Hell, I'm treated like a god here because they've never seen me break a sweat – but you see, I did all my sweating in the trenches, a million times over. I make it look easy, just like you and your buddies make it look easy, because for us, it *is* easy. And third, we work the zoos to look sexy on paper.

"Rob, your CV is a golden passport – send it out to nine places, you'll get ten job offers. And believe it or not, one day your cup will be full, and you'll make your move, just like I did. You'll make lots of money, buy lots of toys, and have lots of fun. Like I said, I've been there. In the meantime, help me with this favor...and we'll make your life a lot more comfortable."

"And it's totally legal, right? I feel like I'm in some drug deal or something."

Carr appeared to look mildly hurt. Smelling (green) blood, he inched forward, and started to go in for the kill.

"I would never, ever, ask you to do anything wrong. Just provide the great care you always do. Pneumonias, MIs, trauma, shock, it's the same shit everywhere. For you it'd be a piece of cake – they don't call you the 'Beast' for nothing.

"You don't have to break into safes or take photographs. Just look around a little and get back to me. Tell me Southside's secret, why they have *my* docs banging down *their* doors trying to get in, and not the other way around. Any day now I'm expecting to get a 'thank you' note from Danielle Green, their director."

"I don't know, John, that's a lot of work just for a few shifts. I'd have to learn a whole new computer system. And for what? To tell you they have better coffee?"

"And if it's as simple as a coffee machine I'll be forever grateful. And you can do this, you could size up an ER in no time flat – how many have you worked in your career, fifteen?"

"Maybe, but why should I? I work too much already."

"We'll make it *very* worth your while. I'm talking serious pocket change."

"Now you're cooking with butane," Keller said, his eyes flickering with interest. "*How* worth my while?"

The director licked his lips and slowly leaned forward.

"It's a simple formula. You get paid from them - and they pay decent - and then you get double that from us. In other words, triple time. Sound good? And we'll pay even for time spent learning their computer system."

"Is it hard getting on staff?" Keller asked, mildly distracted. He was making mental calculations involving money, which Carr noted with quiet satisfaction.

"Not for you. Clean record, double boarded, experienced, willing to work nights and weekends. Man, you're fucking gold. I took the liberty of getting most of your paperwork ready. You just need to sign in a few places."

He removed a file from a drawer and gently placed it front of the ER doctor. Keller stared at it, not moving.

"Help me, Bob, we're getting killed, *I'm* getting killed," the director implored in a strained voice. "I'm working twenty twelves a month and still have to go to all those rubber stamp meetings and do that QA bullshit. I'm dishing out over ten grand a month just in bonuses, and my budget is shot to hell - I just had to put the new ultrasound on hold. I haven't worked this hard since my Charter days. Admin is not happy – honestly, if this goes on much longer, I'll be out on the street."

The director paused, trying to regain his composure. He inhaled, exhaled slowly, and made his final pitch.

"Triple time, Bob," he said softly. "With maybe a little bonus up front?"

Keller started to feign serious thought, then shrugged and looked up.

"Who am I kidding? Okay, my friend, you just got yourself a secret agent."

The two doctors shook hands.

"Just remember to be careful, Rob. If they do catch you, we would have to deny..."

"Holy shit, this *is* a fucking spy movie."

*

Several weeks later, at seven pm, Secret Agent Rob Keller sauntered into Southside's ER and calmly looked around, his face a controlled mask of coolness and mild disdain. He had been in-serviced, taken the obligatory tour three days earlier and had cased the joint well. He'd also memorized the music and lyrics to the song Secret Agent Man. Keller was ready.

The place on the whole seemed pretty decent – clean, nice equipment, nice patients. And tonight seemed okay as well – no one was screaming, there was a half-moon in the sky and no blood on the floor. So far, this had the makings of a good shift.

He walked into the physicians' area and noted that the outgoing day doc was none other than Don Brown, Mainland's ex-assistant director. Brown was both talented and well liked; Carr's shop had taken a serious hit when he had left.

"So, here we are, refugees from across town," Keller said casually, shaking hands. "I've heard some good stuff about this place – is it as good as it looks?"

"It ain't a zoo, if that's what you're asking. It can get pretty busy sometimes, but overall it's okay. Quick turnaround times, friendly attendings, solid nursing. Yeah, you'll like it."

"Anyway, let me get you out of here," Keller said. "What you got for me?"

It was a quick sign-out between two seasoned pros.

"I think I'll like it here," Keller said in a friendly tone. He looked at Brown and squinted his eyes just a bit. "So, I'm curious – what makes this place better than Mainland? It's looks like a carbon copy."

"There are perks. Come with me and I'll introduce you to the staff."

Together they walked into the nurses' station. Brown waved his hands over his head. All movement stopped, as the outgoing day and the incoming night crews looked at them. Keller fidgeted nervously, and briefly looked down. This was for him always the least pleasant part of starting at a new place. New names and faces, new cliques, new quirks. Damn right I get triple for this, he thought, I deserve it.

"Listen up, everyone," he heard Brown saying. "This is Rob Keller, one of our newest docs. He's one of the hot shots from North Central. You'll get used to him...just joking. Take good care of him. Rob, they're going to love you. Two things – first, it's Doctor Appreciation Week so they'll bring you free dinner around midnight; and the bus let's out soon, so don't get too comfortable. See you in the morning."

Bus, what bus, Keller thought, looking around. No one said anything about a bus. He looked up at the patient tracker – mysteriously, three patients had registered in the past five minutes.

With that Brown left. The new doctor and the nurses awkwardly traded glances, sizing each other up. This was a ritual practiced throughout the ER world. Some of the staff smiled at him, some looked at him with suspicion, and one even emanated a trace of hostility. And he caught at least one of them peeking at his left hand. Wow, there are some really cute ones here, he found himself thinking.

Keller debated if it was even worth trying to start memorizing names – that was always exhausting, sometimes brutal. He believed a sin he committed in a past life eternally doomed him to leave a place as soon as he had connected all the names to the faces, only to begin anew somewhere else (sort of like the curse of Sisyphus, ER style). He also reckoned that this would be a short assignment – secret agents never spend too much time in one place, and in any event, he decided not to get too close to the babes. One of them might be a double agent, maybe even a triple...

"So you're the latest North Central hot shot," one of the babes finally said. "My name is Doreen and I'm the house supervisor. As a head's up, we may need you later to tube someone in the ICU. I'll be upstairs."

"I gotta tube on the floors?" Keller blurted out. "What's up with the hospitalist?"

"I guess this one doesn't intubate," the babe said. "Not my problem, doc."

Keller grumpily looked around and did a double take when he saw the tracking board – the three new patients had mysteriously turned into six.

"Darlin', you might even get to deliver a baby in L&D tonight," one of nurses piped in. "And by the way, there's a diff breather in Room One."

What a way to treat a secret agent, Keller indignantly thought as he strode into the code room. They expect me to *work* tonight?

And work he did, non-stop, for hours. There was some tough stuff in this ER, some very tough stuff. Keller at first fell quickly behind – nothing like a new ER, a new computer system and eight patients (two of them level ones) registering in an hour to kick your ass. It took him nearly four hours to dig himself out. By the time he had regained full control of the department he felt used and abused. He leaned back in his chair and rubbed his forehead. The nurses were a few feet away, catching up on their charting. Who would want to work here in the first place, he wondered, it sucks.

"Hey, is it always like this?" he asked.

None of the nurses even looked up.

"No doctor, sometimes it gets really busy," one of them finally replied.

Keller paused a second, then smiled. Guess I deserved that one. Maybe it's time to make some small talk, turn on the ole charm-eroo. And then I wrap up this shift and get the hell out of here. This ER is officially off my bucket list. I'll just tell Carr there's obviously some mass psychosis going on. And I'll compliment the coffee...

"Doc, I'm Alfred from Dietary. What you want for dinner?"

"What are my choices?" Keller asked, looking at the man, who was dressed in traditional stained whites.

"Well, there's fish, Austrian sausage or chicken."

"Okay, what type of fish?"

"I don't know, regular fish."

"Well then, okay. What is Austrian sausage?"

"I don't know, it's Austrian."

Great, just great, the doctor thought.

"Give me a hint, Alfred, tell me what it looks like."

"I don't...wait, you know what your dick looks like after you fucked four or five times?"

"Okay. Yeah, Alfred, I think I'll take the chicken. Thank you."

Just then Doreen appeared and tapped his shoulder.

"It's intubation time, honey, someone's failing BiPap. Can you break away?"

One of the nurses looked up at him.

"Go, go, you got time," she said.

"Lead the way," Keller said, a slight air of resignation in his voice. He stood up and stretched. With that the supervisor gently tugged on his scrub shirt's sleeve and off they went.

**

It was a great intubation. Keller snapped open his laryngoscope with the pomp of a gang leader opening a stiletto. He hunched over the unconscious patient and inserted the blade to move the jaw up and the tongue out of the way. The patient's mouth was large, his neck was long, and his vocal cords (the gates of heaven in respiratory emergencies) practically shot into view. Keller slid the ET tube between them without effort (he disdained glide scopes, on artistic grounds). He himself was delighted, he being the only person in the universe who would ever know how easy this one was. To the staff standing around the bed he knew he now had creds. For a little special effect, he let out a weary sigh. He stood up, stretched and prepared to go.

"His pressure's pretty good, so let's keep him on propofol, and give him one of Dilaudid," he said, trying to sound cool and in command. "I'll dictate something in the chart and check the x-ray for tube placement from down in the ER…"

Keller stopped and noted a doctor behind a large computer screen in a nearby station, sneaking looks at him.

"And *you'll* call his attending, right?" he asked the hospitalist, who nodded without making eye contact. Then he turned to leave.

"Thank you so much for coming up, doctor," someone in the little group gushed. (Hearing that always makes you feel better. It's fun being a superhero.)

A few minutes later Keller and Doreen were headed back to the ER. The rest of the hospital seemed to be asleep, and the doctor felt sort of a magical pleasure walking through the silent halls.

"Now, that wasn't too bad, was it?" Doreen asked.

"It was okay," he responded, trying to sound nonchalant. He couldn't help but steal an extra glance or two or three in her direction. She was very nice to look at, particularly that lateral oblique view. Maybe that intubation was like an omen, he thought, planning ahead, maybe the second half of the shift will be better than…

"Let's go into the chapel and say a prayer," Doreen suddenly said.

They were standing in front of the hospital's chapel, its open door revealing a small quiet room bathed in velvet and soft hued wood. A peaceful light emanated from a ceiling fixture.

"Say a 'what'? You serious?"

"The power of prayer is very much underestimated. Come on."

She took him by the hand, led him inside and closed the door. Everything around them was perfectly still. She smiled at him.

"So what…"

At that moment she kissed him passionately, wrapping her arms around him. Keller was both completely stunned and wildly excited. He gave secret thanks for not panicking or acting totally stupid, and for the new piece of code gum he had earlier popped in his mouth, a longtime habit whenever he intubated.

He was keenly aware of her intoxicatingly sweet smell, and of the exquisite sensation of her breasts, which were pressed hard against his chest. His initial nervousness rapidly melted before the heat of his desire and hardness. Deep inside he knew that he was now in the middle of a mind-blowing fantasy, as excitement, arousal and finally, all out lust surged through him. His hands moved up and down her body. It only made her more passionate. Dimly, he wondered what would happen if they were caught...and then he stopped wondering.

"Don't worry, the cameras don't reach this area," she whispered, gently easing him onto a cushioned bench, expertly pulling his scrub pants down at the same time. She knelt in front of him and looked up, her hands starting to caress him. "You ER docs really turn me on. Lean back and let *me* appreciate you. Enjoy."

And enjoy he did. Keller's mind may have been numbed but the rest of him most definitely was not. Doreen was going crazy on him. Between the wild, upwardly spiraling pulsations of pure sexual voltage shooting through his body, he found himself thinking, over and over, *Good God, this is the best ER shift I have ever had!!!*

***

Mainland's CEO, Susan Kenworthy, icily looked across her desk at John Carr. He was trying hard not to squirm in his seat, having been abruptly summoned to her office. He felt very much out of place here, his normal liaison to Administration being a lower ranking manager who worked in another building. Aside from attending a few meetings which she chaired, none of which required him doing anything more than silently raising a hand on a few, always unanimous, votes, he had never met this woman. Some of the stony-faced VPs seated on either side of her did look familiar.

"Any word from your mole?" she asked drily.

"He says he needs a little more time to complete his research," the director replied warily, concerned by her demeanor. "Don't worry, we'll get to the bottom of…"

"He gets blowjobs when he works there."

Carr's face contorted with shock and confusion.

"Excuse me?"

"Dr. Carr, I happen to have a little spy of my own. The good Doctor Keller gets blowjobs when he works there. Most of the ER doctors there are getting blowjobs."

Carr cocked his head in bewilderment, and nearly fell out of his seat.

"They, they..."

"Yes, 'they, they' 'are, are,' and in the chapel, no less. Perhaps the chapel arouses less suspicion if someone hears the words 'oh my god' coming from inside. At least one of the nurses, maybe more, regularly performs oral sex on them."

The ER director sat there, speechless. He felt totally beaten.

"I don't know what to say," he finally whispered.

"I appreciate your insight and words of wisdom on this matter," the CEO finally said. "So, Operation Deep Throat is officially over. Call Dr. Keller and please thank him for all of his, well, hard work. I do hope he enjoyed his 'research' and is grateful to us - after all, we paid for, shall we say, every drop. Didn't we?"

"But I had no idea," Carr stammered.

"Of course you didn't, and by the way, Dr. Carr, why don't you just pack your things and call it a day. Go back to your zoo. Frankly, go anywhere. Security will be there to help. Effective immediately we have new management. As the saying goes, 'thank you for your service.' And please close the door when you leave."

As he left her office Carr could hear the rustle of papers and the CEO say to her group, "Okay, now where were we?"

****

Carr sat in his office, a half-filled cardboard box on his lap. A security guard waited patiently nearby. So, it's time to get out of Dodge, he thought. Screw this place. Screw Kenworthy, and screw the swiss cheese schedule; let someone else get old and gray trying to fill it.

He put his hands over his face and breathed deeply a few times. So, what did Atlas do when the weight of the world just got ridiculous, he asked himself. He shrugged. And, hopefully, he started to have fun. I could use a good shrug myself.

He reached for the phone and dialed.

"Hey, Danielle, John Carr from Mainland," he said with as much bravado as he could muster. "Thought I'd catch up a little...how are things at Southside?"

Some obligatory ER director chit-chat now ensued. Finally, Carr cleared his throat "Dani, I'll get to the point – there have been some changes in my life. Would you by any chance have any available *night work?*"

*****

Part Four
My Big Beautiful Car

The man in a suit carefully maneuvered his way through the boisterous emergency room, trying his best to avoid touching anyone or anything. This was easier said than done; it was a busy afternoon, and the hallways were bristling with activity, patients and staff going in every which direction. He was looking for someone.

He approached a cluster of personnel in front of Room One, variously known as the Code Room or Trauma Room, depending on the circumstances. The man puffed up a little, tugged on the lapels of his suit jacket, and assertively pushed his way in, entering the inner sanctum. The group wordlessly parted before him, figuring that someone who looked and acted so sharp just had to be a big shot (although nobody really knew who the hell he was).

The man looked around. The floor was littered with discarded towels and bandages, some used tubing, IV equipment and, yes, a few drops of blood here and there. The center of attention was lying motionless on the stretcher before him – all that was visible were his bare, blue, feet, and a tube sticking out of his mouth. A respiratory therapist was rhythmically bagging him. On either side there were nurses and techs. At the head of the stretcher was the doctor, running the show. She was listening to the man's chest, checking for tube placement. She nodded her head and gave the thumbs up sign.

Welcome to an ER code.

The man cleared his throat.

Peggy Ferguson looked up at him, mildly annoyed.

"What's going on?" she asked, squinting her eyes, trying to figure out who he was.

"Where's Doctor Finkel?" he brusquely asked. "You tell me now."

"And who might you be?" she replied, studying an EKG just handed to her.

"I ask the questions here. Where is Finkel."

"Listen, if you don't belong here, you've got to wait outside. We're busy."

"Are you a nurse or something?" he snapped. "I want your name."

"Can't always get what you want, baby," she said, turning her head to study the heart monitor. "Ronda, let's give him ten of regular insulin, and an amp of D50."

"Don't you ever call me 'baby!" the man warned.

"That's right, you're too ugly to be my baby," she responded coldly, turning slowly to look at him. "Last chance, buddy, get out."

"How dare…"

"Paul, get Security stat."

"You got it, Doctor Peg."

The aide pulled his gloves off and walked to a wall phone, keeping his eyes on the man. Emitting a grunt of disgust, the well-dressed man quickly spun around and walked out, trying to ignore the snickers that ricocheted off his back. I'll get them all, he thought.

He walked to a nearby counter. Behind it was Katrina, the unit secretary, entering orders. She started when she saw him.

"Where's Finkel?" he asked sharply.

Somewhat nervously, she indicated with her thumb the doctor sitting further down the counter. Wordlessly the man walked up to him, his rage building.

Finkel noticed him approaching but paid little mind. He returned to his keyboard, pecking away with two fingers. After a few seconds he finally looked up.

"Can I help you with …wait, you're the urologist, right?"

"And you're the one who reported me, aren't you? Aren't you!"

Finkel looked up at the man glowering at him over the counter. Everyone walking by knew the guy didn't belong in the ER – he was too well dressed. (The staff dress code in the ER was, well, scrubs … maybe jeans for the night docs…and sneakers or crocs. Patient fashion trended towards come-as-you-are, with a few really pushing the fashion envelope by opting for the half-naked or orange jumpsuit look.)

Finkel himself seemed dazzlingly dressed up today, sporting his favorite button-down shirt with the sleeves rolled up, and beat-up but unripped jeans. Usually all that distinguished him from his patients was his badge and master cardiology stethoscope draped over his left shoulder. When Eileen, the head nurse, half-jokingly asked him where he was interviewing, he smiled. Just trying to impress the ladies, Finkel whispered, winking at her. Actually, it was coincidence – they were the first things he grabbed out of the closet when he woke up.

A symphony (to some; to others, a cacophony) of sights and sounds swirled around them. The two doctors ignored all of it, as their eyes locked.

Finkel was expecting this. So the guy wants to rumble, he thought. Then I say, let's get it on.

"Yes, I did," he calmly replied. "You deserved it. Now, if you'll excuse me..."

"Fucking *reported* me! You cocksucker..."

"What did you just call...wait a minute, coming from a urologist, is that a compliment or an insult? Hey, dick man, you flirtin' with me?"

Staff politely walked around the two warring docs, doing their utmost to give them the illusion of privacy, as all nearby personnel went into slow motion as they (casually) strained to listen...this was great. Had this been a schoolyard or bar, you'd practically be hearing the cries of "fight, fight!"

Doctor Phillip Matthew was furious. Yesterday he'd been notified of a formal complaint lodged against him for refusing an ER admission while on call. He was now required to appear before the hospital's Medical Executive, Risk Management and Peer Review committees to defend his actions. He was also advised to bring a lawyer, as this was a very serious charge and not his first incident.

At that minute a nurse appeared. The urologist stared at her; she glared back.

"Sorry to interrupt, Dr. Finkel, but Bed Five wants more pain meds."

"Samantha, just three of morphine. I'm sending his butt home as soon as I get the rest of the labs back. And you, Dr. Kutchakokoff, or whatever your name is," Finkel continued, turning back to his accuser. "I'm too busy to get into this. You had your chance to do the right thing, and you didn't. That patient almost died. And I do hope you enjoyed that 'cocksucker' insult, it's the last one you're getting away with."

"You think you're a wise guy, don't you?" the urologist snapped. "You ER guys take the cake, you think you're all big shots - but you're all losers, you don't know shit."

"I know an OR case when I see one," Finkel answered with an air of mild resignation. He sensed the other man was not going to let go of this.

"He didn't need admission!"

"Fournier's gangrene? Lactic of six? White count of thirty? Would you treat your father like that, but then again, maybe you hate him as much as you hate your patients. And by the way, all you had to do was come in, examine the patient and, if you disagreed with me, you had every right to send him home. You were allowed to say he didn't need admission. But you refused, you were lazy or didn't have the guts, and we were forced to transfer him. I assume you know that you broke the law that night, and the Health Department is already all over this place. Happy now? You got your answer, now go!"

A few *yeahs* and *amens* peppered the air. The urologist whirled around and snorted with fury. Then he turned back to the ER doctor.

"It may be hard for you to believe, but I know more about this subject in my pinky than you do in your entire fucking little ER brain. Remember, you and all your glorified first aid *colleagues* are nothing more than pathetic losers who can't get jobs on the outside!"

Finkel did not change facial features, but to those who were quietly following the exchange, it was clear that Matthew's verbal torpedo scored a direct hit. In the bad old days, it *was* a painful truth that many an ER doc was indeed a *has been* or *never was*. Yeah, but that was light years ago, and since then emergency medicine had rocketed to the top of the medical universe, with more than a few of its disparagers going on to ask, hat in hand, for a job there – usually to be politely turned away; for one, not being boarded in this relatively new branch of medicine; and two, lacking expertise in every single field, the one genuine ER requirement. Still, there were more than a few veterans who'd lived through, and still remembered, the days when the term "ER doctor" was commonly used as an insult.

Less than a minute later Samantha returned. "Excuse me again, Dr. Finkel, but Five says that if he doesn't get Dilaudid, he's ripping out his IV and leaving."

The ER doc gave her a *what else is new* look.

"Sam, this is his sixth visit in three months for the same thing. He's even been admitted for this, and has had several million-dollar workups, all normal. If he wants to leave, let him. It's his choice. He doesn't need the ER; he needs to follow with his private doctor - he never has, by the way."

"You know, he just called me a dumb, bleached blonde bimbo bitch."

"My kind of woman," Dr. Finkel murmured approvingly. "And for the record, Samantha, you are not dumb."

"Dr. Finkel, you are such a pig," she smiled at him.

As soon the nurse started walking away, the urologist started again.

"Wow, such life and death issues you deal with. You do this for a living, don't you?" Matthew taunted. "No wonder you're a second-rate doctor who takes care of second-rate people. In other words, you're a loser, a total piece of shit. How does that make you feel?"

"Well, if I had any respect for you or your opinion, I guess I might feel a little upset," Finkel answered, not looking up from his computer. "But I don't, so I feel just fine. Thanks for asking."

"You better watch your back!"

Finkel shot to his feet. Tall and lanky and having grown up poor and in a rough neighborhood, he was not averse to taking and giving a punch. He leaned forward in a menacing way.

"Where you headed with this, motherfucker, wanna go outside? Come on."

"Touch me and I'll have your license!" the urologist hissed, taking a half step backwards. "But let me leave you with this thought – when you get a chance, check out my big, beautiful car in lot 23, the silver convertible with the gold trim. I paid cash for it, more than you make in three years. It's my baby. And every time I drive it, it reminds me that I'm not *you*. Farewell, doctor, and take good care of your beloved creeps. You deserve each other."

Paul the tech walked up. Samantha was close behind, shaking her head.

"Bed Five just ripped his IV out and is leaving. Thought you should know."

"Everyone brings joy into my life, Paul - some when they enter it, some when they get the fuck out. Good riddance to him. And good riddance to you, dick man."

"What a dump this place is," the urologist mumbled back, looking around as he walked away. "Hey, someone show me where the elevators are! I gotta go down to the path lab."

"Quick suggestion," Finkel called out. "Since you're already headed in that direction, Matthew, go to hell."

The urologist scowled and strode away. Finkel shook his head and watched him depart. He closed his eyes.

"Take it easy, he's not worth it," Sam said supportively.

Finkel remained standing, trying to compose himself.

"I shouldn't have let him get to me like that," he whispered.

At that moment, the furious patient from Bed Five, followed by three friends, walked up to him. Blood was dripping from his arm, where he had just pulled out his IV. Staff members, patients and their families nervously scurried out of his way.

"You fucker, you just left me in pain!" he shouted.

"Time to call security?" Sam whispered in his ear.

"No, no, it's ok." Finkel murmured. "I'll handle this."

The doctor looked at the man evenly.

"Mr. Farley, every time someone walks by your room, you're either sleeping or eating corn chips," Finkel said, holding his ground. "I've been more than nice to you and have given you two rounds of pain meds. Now please get back in your room and let us finish your work up."

"No one believes me!" Farley bellowed. "None of you doctors! What's wrong with you people! You hear me, I'm in pain!"

"Over the past six months you've been prescribed over a thousand pain pills," Finkel replied evenly, holding up several sheets of paper listing Farley's prescription history. "Obviously someone believes you."

"Half those pills were stolen by my so-called friends, and my dog ate the rest."

"You must have a very happy dog."

The patient glared at him.

"Are you giving me pain meds?"

"No, I am not giving you pain meds."

"You lowlife scum."

Finkel put both hands over his face.

"Are you done?" he asked.

"I'll get you for this."

Finkel looked at the man.

"Take a number and get in line."

"No wonder you work in an ER, no one else will have you."

Finkel looked up at the ceiling for a moment, trying to collect his thoughts. Finally, he spoke.

"Let me end this marvelous encounter with this thought: when you get a chance, check out my big, beautiful car in lot 23, the silver convertible with the gold trim. I paid cash for it, more than you will make in your lifetime. It's my baby. And every time I drive it, it reminds me that I'm not you. Farewell, *sir*, and take good care of your beloved creeps. You deserve each other."

Farley called his small group into a huddle, and they spoke quietly. Then they turned and walked away.

"Goodbye, loser," the departing patient taunted. "I ain't signing papers, either."

Finkel smiled at the man and saluted.

"AMF yo yo," he intoned.

Farley stopped in his tracks, at a loss for words. Then he shook it off, and waved his little band out of the ER, shooting the middle finger at everyone he passed along the way.

Finkel calmly watched them leave. Curiously (to some, anyway), they seemed to be headed in the direction of lot 23.

Samantha was watching all the goings on, and then she turned to the doctor.

"And so, what does that 'amf yo yo' mean exactly?" she asked, feigning innocence.

"Perhaps the most important words in all the ER lexicon, my dear - *adios motherfucker, you're on your own.*"

They shared a well-earned laugh.

There suddenly was a commotion from the parking lot. Shouting, lots of smashing noises, and sounds of breaking glass. A car alarm shrieked in protest. The nurse turned back to Finkel and smiled.

"And *now* what do you have to say for yourself, doctor?" she asked, a touch of mischief in her voice.

"Ah, Sam, what's a day without being verbally abused. So, what's next on our agenda?"

*****

Part Five
The Train Wreck from Hell

Author's note – this one's pretty intense, and I was advised by two colleagues to leave it out. I just had to include it, for me. The reader can skip it, and the overall read won't be much affected. If you go forward with this story, strap yourself in and try to enjoy – sort of like going on a disturbing roller coaster ride, hoping one day you'll find yourself laughing about it. Maybe.

This is a tale of Dean Miller, twenty–plus year ER veteran, and Marcus Allen, thirty-plus years. These two docs, along with a powerhouse ER crew, worked the graveyard shift at North Central on one particular Sunday night. A third doctor, driving in through fog, was injured and brought to a neighboring ER, having suffered facial lacerations and a probable broken jaw.

There was a new moon, that is, nothing of it was visible. Combined with thick clouds that blocked the stars, plus the fog, this pitch-dark evening apparently was the perfect opportunity for badness to pay its respects.

Tradition holds that everyone has a good laugh after a terrible shift, and the worse the shift the louder the laughs. No one's laughed yet, and it's been a while.

By the way, this is the third toned-down version.

*

And it started out so nicely. The day crew was firing on all cylinders; Radiology and the lab were quick and efficient and admits practically beamed up to beds upstairs. Even the dreaded waiting room, maybe the one part of the hospital where staff always feared to tread, was behaving. This was in-and-out emergency medicine at its best. 'We ought to re-name this place 'treat 'em and street 'em Central' someone quipped, evoking general laughter.

No one panicked at the prospect of having only two docs and an NP show up for the night. Not much was known yet about Malia Younger's condition following her MVA, and most people just assumed she'd burst into the ER at any minute, albeit sporting a few bandages, ready to work. Almost everyone's guard was down. Both Administration and Phil Tannenbaum, department chair, were appraised. They reviewed the census stats from home, reviewed the weather forecasts – crappy conditions often dampen traffic volumes and also convince borderline patients to just wait till the morning to show up. In the end they gave the evening their blessing, figuring they'd roll the dice and hope the day shift's winning streak would continue into the night. Two top-notch docs, Lori Madlong NP, a firecracker mid-level, and a waiting room under control seemed to be enough.

A lazy calm was in the air as the shifts changed. The outgoing people exuded a smug satisfaction at having kicked ER butt, and the incoming group looked around in curious gratitude…at least most of them. The old timers looked at each other and shook their heads when the last of the day crew vanished through the doors. They knew.

The HERN went off. Cardiac arrest on the way. Marcus Allen shrugged, indicated he'd take it, and moved towards the Code Room.

"Dean, they need you now in Twenty-Two!"

Without a word – you never ask why when an ER nurse tells you to see someone "now" - Dean broke off and walked briskly towards the room.

There he found a man in his forties curled up on the ground holding his head, fighting off spasms of pain. The doctor slowly approached, the computer in his brain going full tilt looking for clues and answers. Suddenly the man relaxed, and he lay still. Then he screamed.

"What's going on, buddy? Tell me how you feel," Dean asked, kneeling by his side.

"Electric shocks in my brain," the man gasped. "I can't take it any more…"

And he again grabbed the left side of his head, grimaced and started writhing on the ground again. Dean shook his head and smiled.

"Get me some mineral oil and alligator forceps, please," he said to the tech who had accompanied him. "Sir, I'm going to help you get back on the stretcher…and I'm going to look in your ear."

Four minutes later he pulled a dead insect – death by mineral oil, if you will – out of the man's ear, using the specially designed alligators. As always, he marveled at how terrifying these bugs looked inside the ear when you're shining a magnifying light right at their kisser.

"Do you feel better, sir?" he asked, knowing what the answer would be – patients with this problem felt instant relief when you pulled out the culprit.

"I think so," he said tentatively, and then he rolled over on the stretcher screaming, again holding his head.

Several minutes later, once they got their patient to hold still again, Dean pulled out a second bug from the very same ear. It was nearly dead from the mineral oil and barely moving. Twice was the charm. The man smiled at him and nodded his head, giving him the thumbs up sign.

Dean gaped in amazement at the second insect – he had never, ever seen two of these guys in the same ear. The big one had chased the little one right into it. Damn, figure them odds.

He returned to the Code Room bays. Marcus Allen was at the nearby counter, grimly signing the death certificate. The area was swarming with police officers; many of them openly grieving.

"Man, that was the strangest fucking case," Dean told his colleague. "What a weird way to start the shift. What's the story with these cops?"

"The guy who coded was a police sergeant; he just keeled over at his desk," Allen answered. "Man, I threw the kitchen sink at him. Just couldn't get him back."

"Wow, I'm so sorry. That, and two bugs in the same ear. What a crappy way to start the night." Dean said. "Hope it's not an omen."

"I very much doubt that, Dean. You and your omens."

Almost on cue, for the briefest of moments, the lights flickered - probably for less than a second, but long enough to force the computers to reboot. Dean stood very still and strained to listen. He swore he heard something.

"You hear something, Marcus? Do you hear that hum?"

"I don't know, I can't say what it is," the older man said, cocking his head, slightly impatient. "Maybe it's the generators. Come on, man, it's bad enough that it's a Sunday night."

(Even during the best of times, Sundays in the ER suck, especially nights. God's day off is probably the worst time to work a shift there.

People can't reach their doctor, and try to 'hold out' until Monday, and thus arrive sicker. Then there are the churches packed with standing seniors; there's the partying, overeating, overdrinking and plenty of outdoor stuff; and let's not forget the grumpy staff, who usually resent working that day (especially that night.)

A moment later another arrest was called in. Dean popped a piece of code gum into his mouth; it was his turn. So, they want to play rough tonight, he thought. Well, bring it on, motherfuckers.

While he was tied up running the ultimately unsuccessful (most of them are, by the way, TV shows to the contrary) twenty-five-minute code, three Level Twos rolled in, and one patient in the waiting room was found lying face down, convulsing. Marcus Allen was nearly blown out of the water. By the time Dean returned to action, shaking his head, the older man was barely holding his own.

The ER never again came close to catching up. The daytime grace period was over. Apparently, the powers that be wanted to avenge the day crew's ungrateful walk in the park. And it ain't the number of patients that'll kill you, it's how sick they are – their *acuity*.

The knife and gun club was apparently meeting in town; so was the 2-0-5 crowd; you know, the 'I only had two beers, wasn't doing nothin', and five guys beat me up' people. There was red stuff everywhere.

Five ODs rolled in before 9p, with two winding up in the Big Room, and two others going directly to the morgue. The fifth should have gone to the basement as well, but had to wait in Room 26, covered with a white sheet, until something opened up downstairs (good luck on that). Then there were those who could barely breathe and those in severe pain. More than a few needed full restraints. A tech had already been assaulted and was in CT. And then there was that increasingly sullen waiting room, which was filling up again big time.

By 10p the place was teeming with serious pathology. Heart failure, kidney failure, respiratory failure. Thirty-eight patients registered in the past three hours - a high but not horrific number in and of itself. But most were genuine emergencies of the highest order. They just sucked the life force out of the depleted staff. There was no respite after that. None. Zero.

Tonight, in North Central's emergency department, the superstitious ones deep down sensed that the devil had decided to make a house call. You could almost hear the door handles to each patient room being jiggled.

By 11p, the graveyard ER shift in this non-descript, mid-sized city hospital, albeit one with a crackerjack staff, had devolved into a take-no-prisoners night. By midnight, the docs, nurses and more than a few patients knew that the ER was in trouble. The air was filled with shouts, screams and cries for help. The floors were slippery from all sorts of…stuff, as Life and Death grappled in all-out combat.

The entire staff, docs, nurses, and Lori – who along with a nurse and a tech was dispatched to handle the restive waiting room - worked non-stop, never having time to take a break, get some coffee or even go to the bathroom (holding it in is an ER superpower). They all shot into hyperdrive, leaping from one melodrama to the next, playing speed chess with human pieces, fervently hoping they'd made the right move because they couldn't look back. More than a few still talk about this one. That's the booby prize for having been there.

Optimists and administrators like to call these shifts *character builders* or *learning opportunities*; the doom-and-gloomers call them *train wrecks*; and the fatalists ask, *okay, so what crime did I commit in Hell to deserve this fucking night?* The correct answer turns out to be - all of the above. It comes with the territory. And yeah, it can really suck.

And it wasn't just the number of patients, as bad as that was. There were no sore throats here, there were stab wounds to the neck. There were no toe infections, there was flesh-eating bacteria consuming a foot from within, purple-blue clouds of infection floating under the skin up the leg. There wasn't a good old-fashioned headache…etc., etc.

Of the twenty-something people Dean had already seen, thirteen had been criticals, six of whom coded, and of that number, four were dead. The two worst of these – actually his two worst cases of this horrific night, among the worst of his career to date – involved two chemical plant workers with massive facial, neck and torso burns, courtesy of a chemical explosion. Dean struggled wildly to get an airway on one man, even cutting open his neck to get to the trachea, but to no avail. The burns were overwhelming and included the inner mouth and throat. The patent slowly died in front of him.

The second man was intubated but remained in shock, with unspeakable injuries, and the burn center refused to take him, demanding further stabilization. He too died in front of the staff, one of the nurses becoming so distraught she had to be excused for the night (only exacerbating the personnel crisis).

Dean spent the next several hours fighting the shock and horror of these failures, sometimes even finding himself doubling over with anguish. He was belching up acid and battling waves of nausea from the images and stench of burning flesh that seemed to have taken him over. He spent much of his dwindling psychic energy desperately cramming these horrors into a suitable brain compartment - he had no time to dwell on these cases. He was needed elsewhere. The subsequent nightmares would leak out soon enough.

Everyone was waiting for the pendulum to slow down, maybe reverse course – it's the rule, right? But then there's that other rule: sometimes you get the bear, and sometimes the bear gets you.

Shortly before 1a Dean realized that it was by now too late to even hope for a remotely decent night. He lowered his sights from practicing hot shot ER medicine to simply diagnosing, stabilizing and getting the admits upstairs. *Stabilizing* was the one basic requirement on sending an admit upstairs (unless specifically requested otherwise). But tonight, this was easier said than done. Tonight, he couldn't seem to stabilize anyone – his patients literally worsened in front of his eyes, as if immune to any treatment. Tonight, all of them needed enormous individual attention, the one commodity he had very little of. He could give them at best ten minutes. He'd examine them, jot something down, order some tests, check some lab and run to the next room, playing kick the (human) can down the road, hoping for a break. It was just another night in paradise.

The hospital went on ambulance diversion thirty minutes later, with only minimal effect. Nursing teams from the ICUs arrived to reinforce, again with only minimal effect. Two elderly family doctors came in to see a few of their private patients – in this modern age, they were a dying species, hospitalists having largely replaced them – and that helped a little, as well as boosting morale – *if they can do it, then damn it, so can I!*

The Grim Reaper clearly had a wicked sense of humor. Two upstairs patients were even sent down to the ER for airways and central lines, procedures normally reserved for Surgery and Anesthesia, who remained out of commission, tied up with their own chaos. The staff looked at these bounce backs and could only sigh and say to themselves, 'thank you sir, may I have another'?

At one point Dean found himself careening from one dying patient to the next, at times rationing barely more than five minutes per. He'd seen over a hundred thousand patients in his life, and tonight he leaned on this experience to its absolute breaking point, handing the controls over to his instinct, with no time for intellectual thought or even second guessing. And just when he thought it was okay to exhale, he'd hear his name being shouted out "stat!," and he'd depart the room with the nine-word promise he knew to be a lie; "I'll be back soon to check in on you." Then he'd shoot out of the room, shout some orders to an already benumbed nurse, and run to the next fire (and his next lie), knowing the best he could hope for was to just tamp it down before racing to the next blaze.

ER docs like to say that what separates them from the rest of the medical crowd is that the other guys go from Patient A, to Patient B, to Patient C, ad infinitum (most ER people would say ad nauseum), while in the ER you deal with Patients A, B, C, D, etc., etc., all at the same time. Tonight, they were being screwed by the whole alphabet.

A little after 2a, Dean Miller slumped in the Nurses' Station, panting, recharging. He'd been banished to the penalty box, so to speak, specifically to get some bars back on his battery. He'd just ordered acetaminophen on a headache patient *per rectum* instead of *per os,* and a frazzled rookie nurse dutifully, albeit *gently,* delivered it through the back door rather than leave it on the front porch – in the computer age an errant mouse click of even a few millimeters can wreak some funky havoc.

When Margo, the charge nurse, found out, she shot him the evil eye and pointed her finger. Wordlessly the doctor slunk off to the Nurses' Station, knowing deep down she was saving his ass. That wasn't his first mistake tonight, either, or his worst.

He glumly looked around from within the boxlike enclave, located smack in the middle of the massive department. As formidable as it seemed, it was largely an illusion, its circle-the-wagon layout comprised mostly of desks, cabinets and counters, with every flat surface covered with phones, radios, manuals and bags of over-nuked popcorn. It neatly enveloped them, *protected them* (Dean often fantasized that theirs' was a castle under attack from the barbarian hordes, who tonight were storming the gates.)

He called Mainland's ER to get the latest on Malia Younger and was told she was stable and admitted. The ER doc, who Dean knew to be topnotch and a good guy, said that her chief complaint was actually about missing her shift. *Man, she's tough,* Dean thought, smiling and shaking his head with admiration. On the downside, it means we're on our own now. It's me, Marcus and Lori against the world.

He then turned to watch the storms erupting around him.

Avoiding glares from the man down the hall who'd just received the errant Tylenol, he instead looked into Room 20. There, a recently reversed OD was being placed in four-point restraints, having pulled a knife from his boot – it made for great theater. Playing the spectator, rather than the doc shouting for Security stat, allowed him to assume a critical, almost disdainful, air – *humph, they didn't even search or restrain him before giving the Narcan – everyone knows they come up swinging; it's how they say, 'thank you so much for saving my life.' Marcus, really? What were you thinking...or were you?*

In the pediatric code room directly in front of him, parents sobbed and wailed alongside their murdered teen-aged daughter, run over by a jealous rival in a parking lot. Towels covered large swaths of the floor in a vain attempt to conceal the blood. Dean was the doc on that one, and it really got to him – the younger the patient, the more pain he felt. Adult cases in this roughneck ER seemed so many times to be self-induced, the consequence of greed, drinking, drugging or sex, alone or in combo. And while their problems often presented worthy challenges, he swore that sometimes they just had it coming. As for the elderly, well, be your absolute nicest, do your absolute best and, as a good friend had once told him, give the rest to God. But sick or injured kids? He had few defenses in his arsenal.

He once thought he had it down pat – the key to survival was leaving your emotions at the door, and it had served him well. His good buddy Bob Finkel summed it up best: *never come with the tricks.* It *always* seemed to work, until lately - now it just *usually* worked. Tonight, he'd already teared up three times: the dead teenager; a stillborn he'd scooped out of a car that'd screeched up to the ER; and a ten-year-old boy who'd swallowed a box of tacks so that he could join his recently deceased father in Heaven.

Dean's love affair with emergency medicine had long ago started to fray. The constant melodramatics, the not knowing what was around the corner, had slowly morphed from a friendly challenge into an unwelcome grind. His burnout light, which began flickering years ago, had become volcanic. If there was anything else in the world that really interested him, anything that would pay the rent, he'd jump ship. There wasn't, and that scared him.

His penalty time up, he slowly stood. He'd cheated and had rested for a whole seven minutes; albeit using this time to check x-ray results and tuning up his cheat sheet. A distant memory flickered in his brain – his Uncle Mike once told him how to care for a sick dog. "Just leave 'em in the basement for a day or two," the old man had said, "and then if the dog's still alive, bring 'em upstairs; and if he's dead, bring 'em out back and bury him." Tonight, he realized very guiltily, that part of Uncle Mike lived on within him.

Dean re-positioned his mental blinders and again only focused on the patients in front of him, ignoring all the pleas and screams surging everywhere – if the nurses want me bad enough, they know how to reach me, he reckoned. His lifetime fear of failure, which always trumped his drive to succeed, served him in good stead now. He was too busy to panic or feel sadness for the innocent people whose lives were in his hands. He was doing his all-out best, nearly fifty thousand hours of front-line experience surging through him – he swore to himself not to fail.

The absolute worst thing that could befall him was becoming overwhelmed. That's akin to driving in a blinding rainstorm, and your wheels lose their traction, your steering wheel betrays you, and you start hydroplaning, helpless, knowing this will only stop when you crash, when you kill someone. Dean had seen it happen twice. Both docs involved were now long gone; one went into primary care; the other completely walked away from medicine, having literally run out of the department when faced with a severe trauma. The personal, financial and legal fallout was sad and terrifying to watch. That memory alone forced Dean to take back control.

As he walked past the unit secretary, he instructed her to call administration to have the two hospitalists come down, and that he'd take responsibility for this. They'll help with the easier stuff – they can at least grab onto the legs of the monster, he figured, and lessen the damage. And then he ran to the next leak in the dam, or fire out of control, or… whatever metaphor you choose. Marcus went in the other direction, a veritable wild man himself. Lori left the waiting room patients to themselves and plunged back into the battle. The two hospitalists arrived, anxiously looking around. One of the elderly family docs decided to stick around to help – I'll do what I can, he promised. Soon there was an improbable army of six going all out against the madness – and it began to help.

Amazingly, there occurred a soft patch of time around four. Both ER docs knew this to be just the eye of the hurricane, and they stumbled into their seats, grateful for a brief respite.

Marcus Allen was tired and breathing through pursed lips. The oldest doctor in the group, he always exuded a calming confidence forged from a natural intelligence, vast experience and razor-sharp instinct. This guy had never been known to break a sweat or even get tired. But tonight, the master himself seemed pretty beat up.

Dean looked up at his older colleague, hoping for wisdom. He always thought that if Marcus, who had him by more than a few years, could keep pounding the pavement then why couldn't he.

"Hey, big brother, how goes the war?" he asked trying to sound casual. "Little rough out there, ain't it?"

"I tell you, this place takes the cake," Marcus grumbled, rubbing his eyes while hunched over his computer. "You tune up some sick dude, and two sicker ones take his place. You know something, I've been doing this crap for like thirty-five years, and I swear, sometimes I can't see one positive trace of my life's work. Forget having had any impact. This is getting old."

"Sometimes I think I'm starting to burn out," Dean confessed, not making eye contact. He looked at and initialed an EKG just handed to him by a tech. "You ever think about hanging it up?"

The senior member of North central's emergency department frowned at the question, as if he'd never considered it. He casually sipped his energy drink.

"Nah, I'm just…hey, it's just locker room talk. What's the fun about having a job if you can't complain about it? And it ain't our fault about Malia and her fucking accident; that's one of the big reasons why we're getting killed. This is on Charlie Meyers for not getting us a replacement. He's in charge of staffing. All he had to do was offer a fucking bonus. A third doc would have seen a bunch of this crap and taken the pressure off. So, going back to your question, my answer to you is, yeah, one day I *will* get out, but on my terms – or they'll have to carry me out. But you're right about tonight, it's a busy one…"

"Busy one?" Dean asked incredulously. "I've been averaging over fifteen patients all night, and then that last multiple trauma…"

"'Multiple'? Three lousy people…"

"One of whom died, and this wasn't DOA crap, they were disasters. We should have called for backup right then and there. You know, I was placing an IJ into this guy's neck when EMS dumped one of those traumas onto the next stretcher. Just when my J-wire is halfway down his jugular, a fucking pumper opens up in her arm and she starts spraying everyone with blood - me, EMS, my patient, the nurse, the tech. It was ridiculous!"

"One hell of a visual," Allen chuckled. "I'd have loved to have seen it."

"We should call for help. We'll never catch up now."

"Too late, amigo. Don't worry, we'll make it – the shift's almost two thirds over. Dino, my friend, just follow the golden rule: '*no one dies from here on in.*' Everyone else can sign their ass out if they're not happy. Who cares? They'll be back tomorrow, I assure you. Just treat the sickest."

By this time, both doctors were weaker than they would admit. Normally they'd still have plenty in the tank for that all-important 4a to 7a gauntlet, when it's time to get your act together and make the big decisions. The seven AM promised land now seemed hopelessly distant. The evil tide had rolled in and was defying everyone's prayers that it would roll out. If only that patient spigot could close, they could even catch up. That should have started by now, but it never did. Things were getting worse, the treadmill they were on was only going faster.

(Now for a quick primer on averages - most ER shifts, anywhere, possess a distinctive patient mix and rhythm, with consistent numbers and acuity. Regardless of how they start, they almost always revert to their norms by shift's end. The genteel shops finish up easy to medium, roughhouses such as North Central bad to ugly. Ironically, the wildest of ERs, the ones that garner the headlines, can be the easiest to work, since they have in-house trauma teams who run down to do all the dirty work – and best of all, you get to share the bragging rights.)

Several post-midnight patients had already died, and others were starting to circle. Both general surgeons on call, Anesthesia, and Gyn remained tied up for hours upstairs, with earlier ER patients. They had left strict instructions to not be called under any circumstances unless it was absolutely necessary.

Going on ambulance diversion definitely helped. But there were still drive ups and walk ins, some really in bad shape, and the ever-sullen waiting room had puffed up again (Lori, who had already worked fifteen hours was told to rest in the comfortable chair in the Director's office, the hope against hope being that a solid nap might get her back into action.) Worse still, the ER had long ago run out of available open rooms, and Marcus and Dean had to examine and treat patients who were lying on stretchers in the hallway or sitting on chairs in the corners.

The staff just kept shaking their heads.

Dean rubbed an ache in his jaw and ran his tongue over his teeth, sub-consciously tracing the cracked grooves in them, born from years and years of jaw clenching. Once upon a time, he lived for this. He remembered a recurrent fantasy – he'd be working a supremely busy ER on the brink, just like this, and he would then heroically pull it back, all to thunderous applause. Happy now, he chided himself, sipping out of a Styrofoam cup. You got your wish.

Marcus looked at Dean's ice water with contempt.

"You do know that drinking that unleaded shit is like fucking with ten rubbers. I mean, what's the point? You are just a little tired, that's all."

With that, Allen grabbed a bullet shaped black can, lifted it up in the style of a toast, and drank it down. He reached into the desk drawer, removed another can, cracked it open, again gestured grandly, and drank most of *that* one down. He winked at Miller, as if he were immune to this heinous night, and belched through his nose.

After guzzling the rest of that can, he reached for another and offered it to Dean.

"Come on, man, it'll put hair on your chest. You wanna survive or not?"

"Since when did you start drinking that crap?"

"Maybe a year. Tastes better than coffee, I'll tell you that. Try some."

"No way, just thinking about it turns my fingers white," Dean finally said, forcing an air of casual bravado. He looked up from his computer, shaking his head. "Marcus, we need help."

"No way, I've been in way tougher jams than this," Marcus said sternly, effectively shutting him down. "Last chance, you want some?"

"Nah, I have enough trouble with my BP already. Anyway, what you got going?"

"Same old, same old, except that the charmer in Room Two is starting to crash, and she'll need a tube soon - *and* from the looks of it, she's got the airway from Hell," Allen stated, disgustedly. "Obese, small mouth and no neck. Even her tongue is fat. How can you get that fat when you can't fit food in your mouth? You know, I'd call Anesthesia for help on this one, but they're all tied up. So, you drink your spring water, and I'll stick to the good stuff. I need it."

Allen lifted the can to his mouth and guzzled. Finally, he set it down and smiled at Dean, implying that he was the better man.

"Ahh, all that delicious rocket fuel sloshing around in my belly, it's gotten me through many a rough night," he confessed. He suddenly did a double take.

"Whoooh, did I just get a rush!"

Dean did not share Allen's optimism. He was looking at an ER on a cliff's edge – one or two more train wrecks might literally push it off. Even North Central's ER nurses, who held near special forces status in the building, were walking around mumbling "this is fucking crazy" to each other. Everyone was working at breakneck speed, hoping that they were doing the right things.

Miller's comfort zone was anything under ten patients – now he was juggling sixteen, several of them serious to critical. Three didn't speak English, and (of course) the blue translation phone wasn't working. Another two had the same last name and the same symptoms. Only by obsessively checking his list was it possible to survive without making a mistake. He kept repeating to himself, over and over, *no one dies, no one dies, no one dies...*

After all was said and done, it was just another night in paradise.

Thirty minutes later, Dean's persistent lobbying/nagging paid off, and Allen (very) reluctantly agreed to call the day docs, and instruct them per protocol to come in. One had to employ this nuclear option with extreme caution; partly out of consideration for your unsuspecting colleagues, who would have to clean up your mess, all the while acquiring one of their own; partly to avoid admitting you couldn't handle the night; partly because this would undoubtedly by scrutinized by Admin, Payroll and Risk Management; and finally, because of the Revenge Factor – what goes around comes around. Both of them would likely be getting a 4am call in the not-so-distant future.

It turned out that their reinforcements were quite a bit down the road. Backup number one's phone went straight to voicemail, and he would no doubt invoke some tech-related excuse (bullshit but unassailable – a whole new species of alibis was born with the death of landlines). The second doc was pissed and passive-aggressively invoked the sixty-minute clause.

"Doctor Dean, Tannenbaum for you on line three," Katrina suddenly called out.

"Tannenbaum, already?"

"Yes, as in the big cheese. He specifically asked for you."

Damn it, Miller thought, picking up the phone, *what now*. He pressed the button.

"Dean, this is Phil Tannenbaum, how are you tonight?"

"Pretty good…busy," Miller answered, a bit cagily. "But we're giving as good as we're getting."

"So I've heard. How's Marcus? Is he getting tired?"

"Holding his own, I think he's okay," Dean said; after a pause he decided to fess up, figuring the chief would find out if he had not already done so. "We called for backup, and we went on ambulance diversion."

"I know, it happens. How are you, Dean?"

"Hanging in there. It's been a long night."

"Dean, do you need me to come in?"

Miller shifted awkwardly in his seat. It was common knowledge that Phillip Tannenbaum was a renowned but fading superstar in the emergency medicine world. He was one of the pioneers who helped put the field on the map, and every ER doc alive owed a good part of the respect and salary he or she now received to this man's contributions and innovations. But he clearly was past his prime, at least clinically, and his would not be constructive assistance. If anything, everyone would turn into self-conscious and even more exhausted basket cases.

"No, no we'll be okay sir, but, if need be, I'll let you know."

"I've spoken to the house supervisor, and I agree with your calling the hospitalists down. Give them the easy stuff: lacerations, URIs, UTIs. We also have residents on the way. And if you'd like me to come in, let me know. On another note, Dean, you certainly work long hours, probably more than you should, if you'll pardon my intrusion. Think you'll need a break soon? Remember, you're in this for the long haul."

"I'm fine, I'm fine, but I appreciate your concern."

"Well, do your best, Dean, and please let me know if I can do anything. I'm here for you, and I have your back. Oh, and you'll probably get those reinforcements sooner than you think.

"Remember, Dean, keep the sick ones alive, and to hell with everyone else - *let-them-sign-their-asses-out-AMA* if they want to! Hang in there and hold the place together."

The phone went dead. He stared at it in amazement – Tannenbaum was always so appropriate, he thought, when did he become so human.

He rubbed the ache in his jaw with mild success, grimly realizing how glad he was for having called in the cavalry. Allen, however, had gotten positively grumpy, although it was clear he was in even worse shape. Already running more patients than Dean, he sometimes seemed to be staggering from one room to the other. The older doctor wasn't pushing sixty anymore, he was pulling it. He was also out of shape and had a (closet) smoker's cough that got wheezy whenever he was tired, and his breath now sounded like sandpaper.

Still, though he looked a little rough, Dean wasn't worried much – the older man maybe wasn't what he once was, but he still was a monster force to be reckoned with. I'd still let him take care of me, Dean mused (the highest compliment an ER doctor can ever bestow), a little sad at the inevitability of relentless decline.

The doctors crisscrossed the department incessantly, working at top speed. They briefly reunited again, pretty much by coincidence, in the Doctors' Area, ostensibly to chart and check labs, but mostly to take a quick break. Dean sipped on his ice water, Marcus his rocket fuel. The older man was the first to rise. Dean was becoming a little concerned about him – twice in the last twenty minutes nurses had walked up to him to quietly ask him to clarify or override an order that did not add up. He wasn't one to throw stones, though; nurses had kept him out of jail more times than he cared to admit.

"Remember, the good stuff is here in this drawer. I'd steer away from the black cans, you're pretty much a rookie on this, but the green or orange ones are cool."

There was some commotion in the Code Room, and both men turned toward it reflexively. Then the sound faded away.

"Marcus, Tannenbaum called. He wanted to see how things were, and asked if he should come in."

"The big boy himself, huh…he called? Must've woke up for a diaper change."

Dean regarded Tannenbaum as something of a father figure, someone who'd given him his start, and who protected him when he was beset with personal issues. Also, Tannenbaum was only a few years older than Marcus, so the 'diaper' remark struck him as shallow and petulant. It was well known that he'd never forgiven the chief for bypassing him to choose Charley Meyers as assistant director. But rather than snap back and risk a potentially disastrous confrontation at this time, Dean chose to ignore it. And deep down, he did like Marcus, so he gave him a pass.

"Yeah, I said thanks, but told him we'd survive."

"Damn straight. You know, he's not one to talk. We go way back, worked side by side for years, and I can tell you now *he* was the poster child for burnout. He had a really bad case once, some kid. Phil was never the same after that, it damn near destroyed him. He left for academia and never looked back. Now, you didn't hear that from me. Anyway, before tubing this train wreck, maybe I'll get an easy one out of the way…"

Without realizing it, Dean closed his eyes, and instantly found himself in a carnival in a dark forest in the dead of night. He was standing in front of a merry-go-round spinning round and round to loud music. His patients were on it, glowing, staring at him with frozen smiles, their faces bloody. He heard himself moaning in fear…

"Hey, man, you okay?" Allen asked, prodding his shoulder.

"Yeah, yeah, I'm fine. Sorry, I didn't mean to…"

Allen looked at the triage note, shook his head and smiled.

"Ah, back to the real world: 'three weeks of pelvic pain with a discharge,'" he pronounced. "And tonight she decides to come in – by ambulance, no less. Now, one might ask, 'so *why now, why did you pick this fucking night to torture me?*' But then again, why mess with one of life's great mysteries. You know, wasn't there once a hit song about this, called 'I've been sticking my love in all the wrong places'?"

"It might have been, 'looking for love in all the wrong places,'" Dean absently replied. He was staring at the tracking board, trying to will it to just disappear. "It's funny, one of my earlier patients was a pole dancer, who wore confederate panties during her performances. She presented with a friction burn and wanted her visit billed as workman's comp. Weird shit tonight, huh?'"

Allen looked at him and shrugged. For the tiniest of moments he paused, frowning; then whatever it was, passed.

"What do you expect," he mumbled. "It's just one of those nights."

Dean wiped his clammy forehead with the back of his hand, hoping again that the ache in his jaw was indeed from clenching, and not his heart starting to play a knock-knock joke. He took a deep breath and stood up. His knees crackled in protest.

"Let's go, guys," he said, gently smacking them. "Break's over, let's move."

Allen took another sip out of his black can, noted Dean's disapproval and scowled back at his yawning colleague.

"Listen, Miller, at least what I'm doing is fucking legal, and you know *damn* well what I mean! As addictions go, caffeine ain't a bad one. And yeah, for the record, I have considered getting out, just like you, but it'll be at a place and time of my own choosing…"

Just then Margo strode into their station. She looked aggressively at Allen.

"Doc, it's time. Two's starting to crash."

Allen stared at her, a slightly flustered look about him.

"Chop, chop, let's go!" the veteran nurse snapped, clapping her hands. "NOW!"

Allen started at the noise. He exhaled wearily, and weakly extended the chart in his hand to Dean.

"Yeah, time to go. Lead the way, Margo. Dean, you mind taking this case? I'm not dumping, I hope you know that. It's just that the lady in Two is starting to, you know…"

"Marcus, come on," she hissed. "Fuck it, I'm calling a code!"

She picked up a wall phone, pressed a button and spoke rapidly.

"Marcus, you need me? Dean asked nervously. "I'll run it, or I can just be your second pair of hands."

The older man stopped, turned and shook his head (he seemed so tired) – *no, but thanks.* Then he disappeared into the Code Room, Margo right behind him.

"Go do your thing, man," Dean muttered, his voice starting to trail off. "And if you need backup…"

With Allen and Margo now gone, he reluctantly headed to the far side of the department, so remote from the main action that it was nicknamed Siberia. He did manage a quick look, over his shoulder, and saw a small procession of respiratory, lab and radiology techs trudge into Room Two, followed by the night supervisor. Yeah, the hospital's getting its money's worth out of the Code Team tonight, he thought.

Miller walked down the hallway, stopping along the way to check on some of his patients, as would a general inspecting his troops. He'd look them over, say a few words, make changes on his to-do lists, and move on. More than once he looked over his shoulders, in the direction of the Code Room.

Minutes later he was sitting on a stool in Sixteen, hurriedly prepping for a pelvic exam, a young woman laying before him in the lithotomy position, a female nurse-chaperone preparing an array of swabs to be used. Suddenly there was shouting down the hallway. The door opened a crack.

"Doctor Miller – sorry, ma'am – there's a code in Room Two," a tech tensely whispered, poking her head a couple of inches inside, only her nose visible. "They're asking where you are."

"Tell them I'll be there soon," he replied.

"Sounds bad," the chaperone said quietly, watching the door close gently.

"Yeah, tricyclic ODs don't do so well," Miller whispered, mostly to himself.

"I'm almost done. Ma'am, you're going to feel my hand, and then I'll insert…"

The door burst open. Margo glared at him, her eyes boiling.

"Where's your fucking pager?" she snarled. She looked down at the patient, who cowered on the stretcher. "I'm very sorry, ma'am. Doctor Miller, you're needed stat in Room Two! Stat!"

"Okay, okay, I'm coming. Sorry, I forgot to take it with me."

Margo disappeared, slamming the door. Dean stood up and looked down at his patient.

"I'm so sorry, ma'am, I have to go," he told her. "I'll be back."

"You'll be back, you'll be BACK?" she yelled. "Fuck you, asshole, I've been waiting in this room two hours, and I'm outta here! Somebody get my clothes!"

Dean resisted the urge to do or say something he'd regret but instead exited quietly. He speed-walked towards the code room (he'd quit running to these things years ago), rubbing his jaw, trying to psyche himself up. He knew that if Marcus Allen was having trouble, then so would he, or any doc on the planet for that matter. And from the way Marcus had been describing the patient's airway, he knew he too might once again wind up in a world of trouble. Of his ten worst cases of all time, which now included tonight's facial burn, most involved airways. You can dodge and you can dance, but airway problems are the one emergency you can't fake. You either get the tube in or you don't. Dean remembered them all to the nth degree - all the others he usually forgot by shift's end.

In moments he was touching the glass door of Room Two. He took a deep breath and entered.

Everyone stopped and stared at him, their eyes wide and fearful – was it his imagination? His hand subtly moved to the front of his pants to check on his…and then he gasped violently, almost inhaling his gum.

Before him lay the spreadeagled body of Marcus Allen, surrounded by frantic personnel doing chest compressions, CPR in full swing. The fallen doctor's skin glowed a waxy yellow blue.

Miller had seen this at least a thousand times – he knew instantly that his colleague was dying, if not already dead. The patient on the stretcher, now successfully intubated in what may have been Allen's final act as a doctor, was being bagged by a respiratory tech. The woman was now stable; her savior lay on the ground next to her stretcher. An aide knelt beside him, squeezing air via an ambu bag into his lungs. The room's mood was somber – no chit chat, no pizza talk, no nothing – everyone knew what was going on.

"Let me in!" Miller snapped, pushing through until he stood over Marcus. He dropped to his knees, wincing at the pain when they contacted the floor with a direct thud. He looked at the small crowd inside the room – most were just gaping.

"Unless you have business here, you need to be outside!" Miller snapped. "And where's the damn stretcher? You really want to run this on the floor? Somebody give me vitals!"

"He has no fucking vitals," Margo answered tensely, staring at the small procession of gawkers filing out. "And there's no fucking stretcher!"

"We sent out to Rehab for one," a tech said smugly. "I've said it a million times, we always need an extra gurney just in case…"

"Then I'll tube him right here!" Miller snarled. He lay on his abdomen, propped up by his elbows, his face near Allen's. "Give me a Mac and a size eight…"

There were suddenly excited words exchanged among the people looking at the monitor. Dean looked up and stared in disbelief.

"V-fib!" Margo shouted.

"Shock, three hundred sixty joules," Miller instantly commanded, his eyes fixed on the deadly rhythm on the screen.

At that moment Allen explosively vomited, splattering Dean's face. The half-blinded ER doctor belatedly sprang back and staggered to his feet, bellowing with disbelief. He looked at the stunned group, all the while wiping his eyes with a grimy sleeve.

"Shit! Someone get me a towel, someone suction his mouth, and let's give him…wait, don't we even have an IV line? God, I do not believe this is happening! Margo, is that thing charged up yet?! Fuck. Fuck!"

The defibrillator started to whine, which became higher and higher pitched; it then emanated a low beep. Margo reached for the button.

"Stand clear, everyone!" Dean ordered, wiping his face with a wet towel an aide had just given him. He looked at Margo and nodded. She nodded back and pushed the button.

Allen's body shot up nearly two inches off the floor, as if defying gravity. They all stared at him in silence, then at the monitor, then again at the fallen doctor. The few seconds seemed like hours. Then a touch of pink started to blush his cheeks.

"Sinus rhythm," Margo said quietly. She and Dean exchanged a knowing glance, both aware of how lucky they were. She looked at the screen again. "Systolic is 90."

Marcus moaned, then coughed loudly. He opened his eyes and weakly looked at Dean, terrified, confused. There was blood at the corners of his mouth. A tech passed a just-completed EKG to Dean, who had by then sat back on the ground to stay by his comrade. Margo looked at it over his shoulder. They looked at each other and shook their heads. The charge nurse headed for the wall phone.

Two aides raced in with a stretcher, and on the count of three, Marcus Allen was hoisted aboard, while Dean got up and washed his face at the nearby sink. Then he returned to his friend and gently took his hand. As if by magic there were now two large-bore IVs in each of the patient's arms.

Dean felt someone tap his shoulder. A nurse whispered into his ear.

"I've got to take this call, Marcus," he said. "Be right back."

The doctor nodded his understanding.

*

Fifteen or so minutes later the room was empty except for Dean, Margo, the cath team's advance unit, and the patient. All unnecessary personnel had been shooed back to their posts.

"You did really good, Marcus, you should be okay," Dean said gently. He could hear the sound of the hospitalists outside doing their best in this (for them) foreboding environment. ER help was now on the way. Lori Madlong had also awakened and was back at her post.

"Dean, will somebody tell me please what's going on?" Allen whispered hoarsely. His color was pale, and his skin was cool, but this was still a far cry better than his earlier death pall.

"Too early to say," Dean replied softly, studying the cardiogram for what seemed like the millionth time. "But, Marcus, there's a chance you may have just retired."

He turned the tracing around and held it in front of Marcus. The older man stared for a few seconds, smiled thinly and shook his head.

"Anterior wall with tombstones, how 'bout that? When I do it, I do it right."

"Just relax, Marcus, the cath team is here."

"I guess we all wind up as ER patients one day, don't we?"

"I guess we do," Dean agreed, half to himself.

"Did you call my wife?"

"Beth? Yes, she's on the way. She's a little upset and your daughter's driving her in. You've got a great family, by the way."

"They're the best; I don't really deserve them."

Allen dabbed his eyes with his patient gown and looked at the ceiling.

"It's been a good career. Lots of fun, lots of good deeds, not one lawsuit, not even a complaint. I put my kids through college, paid off the houses...Dean, you think I'm gonna' die?"

"Nah, you have been in tougher jams, Marcus, relax. Save your strength."

"Relax? Those are tombstones in the precordial leads. My heart has fucking tombstones...you gave me heparin, right?"

"Heparin, aspirin, oxygen, hey, we're even using clean needles. Marcus, just take it easy, the ER is stabilizing, and the good guys are on the way."

"Dean, I always tried my best – I never had your brilliance, Lars Anderson's decency or Finkel's toughness, but deep down I know I was okay," the older man whispered.

He seemed to be in pain and was struggling for the energy to speak.

"My work may not have been the most elegant, but I swear I held my own."

"Marcus, you were the greatest – you *are* the greatest. Listen, I'll be right back – I've got to check on a couple of patients. You're in good hands."

"Go do your thing, my brother. I'll guard the stretcher."

They both laughed, Marcus coughing just a bit.

Shortly thereafter, the cath team began bundling up their patient, speaking briefly and respectfully to him. Marcus waved his goodbye as Dean waited outside, psyching himself up for yet another code, now about two minutes out. Miller paused, re-entered the room, and gave his friend a hug.

He walked into the adjacent code room. The Code team, already in place, nodded to him.

"It's showtime, everybody," was all he said.

And as the gates of Hell opened one more time Dean saw, out of the corner of his eye, Phil Tannenbaum entering Allen's room.

**

Dean sat slumped in the Nurses' Station, staring ahead numbly. It was a little before six. All of his and Marcus' cases had been swept up by the cavalry, which included Finkel, Meyers, Aaron Freeman, and the sixty-minute clause invoker, who wouldn't look him in the eye. All that fresh blood made it look easy, and they were kicking ass. Lori Madlong, slightly beat up after eighteen brutal hours but still on her feet, was relieved and sent home, and given this upcoming night shift off with full pay. The entire night crew, from nurses to housekeeping, also received the same when they departed at seven.

Allen had gone straight from the cath lab into pre-op. Phil Tannenbaum was at his side until they wheeled him into the OR. At this point, no one knew anything.

And to think Marcus had no medical problems, Miller quietly said to himself. Well, I guess he did have at least one, he just didn't know about it. He found this last thought uproarious, and he broke into a soft burst of laughter. The moral of this story, he told himself, is that ER is a young man's game after all. That could have been me and, in a few years, it *will* be me. I ain't no spring chicken. Do I really want to work like this until it's *my* turn to crap out on some ER floor? On the other hand, when all is said and done, maybe I'm a whiny, self-pitying bastard who just needs some sleep and a decent pair of balls. And wait…am I now the third or fourth oldest doc in the group…

He shivered slightly and realized that the back of his throat was becoming raw. The pain in his jaw most likely was a submandibular node. I'll accept that, he thought gratefully, thinking of Marcus. I'm just coming down with the plague – at least it ain't the ticker. He started laughing to himself again.

Dean realized he was still holding a chart – he'd forgotten to hand it over, so he figured he'd keep it for himself. For a moment, just a moment, he decided to close his eyes.

***

A few minutes later he awoke. Just as he summoned the strength to stand up and go back into action, he fielded a call from Tannenbaum. The chief heartily congratulated him on averting disaster on 'this most challenging of nights, one that will make us take a good, hard look at our staffing paradigm.' That was code for 'thanks for limiting the body count to those who were going to die anyway.' He too was relieved of his next shift, this upcoming night, with full pay. Add that to his already scheduled next five days (and nights) off, he now had quite the sexy run of nearly a full week's vacation coming up.

They briefly discussed the new changes in the hospital's holding policy…then there was a pause in the conversation. Dean's radar self-activated at the end of the small talk, and he cautiously waited.

"You're a valued member of this department," Tannenbaum finally said. "I've noticed that lately you seem to be straining a bit. Dean, what can we do to get you re-engaged?"

"Has there been a problem?" Dean asked nervously. *Is it that apparent*, he asked himself.

"Not at all, Dean, your work is outstanding. It's my job to keep it that way. Can I help? I'll be honest, I've seen burnout in my time and have had some myself. I'm just trying to prevent that from ruining your career. It almost ruined mine. Tell me how to keep you in this department for the long haul."

"Could I trial thirty-two hours a week, maybe just for a while?" Dean heard himself blurting out. "I'm, I'm averaging close to fifty now. I do know there are staffing problems."

"I'm aware of that, Dean. Believe it or not, I've got a reasonable handle on the comings and goings of the department. And staffing issues aren't even counted as problems anymore; they're a way of life. You live with it.

"So, your request is granted, we'll trial it. You're a key member of the team, and you're too good to lose. My sense is that you'll love the change, it'll revitalize you. However, should you ever want more hours, that would also be acceptable. And it goes without saying that you'll retain your perks and seniority."

Did he really say that? Did I really ask for that?

"I appreciate this very much," he heard himself saying, trying not to let his voice crack. "Thank you."

"It's me who should be thanking you. Call the office when it opens. We're going to re-invent your schedule, and I'm certain it will be to your liking. Do we have a deal?"

"Yes, we have a deal."

"By the way, I can assure you that you will never again get the runaround when calling for backup. Get some rest, Dean. Take care."

Dean Miller took a deep breath and started to open his final chart. So, what do we have here, he asked himself, not looking at the patient's chief complaint. He tried to guess what the case might be. He ran through the litany of usual suspects - chest pain, shortness of breath, sick child, stroke, abdominal pain, fall down the stairs, overdose, splinter in the eye – all bread-and-butter cases.

Who am I kidding, he realized, laying the chart back on the desk. The Marcus Allen episode and this last code had broken the bank. The air seemed thick, and it hurt to breathe. He couldn't shake the smell of burning flesh or Allen's vomit from his hands and arms; they seemed to defy soap and water. His new scrub shirt was already mottled with chilly sweat. Worst of all, an unpleasant mental paralysis had taken hold. Tonight's game was over, he had nothing left.

"Hey, you look like shit," his colleague and good friend Bob Finkel said, sitting down beside him. The man seemed to ripple with energy. "I hear tell you guys had quite the party. So, what do you have to say for yourself?"

"Don't know, guess it was just one of those nights."

"And you came, you saw, and you kicked ass. Come on, brother, give me that case, sign that puppy over. And don't touch anything else. Get outta here while the going's good and just take it easy. You know, the chief and Admin seemed really impressed you held the place together. The downside of all this is that for the rest of this month, probably longer, I've been tapped to work for Marcus – *shit, double shit and triple shit*, I can't believe I'm back on nights."

Dean rubbed his face and said nothing. He clumsily suppressed a yawn. He gratefully handed the chart over and stood up. Finkel looked at it, snorted with mild boredom, and stood up as well.

"So, was that the worst shift of your life?"

"Yeah, I think it was."

"Then congrats are in order," Finkel said with a smile.

"What the hell for?"

"For showing the world how it's done, for surviving, and getting it out of the way. Everyone has the worst shift of their life, you just had yours. And you do know that in a matter of months, maybe weeks, you'll be reminiscing about this shift and having a few 'holy crap, did I really do that?' laughs. All war stories get sweeter with time, don't they?"

"Yup, it's how we get by," Dean softly agreed, starting to feel hope seep back into him – this night was over. "But for the record, I'm really glad you guys showed up."

"And here's another one for the record, Dean. Thanks for getting Marcus back, and for running that circus. You fucking rescued the place. Good work."

Finkel pretended not to notice his friend's eyes tear up and reached into a desk drawer to pull out a long black can.

"And right now, our goal is to get you back to the hotel in one piece…here, my personal stash. It would wake the dead…well, okay, maybe not the greatest choice of words…"

Dean took it and held it in his hand, rolling it over and over. His fatigue was actually painful, and this apparent antidote did seem to beckon, so tempting, so easy. Then he thought of his fallen comrade, smiled, and shook his head.

"I think you've done enough damage tonight," he told it, the look on his face bordering on contempt. "Get thee to Hell."

Finkel studied his friend with perplexed bemusement. Dean smiled and returned the energy drink.

"Thanks for the offer, Bob, but I think I'll just grab a back room, hop on a stretcher, and catch a few zzz's. Oh, and do not send anybody in to intubate me - I heard about your stunt with the med student. And then I'm heading home. Watch the store."

*****

Part Six
I Know Something You Don't Know

It should have been the easiest shift of all time. Tonight was slow even by Wednesday standards, and late June is the slowest time of the year, especially when the weather is beautiful. The lowest census night falling on the lowest census time of year – it doesn't get any better than that. String three of these days together and you're guaranteed to have an irate administrator coming down to visit, demanding the ER director explain just what the hell is going on.

The only glitch was that Charley Meyers, assistant director, along with Lori Madlong, the mid-level, were the only clinicians working. And, damn, they were both tired.

At least Lori came by her exhaustion honestly. She'd already stayed on three hours past her shift's end to help out Rob Keller, aka The Beast, victim of a gas station hot dog (do people really eat those?). Meyers had no excuse – he had screwed up plain and simple and started the night with only three hours of sleep under his belt.

Keller showed up on time and, as usual, had plunged into work. But he soon began to fizzle out. (Actually, a sick Beast could still hold his own against most other ER docs.) In the beginning, neither staff nor patients suspected a thing. Then he seemed to visibly wilt, and he asked for a hep lock so that he could get IV hydration between cases. Myers approved it, and the nurses started bolusing him a few hundred ccs in a side room, usually after two or three rounds of vomiting and diarrhea. Soon, however, all pretense was dropped and they let the bedraggled doctor trudge from patient to patient with his IV pole in tow, saline running wide open. It seemed to work, sort of, though Meyers was wracked with self-doubts about whether he should have allowed this at all – it was wrong on several levels.

But, of course, Keller only got worse, and after liter number three Charley called the fight – his diaphoretic colleague was found in a side room, curled into the fetal position and running a pulse of 110. Over his protestations – ER doctors are notoriously averse to admitting they are human – Keller was duly registered, labbed up and parked in a monitored room. Within minutes, he was in a deep, peaceful sleep, snoring loudly. Myers looked at him and his indestructible youth with envy. He and Lori then assumed Keller's cases. So much for an easy night; their workloads had just increased by a third.

It did take them some effort, at least in the beginning, to plow through Keller's charts. His workups seemed jumbled and convoluted, featuring shotgunning at its "best" – ordering everything so you don't miss anything This is an all-too-common maneuver many ER docs employ when they are: A. tired; B. stalling for time/shift change C. do not know what the fuck is going on and are hoping an answer falls in their lap; or D. as in Keller's case, feel like they are fixing to die.

And then he made the command decision to send Lori home.

Meyers would later explain that Lori – whose work had been exemplary - was already fifteen hours into her shift - and she still had to go home, get what sleep she could manage, and get her kids ready for school – last week before summer vacation. Anyway, there were less than three hours to go – that's a typical waiting time on the weekend. Worst case scenario, he'd call a hospitalist down to help with the minor stuff, or just force Keller to wake up – he'd been sleeping for a few hours and his pulse was normalizing. Or, he could choose both options.

Though he was brutally tired Meyers wasn't worried in the least. Over the years he'd worked solo hundreds of times, and Lori, who was something of a dynamo herself, really had helped clean the place up.

The way things stood now, all systems were go - the department was pretty empty and there was just one patient waiting to be seen.

Just to be safe, Myers began defensive measures to conserve energy. He batched charts by room locale to conserve steps. He asked the staff to get him his suture and LP kits, as well as basic supplies – he often did that himself – and asked that they keep his coffee cup filled. He sat whenever possible – he usually stood for most of his shift, a holdover habit from his paper charting days, when there was no real reason to sit. All this may sound like peanuts in the scheme of things, but it can't hurt and, hey, if you have enough peanuts, you just might be able to feed an elephant.

He was extremely pissed at himself. Despite knowing that *any* graveyard shift at North Central required 110% - you were always only two or three cases away from contemplating suicide - he had *not* gone straight home after yesterday's night's shift, instead going to the gym for a quick workout. But it quickly morphed into a full workout - he rationalized that he was already there, it was Wednesday, and he'd be teamed up with Lori and the Beast. The gamble seemed reasonable on the surface, but it overlooked one minor detail - he broke the eleventh and twelfth commandments for all emergency docs over fifty – the eleventh being, *thou shalt never begin a night shift already tired; and the twelfth, thou shall never break the eleventh commandment.*

He'd returned to his apartment from the gym fairly wired, and he couldn't get to sleep, despite good faith efforts with plenty of food, wine and white noise. A dog down the street, barking erratically, only made things worse. And of course, the more he fretted about insomnia, the more he rolled around in bed with it. A vicious cycle was thus born.

There really weren't any good options now – there wasn't really anybody to call. Going crazy and calling in the cavalry with just two hours to go didn't seem worth it, and chief Tannenbaum's long-standing offer to come in at any time and help out was recognized by one and all to be little more than a noble gesture.

I'll be okay, Charley reassured himself, I've been in tougher jams than this.

He had been but knew this was a self-inflicted wound. Don't even begin to throw a pity party for yourself, he thought angrily, no one forced you into the gym. And now everyone is watching. On the bright side, it's only two and a half hours. So, drink your coffee and get your butt in gear. Forget wait times, satisfaction scores and all that crap, just focus on the sickest of patients. And if the other patients don't like it, let 'em sign out. Just concentrate on the sickest, he told himself. You've had a bunch of nights like this - one more won't make a difference.

Meyers had a love/hate relationship with twelve-hour shifts. They really were starting to kick his ass. The supreme virtue of the twelve (the only one, actually) is that you can work less of them. In his younger days he'd batch eight or nine together and then go off on a beautiful vacation. Uh, not anymore. There were eight-hour slots to be had, but that entailed working six extra days a month so he could get his hours – and that was a non-starter. Now he had to baby himself both the day before a twelve and the day after it. He figured when his cup got full enough, he'd do something about it – he was getting there, but not yet.

So here he was, self-caffeinating, pacing himself and frowning at the life and death decisions he was routinely making, and trying not to look the way he felt.

His present situation reignited smoldering infernos of anxiety – his personal demon made an appearance, grinning at him through the flames and screaming that he was a charlatan, a fraudster who'd lucked out and cherry picked his way throughout his career. Well, tonight just might be the time of your unmasking, it laughed. And you deserve it!

Everyone screws up royally at least once every ten or fifteen years, Meyers calculated, and I've only done that once that I'm aware of. So I figure I'm overdue for at least another one or two more biggies coming my way. Then the younger guys will have plenty of ammo to push me out. What was I thinking when I hit the gym?

Meyers gulped down his fourth coffee, garnered his remaining strength and energy, and plunged into action. He didn't let himself daydream or overthink a problem – he let his instinct and gestalt, forged by 150,000-plus patient encounters, take over. He just plowed ahead, neither looking up nor back. For over one hour he was a rocket, earning the admiration of those working with him. But then the rocket slowed down a bit, and its trajectory blunted. He caught himself on two minor mistakes; no harm, no foul… but he knew it was time to rest.

He now allowed himself to look around, and he smiled with self-approval – he'd done it, he'd made a decent dent. He smiled even more when he studied the tracking board – since he began his counteroffensive, only one new patient had registered. One of the great miracles in emergency medicine, the closing of the new-patient spigot, had just taken place. And just in time - Charley felt himself starting to sweat, though he felt cold. He'd just seen two patients from a minor MVA; he wrote 'em up, wrote some orders, and then opted for a strategic retreat. It was time to take a break before something slipped through the cracks – and his unsuspecting patients deserved better than a weary doc managing their lives, powered solely by momentum.

He ran through his list of patients yet one more time – a stable OD, a stable psyche, two COPDers, a belly pain, the two MVAs (one easy, one so-so), a migraine going home; and a ninety-year-old post-fall, getting her car wash CT, reasonably stable (ninety-year-olds are often reasonably stable, as long as you don't look too hard). Keller was doing great and going home at shift's change. Nothing major going on. Most important, there was but one person in the waiting room. It was now or never. He made his move.

He walked into the nurses' station. Two of the nurses, Skye and Samantha, were huddled in front of their computers entering data, their eyes squinted, their cheeks bulging with popcorn. Nearby, Katrina, the unit secretary was looking at photos on her cellphone. They looked up at him and smiled. Overseeing everything was the charge nurse, Margo, queen of nights, standing outside the code room, leaning against a wall. She gave him a little wave.

"I'll be in the doctors' office for a little while, doing some research," he announced.

"And what are you researching this time?" Katrina asked, not looking up from her phone.

"You know I can't tell you, it's classified," he replied, turning and walking away. "If you need me, call me. Margo, how are all the problem children doing?"

"Mostly sleeping," she replied. "Enjoy your research, baby."

Dutifully, Myers shuffled down an ER corridor, made a few lefts and rights, and wound up in front of a door with a small sign that read, "ER Director." Digging into a pocket he quickly found his key, and let himself in.

The small room was quite sparse, featuring little more than a desk cluttered with papers, some as old as ten years; a desktop phone and dusty lamp; and a beautifully plush easy chair. It was common knowledge that over ninety-five per cent of all visitors entered this room just to sleep in this chair, which didn't even face the desk. Myers preferred not to think about the other five per cent, opting to forever think of this soft throne as virginal, used only for beautiful naps.

Leaving the lights off, the doctor used butt memory and backed himself into the chair, nestled in and leaned it all the way back. He stared contentedly into the blackness, but as his eyes adjusted, he recognized the faintest blue glow emanating from a desk-level socket, welcoming him. Meyers knew it well, and waved hello, two old friends meeting up once again. He flashed back to a dream he had years ago about it. In the dream it wasn't a light, but a portal, a pathway to another dimension, to another place, to... somewhere.

He never got to find out how it ended, or what it meant, if anything, or what awaited on the other side, if anything. But he always remembered this silly little dream, at least when he was here, and it always made him smile.

When he closed his eyes, he knew sleep would come easily – he had already forgotten his patients, and his brain was swimming with fuzzy illusions. He had the sensation of speeding or sliding somewhere. His last wakeful thoughts were, *let's do it, let's go for a ride!*

*

Myers woke with a start, still coated in a thin layer of cool sweat. Someone was knocking at the door. Immediately he shot up, rubbed his hair down, tucked in his shirt and checked his zipper. Looking up, he noticed the blue light was blinking. That's odd, he thought, as he turned on the overhead light and opened the door.

"Sorry to bother you, doc," the tech said. "CT results are back."

"No, no, you didn't bother me, I was doing paperwork. Be right out."

**

As the doctor walked down the hallway, he tried to remember his dreams but couldn't. Instead, he brought his patient roster into focus, but he just couldn't shake a very strange feeling. He was shaking, and ...he could swear there was something in the air.

Reaching the main ER, he looked around and contentedly grunted – not much had changed, and there was just that one new name still on the tracking board. Margo was by the desk and she waved hello.

Katrina was talking about yesterday's suicide, a young man known to several of the staff. He'd hanged himself, and was clearly dead on arrival, but they spent over thirty minutes trying for a Hail Mary save. Myers was touched by the case, not because it was exciting – it wasn't – but because of the palpable sadness surrounding it. The code room was flooded with family and friends, one punching the wall, others lying on the floor, sobbing. Several staff were visibly shaken. Usually Myers, like most ER people with any degree of longevity, could stoically sail through even the most evil of situations. But last night got to him; that bugged him, and he didn't know why.

Perhaps that's why he wound up in the gym hours later, feeling the need to purge himself of uninvited feelings percolating deep inside. As he'd gotten older, he'd become more sensitive, and he still wasn't sure if it was a good or bad thing.

"I used to babysit him, he had it so rough," Katrina was saying dully. "You live a little, do a little bit of this and that. Then you die and probably go back to where you started from. Why? Doc, you're smart. What's the frigging purpose of all this?"

"I'm not sure we're really supposed to find out," he heard himself saying softly. "Lots of smart people, way smarter than me, have looked into this and most have come up empty. Some people think they've got it figured out and we call them philosophers. Some of them even add rules and regulations and call it religion."

"Yeah, I guess," Katrina said, mulling over his words. "Although, what Jimmy did last night was way too violent, don't you think? I mean, if you really have to do it…"

"Yeah, there's got to be a better way," Paul the tech added. "Doc, what's the best way to kill yourself - carbon monoxide, fentanyl, potassium?"

"You know, I don't really worry about that stuff. At my age, Paul, I just have to run for the bus."

"I like that," Margo said with a laugh.

"I still can't believe he's dead," Katrina continued, her voice breaking. "He was so adorable, and so many bad things out of his control happened. Now, he's gone."

Myers sat down, straddling a chair, and smiled at the secretary.

"Maybe he's not gone, ever think of that? You know, when we die - and we all die, 150,000 people every day - what's the first thing people say when they look in the casket - *'that's not him'* or*, 'he's somewhere else.'* They're actually right on. Jimmy *is* somewhere else. His life ended, as will ours, but his soul journeyed home, as will ours. Remember, we're all a mixture of just two things: a collection of moving parts, standard issue to all living things; *and* a soul, which is a gift. The parts will break down and rot away - we really are nothing more than refrigerators with souls. Remember, doctors don't cure, they just stall - but you can't kill a soul, and it goes home when our worldly tour wraps up. That's what Jimmy's did, and that's what ours will do. Granted, he had a crappy time here, and he chose a crappy way to finish up, but in the vast scheme of things it's probably okay. He made it back, he's present and accounted for. Simple as that."

"You mean, he's with God?" Katrina asked, wiping a tear away. "Like, right now You mean that?"

"Of course," the doctor answered matter of factly.

"Doc, but you're like a scientist," Paul said. "You really believe in God?"

"More and more with each new discovery," Meyers said. "Einstein may have discovered relativity and all that time and space stuff, but he didn't *invent* them. He just figured out what God created. The astonishing laws of the universe are too precise and perfect to be random coincidence. Most scientists believe every law of science - gravity, relativity, astrophysics - was present at the moment of creation. What scientists really do is figure them out. The *Creator,* or God if you prefer, must really get a kick out of that."

"So what's God like?" Paul asked. "This I gotta hear."

"I've never met God, though I highly doubt you'll find an old white guy with a beard. But don't worry. I'm sure you'll approve when you get re-acquainted at your journey's end."

"So, what does God want from us, do you have any idea?" Skye asked.

"He wants you to take good care of your soul; it's on loan to your mortal body. Do that, and everything falls into place."

"That's it?" Samantha said. "Caring for your soul?"

"Absolutely – and it's not that hard."

"Oh yeah, how?" Sam asked. "Okay, give us a hint."

"Well, for starters, create more energy in your lifetime than you use up. Finish with a surplus, and you've made the universe, well, a better place."

"Sounds complicated," Katrina said uneasily. "Any specifics?"

"Thou shalt be kind, thou shalt be gentle, and thou shalt be generous, how's that for starters. Of course, that's easier said than done in this crazy world. Just look around the ER."

"Touché," Margo said with a smile. "Well, aren't you the philosopher king tonight."

She looked at Myers, her face reflecting a mix of affection, curiosity and suspicion. She turned to her crew.

"Anyone else in the mood for some enlightenment?" she asked them. "Ask away. Going once, going twice…"

"Sure, why not, you're probably the only one who doesn't know the story," Skye said quietly. "Doctor M, I met this guy on vacation. We fell in love and became inseparable, like we were one person. It turns out he lives less than an hour away, and he swore he'd call me. It's been over ten days, and nothing. Comments?"

"Well, Skye, many a tale *has* been written in red wine. I'm sorry. Enough said?"

There was a moment's pause as the group digested the words.

"Well then, okay," the nurse finally said. "Thank you, I guess. Actually, that was my hunch."

There was another pause.

"My son and his wife hate each other; they fight every day," Steve the X-ray tech blurted out. "They have shitty jobs, shitty lives and no money. Every day is a crisis. We help out when we can, we even let them live in our finished basement. They'd be out on the street if it wasn't for us. And you know what? Not only are they ungrateful, it's like they resent us; for what I really don't know.

"So, they're stuck with us, and each other – if they went separate ways, they'd be homeless and penniless within weeks," Steve continued, his pent-up emotions boiling to the surface. "And, of course, now they're having a kid, to 'patch things up,' who, of course, *we'll* have to support. What's your take?"

"They sound more like cellmates than soulmates, it happens all the time," Myers said gently. "And they may just find their own way, but I assume things will get worse before they get better. And yes, cellmates have been known to have sex."

The doctor looked around.

"Okay, my turn," a third nurse finally said. "A good friend of mine has a daughter who calls maybe once a month, and visits only on Christmas, and sometimes on the Fourth. It all began after she got married and moved out, not that far away. Her parents gave her everything, dance lessons, music lessons, summer camp, the best cars, clothes and gadgets, you name it. Now she doesn't have any time for family, it's like they embarrass her. We had to find out from a friend that she's pregnant! And there was never even a big fight. What gives?"

"Maryanne, when you raise a princess, don't be surprised when she grows into a queen. It certainly sounds like she has and, frankly, that's how some queens are. I'd hang in there. Things could improve but, realistically, I'd modify my expectations if I were...your friend."

Myers stared at each of them, then looked away. The room was silent – even the now-alert OD in Room Two seemed to ponder his words. The staff shifted uncomfortably where they stood or sat. Myers just sat there, trembling slightly, staring ahead, still mildly diaphoretic.

Margo was the first to speak.

"Doc, do some more research," she said gently, reaching for his hand. "We'll order some stuff and call you with the results. There's nothing serious out here. Come on."

"What about the patients," Myers whispered. "What about the CT and X-Ray results, and did Respiratory give that third treatment?"

"X-rays normal, breathing treatment given," Katrina replied. "And the surgeon, Doctor Cooper, was upstairs when the belly CT came back. Margo called her, and she'll see the patient upstairs came and write orders - hot appendix. She also put the ninety-year-old on Observation."

Margo tugged on his hand. The doctor offered no resistance.

"Well, just for a couple more minutes, I guess."

Margo led him gently through the quiet hallway towards his room. When they reached the door, he stopped and looked down. Very gently she reached for his face and turned him towards her.

"Okay, my turn," she finally said, looking deeply into his eyes. "We've worked together for all these years. We know each other cold, we finish each other's sentences, we laugh at the same jokes. And I know you like the way I look. Why haven't you ever asked me out?"

The doctor's eyes seemed to flash, and there was an unusually long three second pause.

"Because every relationship I've ever had blew up," Charley blurted out, his voice strained. "Girlfriends, my ex-wife, even my ex-jobs, everything ended badly, sometimes very much so. Margo, I cherish our times together, but I get so scared. The group offered to switch me to days last year – you know, seniority stuff - but I love my nights with you and said no. I feel pain when I'm not with you. I couldn't live with that and would rather go on having just this little piece. This is my fault, my problem. And Margo, it makes me so sad, it makes me feel so pathetic, to think that you will always be the great 'what if' of my life. I swear it makes me want to cry – I just don't know how."

The doctor shivered and broke eye contact.

Margo looked down, biting her lower lip and softly shaking her head. Then she looked at him, smiling thinly.

"Get some rest, Charley."

They faced each other for what seemed like forever. Charley Myers turned to leave, but not before Margo saw, or could have sworn she saw, a teardrop fall onto the doctor's shoe.

She opened the door and Myers slowly walked in. The door closed behind him.

Myers turned off the light, looked through the darkness and nodded at the welcoming blue glow, now calm and steady. Within two minutes he was in a deep sleep.

***

…and twenty minutes later he awoke on his own. He strode into the ER and took complete control, sending every patient home, including one slightly bedraggled Dr. Keller. A serious trauma came in, shortly before his reinforcements were due, and Myers expertly intubated the patient, put in the central line, and inserted bilateral chest tubes – *and* got the patient back. In the world of emergency medicine that is the epitome of coolness – you can't get any better.

Minutes later the day people arrived to a messy, bloody ER that was not only under control, it was pretty much caught up (actually, a messy, bloody ER under control *and* caught up is major). The triumphant night staff started high fiving each other as the incoming staff looked on with envy at having missed the fun. And after taking report, as if launched from starting blocks, the day nurses and two fresh docs blasted into their shift, racing from room to room to see the new patients.

Charley Myers gathered his belongings. He started fantasizing about a steak, a baked potato, a glass of wine and…something else.

"Great work, Dr. Meyers," one of the night people called out. There was playful applause.

The doctor set his bag down, pointed with both hands to all his friends, and slightly but perceptibly bowed in their direction. Then he turned to leave.

"See you tonight, everyone," he called over his shoulder, approaching the ambulance bay exit doors, now bathed in the early glow of dawn. "You were all fantastic."

Suddenly a voice called out after him. Myers stopped and turned.

"Hey, Doc, you gonna tell us any more secrets of life?" Katrina practically shouted.

"Secrets of…excuse me?" Myers asked, more than a little befuddled.

"Heaven? Eternity? Like, do we hear Part Two tonight?"

Myers stared at them blankly, and then beseechingly at Margo, who had walked him out. She touched his arm and licked her lips. They were alone in the warm, enveloping morning air. She was taking deep breaths.

"What are they…?" he asked her.

"I'll tell you later. Have yourself a great sleep, but more important…how would you like it if I came over for a bit and tucked you in?"

Margo recognized the flash in his eyes because she was expecting it. She calmly waited and witnessed another monumentally long three second inner struggle. And then Charley gratefully nodded. He seemed to be at peace.

"Yes, yes. See you soon, please?" he asked hopefully, his face bathed in the morning sunshine.

It was Margo's turn to nod. She too was glowing in the golden light.

"Charley, do you have any idea how great this is going to be? See you soon."

*****

Part Seven
La Noche De Amor

It was a pretty decent night, and now the end was sort of coming into view. The two docs were just hanging out in the doctor's station, enjoying the world around them. It was their home away from home and, though they'd never say it out loud, they (usually) loved being here.

"Look!" Bob Finkel exclaimed. "Something's afoot, I tell you. And I happen to know exactly what's wrong with that foot."

"Do tell," Dean Miller mumbled, yessing him. He was hunched over his sudoku puzzle, furiously scribbling numbers, going in for the kill.

Finkel was intently observing the women huddled by the unit secretary's desk. Something indeed was going on. Dean Miller, the second doc working the graveyard shift, paid them no mind, his eyes wildly zigzagging (puzzles are great for people with ADD). Suddenly, he grimaced with outrage, having crashed and burned three answers from victory. Holding his pen as one would wield a weapon, he started hissing "die!" over and over, and scratched lines of hatred all over the page. Only then did he finally gaze up at the women, and his grumpiness abated a tad. Harry, a medical student assigned to Finkel for the evening, sat within earshot, secretly craned his head and stared forward, always maintaining a respectful silence.

"Yup, something's up," Miller finally whispered. "Hey, that's Skye crying, what gives? She's been acting weird all night. But more importantly, how are you going to break the fast later when you're paroled?"

"Me, I'm hitting Tony Baloney's, you know, that twenty-four hour deli, and load up on fried chicken and all the *accoutrements*, no ifs, ands, or what the fucks," Finkel answered quietly. "Washed down of course with a touch of gin; well maybe more than a touch."

"I'll accept that; gin is like sex…a touch is never enough," Dean replied approvingly. "Ain't that right, Harry?"

He turned to Harry, who vigorously nodded, blushing at having been caught listening in, but secretly delighted to have been allowed into the conversation.

Dean studied the women. "So, uh, what gives with Skye?"

"Ahh, that's what I'm getting at, brother," Finkel said quietly, carefully looking left and right. "Her *fiancé*, who she's been dating for nearly three whole months, nearly kicked last night. Full arrest. They brought him to Southside. Keller was moonlighting there, again – he loves that place, what are they doing there, giving him blowjobs or something? Anyway, he took the case and got him back. Told me it looked like Brugada, like that dude had the classic EKG."

"Brugada Syndrome?" Harry asked. "It's a heart condition, right?"

"Actually, real-life cases are the best way to learn, so read up on this and present it to us tomorrow," Dean ordered, going back to his puzzle book, searching for just the right one. "Yeah, you can't fight Brugada; you're fine one minute and then *bam*, you're dead. Harry, remember, by tomorrow you are to be a jedi master on this."

The med student vigorously nodded his head.

"Anyway, poor, poor Skye," Dean solemnly continued. "And, of course, poor, poor *fiancé*...so, blowjobs at Southside, you say. You know, we could try that here – what a great morale booster."

"Harry, go see someone," Finkel commanded, not taking his eyes off the women.

"Yes, sir," the student immediately replied. He walked to the chart rack, picked up the next to be seen, and scrunched his face.

Again, Finkel looked around furtively. "And get this. It happened while they were having sex. *And* it turns out that this guy's brother had the same thing happen to him about a year ago, while *he* was having sex - I mean hopefully not with Skye, that's banjo territory, don't you think? But it sure as hell sounds familial, and that's Brugada until proven otherwise. Unless of course it was Skye's fault, because I've got a hunch she just may give soul sucking, brain melting, you-are-meeting-your-maker orgasms."

There was, well, a pregnant pause after that one.

"Wow, I don't even know what to say," Dean finally said. "Now I sort of hope he dies so I can date her."

Harry intruded upon their reverie. He was cradling a chart.

"Rectal pain. Am I okay to see that? You know, I'll just take the history."

"Absolutely, and you can even stick your finger up there. Harry, maybe this is your moment to shine, sort of. Ace this one and you'll soon be flying solo. Take that nursing student with you. They also have to present cases, but ask Margo first. She's the night boss. And then, go do your thing. Read the notes, take a good history, poke his butt, and report back to me. And do me a favor, touch his belly also, okay?"

Harry nodded gratefully, turned and respectfully approached the cluster of women. He whispered something to the night charge. Margo looked at Finkel, who nodded; then she shrugged and gave her approval. She pointed at her student and said, "Rose, go with Harry on this case. Then you can write a care plan on the patient." Rose and Harry looked at each other and smiled. Soon they were marching into battle, walking close to each other. They headed for Room Seventeen to see the rectal pain.

Miller had been in deep thought. It was now time for a pronouncement.

"Soul sucking orgasms, is that a fact," he finally said, his eyes riveted on the group, Skye in particular. "Well done, Bob, you have forever changed my perspective about that nurse, and way for the better…ever notice how much extra credit we give to hot women? What's wrong with us?"

Suddenly, Miller's eyes were torn away at the sight of Finkel pulling something out of his backpack.

"And of course, thoughts and prayers for the *fiancé,* thoughts and prayers always," Dean said, his eyes riveted on a huge bag of potato chips.

"Wow, so touching. Did you really mean that, Dean, or did you just say it?"

"Nah, I just said it. Need any help with those chips?"

"Your compassion is duly noted. It'll go into the minutes that you were both shocked and appalled by what transpired last night. Hold out a cup."

"You know, Bob, considering Skye's superpower, I am going to posit my new theory, that after all is said and done, when it comes to great sex, there are many, many worse ways to leave this planet. Maybe it wasn't Brugada after all."

Finkel nodded and pulled the bag open. He first pulled out two large, perfectly shaped salt and vinegar kettle chips and gave one to his partner. Each raised the chip a bit, toasted Skye and all womankind, clinked their respective chips, popped 'em in their mouths, and started making crunching sounds. Then Finkel filled both their cups.

"You're right, there are many worse ways, and I sure as hell see a Nobel in your future," he mumbled. "Wait, did you really say 'posit'?"

"I most certainly did," Dean answered, again holding out his Styrofoam cup, which his friend promptly refilled. "Sounds like the *fiancé* didn't know if he was coming or going. So, then what happened?"

Finkel chewed a little faster, and when the crunching grew less audible, he resumed his tale.

"Anyway, Keller gets him right back – you know, I just might let that puppy take care of *me* – and he makes some quick calls. Now, either there was a full eclipse of Jupiter, or the stars were in perfect alignment, but the OR *and* Anesthesia teams were in-house, on-call Cardio was rounding in the unit, and the *fiancé* hadn't eaten anything for the past six hours, except maybe Skye of course. Keller didn't even have to float a pacer. He just slapped on the pads and shot him upstairs. How lucky can you get?"

"Some guys have it made in the shade," Dean agreed. "Me, I usually get some drunk on thinners who just ate, and they tell me, 'float a pacer and babysit him 'til the morning.' Funny how in the middle of the night I become the world's greatest cardiologist, not to mention the world's greatest plastic surgeon if I'm calling with a facial lac. And may I confess that floating a temporary pacer is my absolute least favorite procedure. There are just too many steps. What thinkest thou?"

"I personally hate central lines these days, which is a tragedy because they used to be my favorites," Finkel confided, not taking his eyes off the women. "Now they make you dress up like a fucking cosmonaut before you start, and then they cover the patient from head to toe in white paper like he's being embalmed.

"But staying on subject, Skye looks - medically speaking of course - quite edible tonight, wouldn't you say? Did you know that great oral sex has been shown to burn up at least two Weight Watcher points? This has been thoroughly documented, so I've been told."

"I'll remember that for my next diet."

Miller looked up at Skye, his mind now consumed with non-medical thoughts. He crunched on some chips, let out a deep breath, then stood and walked along the string of desks and counters to the wooden patients-to-be-seen bin. He reached inside and grabbed the next metal clipboard (actually, in the age of EMR, clipboard charts aren't really charts, but rather serve three functions: part glorified notepad; part making one *look* like a real doctor; and part self-defense, to shield against physical attacks.) He opened it to look at the presenting complaint and did a double take.

"God, shoot me now," he said, slowly walking away. "And this one's married to a board member, no less. I'm a dead man. Anyway Bob, thanks for the health food, it may have been my last meal."

"Don't mention it," Finkel called out. "And whatever you got in that chart, I don't want to know. I can only say, 'better you than me.'"

Meanwhile, Samantha and Karlita, night nurses, Margo, the night charge, Carol, a loaner nurse from the ICU (she loved the craziness of the ER and always volunteered to work there), and Monique the Radiology tech, gathered around to comfort the sobbing Skye, a new grad. Katrina the secretary, who remained seated, looked on sympathetically. She'd just taken a phone call from the Southside ICU and passed it to the bereaved nurse – per the Southside intensivist, her *fiancé* was stable but still critical.

"Hang in there, hon," Margo said soothingly. "It's okay."

"No, it's not okay," she said softly, burying her face in her hands.

"He's so young, no?" Monique asked. "What happen?"

"He fainted, that's what I thought. Then I realized he wasn't breathing. I killed him. I killed him."

"You keeled him, Skye, why would you do that?" Monique asked. "I thought you liked him."

This is re...ridiculous," Samantha said, exasperated. She was watching Miller reluctantly peruse the new chart in his hands, turn it over, make the slightest movements to sneak it back in the rack, then slump with resignation and firmly clutch it, his inner conflict forever a secret only to her. Sighing, he looked around, saw her and headed in her direction. She acknowledged him, but put up both hands and shook her head, *no*. Apparently not in any particular rush, he stopped, yawned, and leaned against the counter. Slightly uneasy at how easily he'd caved, Samantha turned back to the sobbing nurse.

"Come on, what really happened, Skye?" she asked, a touch briskly. "I gotta go with Dean to see a patient."

"Well, we'd just come back from a camping trip; we'd just walked through the door," Skye said haltingly. "It was a great trip, rustic all the way, no electricity, no bathrooms. But it was great. We even saw the northern lights. Anyway, Clark felt a little frisky... I guess a lot frisky. The minute we got home he led me straight to bed. I begged him to give me a few minutes to get presentable, but he was, well, horny as hell and we went at it."

"I can see that being romantic," Karlita mused. "Go on."

"And suddenly Clark went down...*there*. I told him, 'oh, no no no!'"

"Even more romantic," Carol said approvingly. "Only I'd be saying, 'yes yes yes.'"

"But I wasn't ready," Skye protested. "We'd just gotten back from camping. Those icy streams, it was just too cold...we never even took off all our clothes. I mean, we did manage to mess around a little in the sleeping bag, but it took, well, creativity."

Sam and Karlita exchanged smiles. Margo looked on with mild amusement.

"I swear, I'd figured I could take a lightning quick shower when we got back. He just didn't give me a chance. Then during, you know...he stopped moving."

"And you think that caused his cardiac arrest?" Karlita dryly asked. "Doesn't that seem a bit far-fetched?"

"I killed my fiancé," Skye whispered, burying her face in her hands. "And my last words to him, the last words he heard in his life, were 'no no no.'"

"You know, lots of guys really like that," Samantha said with a tinge of annoyance. "That 'washed and ready to eat' stuff may work for lettuce, but otherwise it's bullshit. We are women, and we come in different sizes, shapes and tastes. Get over it."

"Did you just say, 'get over it'?" Karlita mused, to no one in particular.

"We're taught to be embarrassed from day one," Sam continued, stifling a chuckle. "Since the beginning of time we've been told to come off like some flower, or a lemon, or even a test tube. Well, fuck that...no pun intended. Skye, you have nothing to feel bad about...except of course Clark. He *will* make, it, right?"

"I hope so," the nurse answered tearfully. "They put in a pacemaker."

"Don't theenk bad theengs about yourself," Monique advised kindly.

"She's right, you know, shit happens - we see it for a living," Karlita added.

"My boyfriend sort of enjoys that, you know," Carol said. "He won't admit it, but I can tell he likes it when I shower in the AM and we mess around later, if you know what I mean. Don't you worry, Skye, he'll be back on top, or bottom, in no time at all."

"I don't know," Skye said. "I mean, I just didn't have time …"

"With all due respect, I think you're making way too much of this," Margo said maternally. "Come on, honey, what timeframe are we really talking about…you know, not washing? This is a first for me, by the way. I can't believe we're having this conversation."

"Men do not die like that," Monique agreed. "So how long was eet, really?"

"Yeah, this is getting silly," Karlita said. "Skye, lay your cards on the table. What was the timeframe of you not taking care of business?"

"Don't yell at me, let me think," Skye answered nervously. "Remember, it was really cold."

She looked up, counting with her fingers. Katrina busied herself shuffling papers, feigning distraction. The other women stared at her blankly, holding their collective breath. You could hear the drumroll.

"Like, nine days? Definitely not more than ten."

There was a real pause.

"Really?" Karlita asked, a frown on her face. She and Sam started doing mental calculations. Carol and Katrina looked at each other helplessly. Margo touched her lips and looked at the floor, shaking her head. Monique intensely stared at the young nurse, scowling.

There was another pause.

"Assasseen!" Monique suddenly hissed, pointing her index finger in Skye's face.

Skye began to wail. A few people looked in their direction. At that moment, Dean who was getting tired of waiting, walked up. He looked at them and tilted his head toward Room Six, the unofficial gyn room (Six is for chicks, the motto went).

"I need a chaperone…uh, Skye, you okay?"

"She heard some bad news about a friend," Margo said. "Carol and I were just going to take her to the break room. Sam, go with Dean."

As Carol and Margo led the snuffling nurse away, they passed Dean, who turned to them, his nose in the air.

"Hey, one of you smells really good."

With that Skye began to wail again. Karlita looked at him sternly and shook her head *no.*

"What, what did I say?" Dean stammered. "Hey, it sure beats Room 13, it's like a fucking elephant burial ground in there."

Skye began to wail even louder. Karlita, Carol and Margo all snarled at him and led the young woman away.

Dean turned to Sam, totally perplexed.

"Exactly what did I do wrong?"

"Don't worry about it, Doc," she said. "Let's go."

Monique turned to leave.

"I go to the chapel now; light a candle. Poor leetle Clark."

Dean turned back to Sam.

"The world has officially gone crazy. There's a gotta be a full moon out there, right?"

The nurse shrugged, and they started walking down the hall. The ER was fairly decent now, with not one unstable patient in it. Actually, there had been several up until an hour ago – they'd either been sent upstairs to the floors and ICU, or downstairs to the morgue. (Sanders the pathologist liked to call his turf the ECU, as in eternal care unit.) Everyone seemed relaxed and enjoying the moment, except maybe Skye, all the while knowing that at any time, this blissful paradise could pop like a bubble with the next radio call, in line with the unspoken mantra that defined their world: *'eat, drink and be merry, for in ten minutes you're gettin' your ass kicked!'*

They walked past Bob Finkel, who yanked up one of his pant legs and raised a thumb.

"Care if I hitch a ride with you? I'm headed to Eight, some minor shit. Dean, what you got?"

"Well, it would seem that this lady has a wayward tampon, if you get the gist."

"Ahh, a rescue mission," Finkel mused. "I see someone had an 'oops' moment."

"Don't give him any ideas," Sam warned.

"What in the world could you possibly be talking about," Finkel said, his face a mask of hurt. "We're talking medical stuff here."

The trio ambled down the hall calmly and resolutely, nodding to various staff along the way. A nice night for a walk. On the way, Harry and Rosie scurried up to them. They formed a small group in the hallway.

"Doctor Finkel, Doctor Finkel," Harry said, carefully approaching. "Can I present? We may have something."

"Outstanding," Finkel calmly said. He made note of Rosie hanging on to Harry's every word. "What's your patient have to say for himself?"

"He's a man of few words. EMS told us most of the stuff."

"Sounds like one of ours. Proceed."

"The patient is a fifty-two-year-old man who was in his usual state of health when he…"

"Harry, how's the guy's belly? Is he dying?"

"A little tender in the lower parts, and we don't think he's dying."

"Okay, that's a start. Abnormal vitals?"

"No. He was in his usual state of health…"

"Nice case. And you're certain, he's not going to die."

"I don't think so. He was in his usual state of health, when he started having rectal pain…"

"Great presentation, so how do you want to work it up?"

"Uh, rule out intestinal obstruction."

"Okay, now you're talking, so go back and finish up the physical," Finkel said, looking at the wall clock. Dean and Samantha looked on impassively. "And order some tests. Okay?"

"Like an x-ray, blood work and some urine?"

"Knock yourself out, but if you see any H's or L's next to any of the results, you come get me right away. And don't forget to stick his butt."

The students scurried away, their shoulders practically touching..

"The Master Teacher has spoken," Samantha intoned. "You should write a textbook, you know that?"

That moment, Paul walked up to Finkel. The tech was laughing.

"Doc, the guy in Bed Sixteen wanted another blanket. He said if I did it for him, he'd give me a blowjob. He said the exact same thing to Earnest, the security guard."

Dave from X-Ray overheard this. He stopped his portable machine.

"You know, I did a chest on that guy, and he wanted to give me a blowjob."

"Wait a minute, wait one goddamned minute," Finkel said sharply. "He offered all three of you a blowjob? I was with him for like fifteen minutes and he didn't say shit to me!"

"Fink, I've never seen you jealous," Dean said. "This is a whole new side of you."

The scorned ER doc turned petulantly to the little group. He slapped his chest twice.

"Hey, what's the matter with me! What's wrong with me, I want to know!"

"Oh, not to worry, Doctor Finkel," Sam said maternally. "I'm sure if you ask him nicely enough, he'll give you a blowjob, too."

"Ah, screw it, I'm breaking up with that guy. You can't trust anyone these days."

"Breaking up is hard to do," Samantha tenderly added. "But don't worry, doctor, drunken ER patients who give blowjobs are like streetcars – one gets away from you, another will come along in ten minutes."

"It wouldn't have lasted, anyway, he wasn't my type" Finkel replied, scratching an ear. "I'll just have to work on my lines."

The small group then resumed their stroll. Samantha contacted Karlita via the pager and instructed her to keep a close eye on the students.

Dean cradled the chart under his arm and began to reminisce.

"You know, I went on this blind date about two years' back. Man, was she hot. Wanna know something? Turns out that the day before, this hot looking date of mine was a hot looking ER patient of mine, in our very own Room Six. She had the cap of some body spray stuck way up there. Said she fell on it…"

"Fell on it?" Sam snorted. "Really. How very Olympian."

"It was a strange case. The cap seemed to have self-rotated, and it covered her cervix. I could not pull it out. Call it magnetism, call it suction, call it breech, but that baby did not want to come out. It took me a half hour before I could fish…"

"Here we are," Samantha said brusquely. "In we go. And Dean, you behave, or I may have to kill you."

"Of course. We will keep this professional, treat it matter of factly, and preserve her dignity. Okay? Oh, and for the record, Bob, that was the worst date of my life. We could barely look each other in the eye. I didn't bring it up, and she didn't bring it up, but it was always there, like a three-hundred-pound gorilla standing in the room."

Finkel started to say, "More like a three-hundred-pound body spray …"

"Get in, doctor," Samantha said curtly, opening the door and pushing Dean inside. She shot Finkel the look of death. "You're such a bad influence on him."

"Me, what'd I say now?" the tall doctor started to protest, as the door closed behind them. They heard his muffled voice mutter something like, "You know, it's a good thing you're all so cute, because you're all so crazy."

*

Sitting upright on the stretcher before them was a dignified, stylishly dressed woman, arms at her side, calmy looking at them. Dean resolved to keep this interchange brief, soothing and matter of fact.

"Good evening, ma'am, I'm Doctor Dean Miller and this is my chaperone and your nurse, Samantha."

"And good evening to both of you, I'm Lorraine Henley."

Dean was impressed by her bearing, and said to himself, if only they were all like this, dignified, fashionable and elegant. He gestured at the stool in front of her stretcher.

Samantha intently stared at the chart.

"May I please sit?" the doctor asked.

"Doctor Miller, this patient…"

"One minute, Samantha. May I?" Lorraine nodded her head graciously and with her hand beckoned the doctor to sit down.

"Thank you," Dean said, easing himself onto the stool, pleasantly relieved at the positive tone of the encounter. "Now, may I speak plainly?"

"I wish you would."

Dean felt Samantha tapping his shoulder. *Later*, he said to her silently, *later*.

"Well then. Lorraine, the chart says you have…"

Samantha tapped his shoulder harder. Dean ignored it. She squeezed it; he winced and glared at her and shook his head, visibly annoyed at the attempted interruption. *What's with you?*

At that, the nurse shrugged and smiled broadly at him. The doctor squinted at her, then turned back to the patient, slightly off rhythm now.

"Mrs. Henley, it seems you have, well, a trapped tampon in your vagina. Not a problem. You'd be surprised at how often I see this. We'll take care of it. So, how long has it…"

"I beg your pardon?" the woman said, a bewildered look about her. "What did you just say?"

"I'm glad you're taking this well. Obviously, it must be a little awkward. Certainly, the last thing you expected today was to be in the ER getting a pelvic exam. Don't worry, this will be fully chaperoned…"

"A pelvic exam?" she asked tensely.

Dean flustered a bit – he thought he'd asked a proper question in a proper manner, and to him this was not a proper response. God, I hope I didn't embarrass her. He looked up at Samantha, who was rubbing her face with both hands, and then cautiously turned back to his patient. Be gentle, he thought, she's distraught. (And her husband's on the board.)

"Lorraine, I know you don't want to be here, but here you are. It's not your fault. The chart says you have something in your vagina, or at least the sensation of that…you know, something that just won't come out. Like I said, we'll find it, get it out, and get you home, pronto. That's my promise to you. Just give me a brief history of what…"

"How dare you!" she snapped. "Have you gone mad?"

"Please give us a second," Miller asked, his voice now starting to quaver. He stood and approached Samantha, who looked at him dryly. She made a slight motion with her hands as if shoveling something. He nodded his head towards the door.

"We'll be right back," he told her.

"Take your fucking time! Are you really a doctor?"

Ignoring her last remark, Dean shuffled out, snowplowing Samantha in front of him. The two stood in the hallway looking at each other. Dean was starting to perspire. Sam looked at him with a catlike smile.

"I think she's shy," he nervously whispered. "Is there a more genteel way to refer to a tampon?"

"I personally call them sponge monsters or coochie Q-tips," Sam whispered back. "In Europe, they call them vampire mice. Now, if you will listen to me…"

She's worthless, Dean thought, turning to go back into the room. Samantha followed, again shaking her head. He approached his patient, whose arms were now folded tightly across her chest. Her look could only be described as molten. A little voice inside Dean's head whispered, in an annoying singsong manner *husband on the board, husband on the board, husband...*

The doctor wiped cool sweat off his forehead. He started to feel a bit queasy.

"Would you let me examine you?" he helplessly stammered.

"I wouldn't let you examine my dog," she snapped, gathering her things. "Don't you touch me."

Stay calm, stay calm. Why did you pick up this fucking chart?

"Then why, why may I ask, did you even come to the ER? Remember, *you* came to *me*...or is it, ohhh, maybe somewhere else? I can even get it out of there. Don't worry, we won't judge."

"I came here for a rash, you fucking asshole!"

"Where?" Dean weakly asked, helplessly looking at her crotch.

"Not there, you pervert, on my arm! Can't you read? No wonder they hate you ER people!"

"Uh, Doctor Miller, we need to have a word. Now!"

"Not now Samantha, this woman needs...Mrs. Henley, did you say *arm?*"

"It's in the chart, bozo. Or is illiteracy another one of your board certifications?"

"I do not appreciate your tone. It says here, plain as...."

Dean looked down at the chart, and his eyeballs bulged. He saw at once that he was holding the clipboard upside down – the errant sponge monster was in Room Nine, not Six.

"Well, uhh, I guess that wraps up Part One of the exam," he mumbled. "I'll be back to complete the case."

"You do know that by tomorrow you'll be sitting on a park bench feeding pigeons."

Dean quickstepped backwards, until he bumped into the wall, and then sidled out until he reached the door, which he cracked open and slithered out of. Samantha was right behind him, and carefully closed it. The doctor was breathing heavily. He was leaning his face against the wall.

"I can't believe I did that," he hoarsely whispered, his hands raised on the wall, his nails noisily leaving visible marks as they dragged downwards. "What do you think, Sam? How did I come across?"

"Well, in keeping with the spirit of things, 'douchebag' sort of comes to mind. By the way, I think your 'professional'' shtick needs a little work…"

"God, what have I done?" the doctor agonized.

"And yesterday you glued that trooper's eyelids shut," Sam continued. "You know, he had to be restrained from shooting you. What gives?"

"He moved. Just as I dropped the glue onto his eyebrow, he moved! But if you must know, I felt like shit yesterday and I feel like shit today. I'd like to think of all this as a big coincidence but still, I'll be glad as hell when this shift is over."

"I bet you will. What next, Doctor Dignity?"

"Let's see the lady in Nine."

As they trudged off toward Nine, Paul the tech called Sam on her beeper. She held it up to his ear so they could both listen.

"Bed Six hit her call button. She wants me to tell you she doesn't want Dean for a doctor anymore," he said. "I told Doctor Finkel. He says he'll see her. She called Doctor Dean a few names, by the way."

"Whatever," Dean said gloomily. He traced lines going up and down, then horizontally, across his scrub shirt. "Which way do you think the stripes run in prison?"

"You'll find out soon enough, my dear," Samantha replied. "I'll say one thing, when you screw up, you do it right. Now let's party in Nine."

**

Harry and Rose stood before their patient, a well-groomed man with a waxed handlebar mustache. He lay on the stretcher, arms crossed over his chest, upper body angled at thirty degrees. He stared at the ceiling, not saying anything or making any eye contact. The two students looked at each other.

"We've been here five minutes, Rosie, and he isn't talking; he's not even moving," Harry whispered. "I know he's breathing, but what do you think we should do?"

"Why don't you just start the exam?" someone asked behind them.

They whirled to see Karlita. She nodded her greetings and led them into the hall.

'He's not much of a talker," she said. "His wife came home and found him rocking on the floor, holding his abdomen. Funny thing is, his vitals are stable, his CBC is back already and that's normal too, so there's probably no infection. I touched his belly, it's only a little tender. The whole thing is weird."

"What did his wife say?"

"Oh, she's a bitch, wouldn't even talk to EMS. She called me a…well, guess. And after they put him on the ER stretcher, she told us to fuck off and said 'this ain't his first rodeo,' whatever that means. She stormed out of the room, and I hear she then registered *herself* as a patient. Dean's seeing her now."

"What do we do?" Harry asked her.

"Gotta do something, we can't sit on him all night," the nurse replied. "You never know when it'll get crazy in here again."

"So I better start, huh?" the student asked her.

"Do your thing."

Harry re-entered the room and positioned himself, as taught, on the patient's right side. He had often seen Doctor Finkel do full body exams and had committed them to memory. He could feel Rosie's eyes on him.

"Hello," he said. "Sir, I'm going to give you a more comprehensive examination."

The man with the handlebar mustache stared silently at the ceiling, not moving.

"Sir, you're going to be feeling my hand. Can you say anything to help us? It may be a lot easier for all of us if you tell us what happened."

The man with the handlebar mustache turned his head and looked at them.

"I fell," was all he said.

***

Thirty minutes later Dean slumped in his chair at the doctors' station. Samantha stood nearby looking at him, still shaking her head. The patient in Room Nine had turned out to be a bit difficult – rude, and demanding pain meds from the outset, claiming allergies to all non-steroidals and Tylenol. Dean was a little beat up by now and in no mood for confrontations. Though he usually accepted jousting with seekers as just part of the game (sometimes it was even amusing) this time he gave her something just to keep her quiet. That riled Sam a bit, but she grudgingly went along. The tampon-ectomy was a success, and here they were, back in safe territory…just for a moment.

Finkel walked over and sat down.

"I just saw your girlfriend in Six. She was asking for lots of stuff about you - name, rank, dick size, she wanted all the goods on you. You sure know how to impress them ladies. And now, I humbly ask this in payback – can you talk to the patient's wife in Eight before I kill her? Her eighty-year-old husband trips in the kitchen, lands hard, and now has a humeral neck fracture. No big deal, right? But still, it's his dominant arm. He's confused on a good day and doesn't even remember what happened. Nice guy, though. He's slinged and swathed, and instructed to follow with Ortho, not that they'll do anything different.

"The problem is his wife. They've been married for a thousand years and have at least a thousand kids, all of whom of course have gone home. She seems with it, and it should be a breeze taking care of him. I mean, she already does almost everything for him, but for the life of me she doesn't understand the discharge instructions, it's like I'm speaking Martian."

"Yeah, sure," Miller answered. "But I'll tell you up front that my communication skills are somewhat lacking tonight. Sam, care to keep me out of jail again? Let's see how badly I can mess *this* one up."

A minute later they were in Eight, facing off against the Lombardos. The wife, a short sturdy woman, stood next to her seated, much larger husband – their heads seemed to be at the same level in this setting. The woman eyed Dean warily, which Dean found disconcerting (what the hell did Finkel say to her, he wondered, exchanging a curious glance with Samantha.) Mr. Lombardo, on the other hand, was all smiles, occasionally chuckling to himself.

"It's always something," he said pleasantly. His nose was dripping, which his wife, without looking, expertly wiped clean with a paper towel.

"Heh, heh, heh," he chuckled.

"All right, then," Dean said pleasantly, diagnosing an empty train station. He turned to the woman.

"Good evening, my name is Doctor Miller, and this is Samantha. Doctor Finkel has asked us to further expand on the discharge instructions. Let me start by asking if you have any questions."

"Yeah, what's going on? No one told us shit."

"Well, all right then. Your husband broke his arm, and the treatment for this injury is a sling. Really not much more than that. You follow up with the bone specialist in a few days. In the meantime, you just have to take special care of him because he won't be one hundred percent. We'll write this all down for you. Easy enough?"

"I have no idea what you just said," Mrs. Lombardo said. "The other doctor said his arm's not broken, it's fractured. Don't you know anything?"

"'Fractured' and 'broken' are the same thing, ma'am."

"Whatever."

Her husband chuckled.

"Just take care of him," the doctor finally said, trying hard not to engage.

"So what does that mean?"

"It should be easy. Wash him, toilet him, help dress him…"

"I won't do that."

"Won't do what?"

"Take care of him."

"It's no big deal. You've been married for many years; you've raised a big family together. This should be a piece of cake. Mr. Lombardo, tell her it should be easy."

"It's always something," was the cheerful response.

Dean briefly fought off the urge to tape the man's mouth shut, not to mention his wife's, but thought the better of it.

"Are you going to do it?"

"Nope," she said.

"What the hell do you mean by 'nope'?" Dean asked hotly, only to feel the wrath of Samantha in the form of a well-placed pinch. He was starting to feel anxious about his other patients, not to mention his self-inflicted disaster in Bed Six. Be nice, he commanded himself, and get the hell out of here. And yes, the world has officially gone crazy.

"No. I won't do it."

"Why not?" Dean asked wearily. "Please tell me."

"I cannot clean him *down there*. I, I won't."

"Heh, heh, heh."

"Why, please?" Dean heard himself asking. "I mean, if I may say so, you've been married for a great many years, had a big family. Clearly you know the, well, what's involved. Mr. Lombardo, tell your wife it's okay."

"It's always something."

"Doctor, I didn't even touch it when it was alive!" Mrs. Lombardo blurted out.

The doctor and nurse seemed frozen in place. Their eyes slowly turned to Mr. Lombardo, who looked at them.

"Heh, heh, heh."

"I really don't know what to say," Dean murmured. "Except that I'm going to shoot Finkel."

Sam looked at him and winked.

"Heh, heh, heh," she answered, and then she turned serious. "Dean, go to your room. I'll take care of things."

****

Minutes later Dean trudged back to the nurses' station, having rounded again on his patients, who all seemed to be doing quite well. The whole crew was hanging loose, and everyone appeared quite jovial, including Skye and Samantha, who winked at him. The beloved graveyard lull – no new ambulances and a fairly empty waiting room, so rare in busy ERs, sort of like a double rainbow, as magnificent as it was transient – was in full swing.

Random bits of conversation filled the air.

"...so my teenage son freaks out after I took his tablet away – hey, he snuck money out of my wallet. *"I wish you had swallowed me that night!'* he yells. Well, I'd simply had it. So, I yell back 'and I should have!' You ever wish for a do-over?"

"...you know that pig gyn doc Murphy, the one who calls his patients 'pussies'? He always loves to say how you can tell if the girl's been cheating – they ask for the date they got pregnant, because they're '*sentimental.*' He says that means there's been more than one guy, so they have to go check their calendar. Anyway, guess who walked up to me after she had her ultrasound and asked me that very same question, so *she* could cherish the day forever? Pamela Murphy, his wife! Poetic justice, don't you think?"

"…last week we had this couple, they both had to be in their late seventies, easy. According to the husband, she had a 'itch' *down there.* So we asked her if she's noticed any unusual smells or anything, and she says 'go ask him, he's always down there.' So, we did: does it smell different, look different, anything, you know? He looks at us and says, 'nah, that candy box is smellin' good, lookin' good, and feelin' better than ever!' And she was just lying there, wearing the biggest shit-eating grin you've ever seen. Ain't that the sweetest thing?"

Dean nodded to Sam and walked over. Then they both walked into the adjacent doctors' station, where a small group was standing in front of a computer screen, staring at an abdominal x-ray image. You could hear the "oohs" and ahhs." Finkel was pointing to something and playfully grilling Harry.

"So, what is that, a Kirby or an English?" he demanded.

"I would say English, it's longer and thinner."

"Harry, you're getting pretty good at this. You should become an ER doc."

Finkel turned around and smiled when he saw his good buddy.

"Hey, brother, check out this x-ray - Harry ordered it. This gentleman must be related to that 'hot date' of yours – he *fell* on it!"

Finkel stood up and faced his small audience, putting on his serious face. Dean and Samantha craned their heads forward, smiling. This was a great show.

"Now, everyone listen up, this is for real" Finkel said. "You are going to keep quiet about this, and never betray this patient's identity. This *is* for real - spill the beans today, you'll be serving them with franks tomorrow. Remember, what happens in his butt stays in is butt. You all hear me?"

All present mumbled their agreement. Someone snickered. Samantha quietly took a few steps back, turned around and slipped away.

"None of that, no laughing," Finkel emphasized. "I don't want any one of us getting hurt over this case. Eileen and Margo will be calling all the nursing and support staff to reinforce this, and Tannenbaum and Charley Meyers will be calling the docs, to make…"

"Fucking shit!" Jack Ferrante, the on-call surgeon, yelled out when he walked up to the computer screen. Most non-essentials scurried away. "You weren't lying!"

The surgeon stared at the screen in frustration and shook his head. Then he walked over to Finkel and whispered in his ear. They had known each other for years and were friends.

"Did you try to remove it, Bob?"

"Yeah, it's out of reach. Sorry, Jack. Sad to say, the guy needs a cucumber-rectomy."

"Damn, I'm supposed to go out of town this morning. Can't you move this dude?"

"Jack, if I tried to transfer out a guy with a pickle halfway up his ass, they'd laugh me out of town, and then tell me what to do with the pickle."

"No other options?"

"Well, we could put some garlic and Greek yogurt up there and make tzatziki sauce."

There was a second's pause.

"Don't forget the dill," Ferrante added dryly. "Katrina, please call the nursing supervisor. Wait a minute, this Romeo guy, he's the one on the hospital board, right? As in *the* Edgar Henley?"

"The one and the same," the secretary answered, entering orders. "He says he fell on it, by the way."

"Yeah, yeah, they all do. Listen, tell her, tell everyone, to fast track this case big time. We gotta get lover boy home fast, before word gets out – he's a big shot, after all. You know, Bob, this just might work, I may get to go fishing after all. I am such a fucking genius. Okay, time to say hello."

"Your fishing hole awaits," Finkel said with solemnity.

The surgeon sighed, approached Harry and patted his shoulder.

"Nice pickup," he said. "Hey Katrina, where's the rectum?"

"Rectum's in Seventeen, doc," she replied, not taking her eyes off her computer screen.

The medical student, trembling with pride, watched him leave.

"Yeah, Harry, you'll be flying solo pretty soon," Finkel said. "Good work.

"There was a smattering of 'here, heres' murmured by a few nearby eavesdroppers. Rosie stood closer to her man and quietly touched his lab coat. Soon the crowd dispersed, everyone secretly planning how they could somehow talk about this case *discretely.*

Samantha quietly returned and waited for the crowd to thin out.

"Cute x-ray," Dean said approvingly, sitting down heavily in a chair. "And so very vegan. You sure get the great cases."

"I'd look twice before plopping down like that," his good buddy cautioned. "You never know what's lurking beneath. Chips?"

He passed a large cup to his friend.

The two doctors each worked at their respective computers, checking results, ordering labs and tests, all the while thinking to themselves how most unusual this night had turned out. Samantha walked over to Dean and looked over his shoulder, smirking just a little at the x-ray image.

Dean turned and offered the cup to her. Finkel looked at them looking at each other and took the opportunity to slip away.

"How romantic," Samantha munched. "By the way, I spoke with Lorraine Henley. She won't surface your little faux pas if you can keep everyone's mouth shut about her darling Edgar."

"That can be arranged. Many thanks, Sam. And tell me, how'd you take care of the Lombardos?"

"Oh, I made a quick call, someone'll be in to see them at seven o'clock. It's not that far off. Social Work and Home Health Care will get involved."

"Many thanks, Sam, you're the greatest."

"I know."

"Interesting, and even Skye looks happy now. What gives?"

"She had a nice talk with the ICU doctor about Clark. Plus, Carol and Karlita explained to her the virtues of a PTA bath. She's now fully in-serviced, and should be fine from here on in."

"What is a PTA bath?"

"Pits, tits and ass."

"I beg your pardon?"

Samantha gently touched his shoulder.

"Doc, you don't have to go through every door. Let it be."

They both stood up. Each had places to go and people to see. They looked at each other with a tinge of sadness, knowing that their private adventure was over.

"See you, doc, it's been a lovely date – great conversation… could've been a bit more action, though. Still, people are gonna talk. And I say, why not."

"And how does the song go, 'Let's give 'em something to talk about'?"

She winked. Dean winked back.
"Heh, heh, heh," they whispered in unison.

*****

Part Eight
Harry Loses His Virginity

"Harry, take this patient," Finkel commanded his medical student, pointing to a clipboard in the wooden tray between them. "Your first complete case, how about that? Head to toe, inside and out, history and physical. But don't worry, it's easy – my grandmother could work it.

"I got two ugly traumas rolling in, and of course both surgeons are stuck in the OR with criticals; and of course, Anderson's upstairs tubing someone – when will those hospitalists learn how to clean up their own mess? But I digress - in a very short while I will be getting destroyed. But hey, today's been easy so far, wouldn't you say? Saturdays are like that. You get some decent down time, and then, pow! the pendulum swings back and gets you right in the ass. It's nature's law, you know, all ER shifts average out."

With that the tall ER doctor stood up and looked sternly at his now-frozen student, who was looking at him with bulging eyes, every bit the deer dumbly staring at you while standing in *your* lane. The veteran doc seemed to soften a little.

"Come on, Harry, you're a fourth year, you had to go solo eventually, right? You even said you wanted to, remember? I did it, everyone did it, and after this you're not a virgin anymore. You can do it, just don't kill anyone. *Please*?"

Finkel paused and cocked his head, eyes squinting, his ears straining to….

"Sirens. I can't hear 'em, yet, but I can feel them, they're in the air. They're coming. Gotta go soon, my friend," he murmured, stretching his back and cracking his knuckles. A most unusual calm seemed to envelope him.

"Hey, Harry, did you know I used to live for this? Seeing all that red stuff really turned me on, it was so much fun…and then, it stopped being fun. It's even a little scary now. It's weird – the better I get at these traumas, the more scared I am of them. Some switch in my brain turned off, or turned on, or something. I don't have a clue what's going on. And, of course, in the good old days being covered with blood wasn't considered sloppy. No, no, no, it was chic, so cool - it might even get you laid. Now they yell at you if even a drop hits the floor, it's like you just spilled wine on the carpet.

"I'm changing, man," the doc continued. "Don't tell anyone. I don't like gory traumas anymore, I don't even like cardiac arrests. Worst of all, I think I'm starting to like my patients, some even a lot. You think that's weird? I do. I'm afraid to tell anyone. You I can talk to, it's like confessing to a fucking statue."

Harry continued to stare, not moving. The air suddenly started, almost imperceptibly, to gently vibrate from the furious sounds of onrushing sirens. The department hushed a bit, as muscles tensed and eyes reflexively turned towards the ambulance doors, which shortly would burst open with paramedics delivering mayhem.

Both code rooms by now were bristling with trauma teams – personnel culled from areas all over the hospital – waiting. Finkel sighed, reached for his code gum, and started walking out of the doctor's station. He took one last look at Harry, who still had not moved. The doctor placed his hand on the student's shoulder.

"Harry, you're smart, I swear you know more shit than me. You even know the clotting pathways, whatever they are. Just remember these two rules – first, ninety-five per cent of *everything* is in the nursing note and the history you take. You usually can figure out what's going on, and know what you have to do, before you even touch the patient. The rest is just for show, so put on a good one – and never let 'em see you sweat or act indecisive, even if you don't have a clue as to what's going on. Second, maybe even as important, in our field you can do anything you want, anything, just *as long as there is no problem.* Hey, bring along that nursing student you're so sweet on. She'd love the...."

The ambulance doors seemed to explode. The doctor gently slapped his cheeks, every bit the boxer stepping into the ring.

"And now...showtime," he said softly to himself. "Bye, Harry."

Finkel vanished.

The tense calm had shattered into organized chaos. Lots of raised voices, some shouts, some laughter, and over everything the student heard his mentor machine-gunning orders, sidestepping from one patient to the other, and then back again. He craned his neck and managed a peek – Finkel's trauma gown was already speckled with blood.

*

Harry practiced deep breathing for about a minute. Finally, he wiped his forehead and slowly stood up, noting how wobbly his thighs were. Don't fall, he warned himself, don't break anything.

A beat-up metal clipboard, now mostly used for show and taking some basic notes, glared defiantly at him from the to-be-seen box. It sported a yellow dot on the front, indicating medium acuity. Harry glared back – I can, I *will,* do this, he thought – and gathered his courage. He grabbed it much in the way a fullback would take a handoff and forged ahead.

He swaggered – actually it was more like a *faux* swagger – towards Rose, a young nursing student copying vital signs into a chart, under the watchful eyes of a nursing instructor, Sarah Kennedy, who was trying not to look bored. The hallway was fairly empty, most personnel having diverted to the trauma bays. When the students' eyes met, both of them stopped. The instructor, herself a veteran of the ER wars who'd switched over to teaching, looked at them and couldn't help but smile. Rose turned to her with pleading eyes. The instructor nodded *yes*, and then she gratefully headed towards Trauma One to check things out.

"I'll go see if they need me," she called over her shoulder. "Rosie, stay with the med student and present to me later."

The young man and woman nervously looked at each other, then away, and then back again at each other, oblivious to the commotion just around the corner. Harry tilted his head slightly, and his eyes asked her if she'd accompany him. She blinked yes, let's go. They carefully began walking to Room 16, as if walking onto a dance floor.

"Harry, where's Doctor Finkel?" Rose asked, looking around. "Shouldn't we wait?"

"He had to go take care of the traumas, so I guess I'm, uh, sort of in charge until Dr. Anderson returns. I'll take this case. Yup, Saturdays can be like this."

"Oh God, I'm so proud of you…are you nervous?"

Harry looked down at his shoes, contemplating an answer.

"Not really...well, just a little. Yeah, I guess I am. I'll just take it slow, and I'll be thorough. As they always say, 'it's all in the history...'"

"Harry, you sound just like an ER doctor. And you're gonna do so good."

After a fierce inner struggle, pitting hormones against a lifetime's collection of insecurities and rejections – it's really rough being a nerd, at least for the first half of your life - the gods of lust and love prevailed, and Harry made his move.

"Rosie, when you're free, like around five, would you like go to the cafeteria and get something to eat?"

"Yes! Someone told me they have tater tot casserole today. *And* four-cheese cream of broccoli soup. It's so thick the spoon stands up in the bowl."

"Wow, my favorites," Harry agreed gratefully. "That's perfect. Well, off we go, it's showtime..."

Their pace slowed, more than a little, when they saw the two thickly muscled correction officers, each with a slung rifle, standing in front of their destination. They turned to face the students, who now were more than a little flustered. Harry checked the room number and grimaced. This was it. Room Sixteen. Feeling the eyes of Rose on him, Harry steeled himself, and nodded at them respectfully.

"Good afternoon, gentlemen," he heard himself saying.

"And a very good afternoon to you, doc," the older of the two replied. "We got a present for you. Ready?"

Harry, who'd been hoping for something nice and easy, grimly nodded. The guard grunted and rapped twice on the closed door with a nightstick.

"Doc and the nurse are here," he called out. "Is 'lover boy' decent?"

"Send 'em in," came the muffled reply, followed by two raps from within.

"He's all yours," the guard said with a flourish of his hand.

The door slowly opened, and the two students tentatively entered, followed by the senior guard. Harry and Rose were both wondering how to take that 'lover boy' remark. Each simultaneously took a quick breath and exhaled as they embarked, together at last, on Harry's first case.

Both stopped in their tracks the moment they walked in. The remaining outside guard closed the door behind them.

There were two other huge guards inside the room, each heavily armed. Sitting on the gurney, shackled from top to bottom, was his very first patient. The man, a Mr. Hercules Jones, was gigantic, maybe the largest human Harry had ever seen. He glowered at them and then turned away.

Their silent hopes for a fun, easy case having now evaporated, the students came face to face with grim ER reality. It was accepted knowledge that a prisoner's corrections escort was directly proportional to how much of a badass he was. The older ones arrived with older guards who often were in worse shape than their charges. Just yesterday a senior guard, two months shy of retirement, had gone into a dangerous heart rhythm restraining a prisoner and had to be admitted. This inmate, who looked like Godzilla dressed in pumpkin orange, surrounded by heavily armed men with fingers on or near the trigger, was obviously a really bad hombre.

Harry fought his instinctive urge to back away. He had been expecting a young lover, or something – the chief complaint had read "Requesting HIV counseling" - and his mind reeled in confusion. He contemplated waiting for Dr. Finkel, as his first case suddenly seemed a bit challenging, nothing like his initial fantasies of a rash or discharge. But the guards, and Rose, were staring at him, so he began his march down the first clinical journey of his fledgling career. God, don't let me kill this guy, he thought. Wait, forget him. God, don't let him kill *me*. (And Doctor Finkel's grandmother could take care of him? I wouldn't want to meet *her* in a dark alley either.)

"Okay, so what's going on?" he heard himself say, trying to affect a slightly bored machismo.

The guard who seemed to be in charge approached.

"He was having sex with another inmate. When you catch 'em you got to bring 'em, it's some rule. You have to offer them counseling. They decline - they always decline - you sign these forms, and we're out of your hair. The other guy was half his size - you had to see it to believe it – he went to another ER, another rule."

Harry gathered his thoughts. *Okay, I will not let Dr. Finkel down.* Garnering what he could of his resolve, he clenched his jaw and slipped his ID badge into a pocket. Rose did the same – one of the first survival rules you pick up is staying anonymous with prisoners, drunks, and anyone who is even a trace menacing. And now, emboldened by his personal SWAT team, the medical student straightened his posture and sauntered up to the seated man, the nursing student right behind him, inches away.

It was most unusual. The giant sat perfectly still, hands bound to waist irons, his feet chained to each other, staring straight ahead, possibly the scariest man he had ever seen. His muscles had muscles, and his tattoos were downright satanic. On either side the guards, one holding a short-barreled shotgun, the other with what seemed to be an assault rifle slung over a shoulder (both carried sidearms, small clubs, mace and tasers as well), didn't take their eyes off him. There were a few sheets of paper on the counter next to the sink.

Harry glanced again at the nurse's note, praying it would give him further insight. That prayer crashed and burned. Aside from those three meager words – "requesting HIV counseling" – the rest of the note was prison info, date of birth, current meds and allergies, etc. Oh well, he concluded, I'll just have to take a better history, and then do a great physical.

Borrowing a technique he'd learned from Finkel, he decided against any introductions. Now take command, he thought, and show him who's boss.

"So, what brings you here today?" he asked firmly.

The huge man stared straight ahead, not moving. Above the door a mounted television silently showed a police reality show – a car chase was in progress. Wonder who's he rooting for, the student thought.

"I asked you, what brings you here today," Harry repeated, a tinge of anxiety uncontrollably sneaking into his voice. "I need to hear it from you."

(Harry wasn't really sure if that was true but it seemed like the right thing to say.)

No answer, no movement.

"Come on, Jonesy!" the officer in charge snapped at his ward. "I want to get out of here. Answer the man!"

Again, silence. The guards shifted on their feet sullenly. Their leader again spoke.

"Doc, he was having sex with this little guy in the shower. No one was hurt, there were no problems, it happens every day. They just got caught. Can we just get out of here, like soon? Our shift ended twenty minutes ago."

"Give me a few minutes," Harry heard himself saying confidently. He was inwardly stunned at how easily he made the words come out, and even more stunned that these huge guards shrugged and acquiesced to him immediately. Rank does have its privileges, he thought, slightly amazed. He felt Rose ever so subtly touching his jacket sleeve. A tidal wave of testosterone washed away his fears – *he was in charge.*

"So, Mr. Jones, it seems that you were having sex. Was this protected sex?" Harry could make out the large man twitch ever so slightly. He had elicited a reaction, and this seemed to him to be a small victory. Harry had won the first round. He decided to pursue his quarry.

"Was it consensual sex? Did he force himself on you?"

The giant sitting on the stretcher turned his head – he moved again! – and glared at him. Harry glanced at the guards, who were watching the proceedings warily.

"I mean, are you in a relationship with that man?" Harry continued. "Like, are you married to him? You do know that it's legal these days."

"No," Jones answered in a clipped voice. The guards grew even more tense.

"Doc, come on," the lead officer implored.

"I mean, are you in love with him?"

"Doc, it was a dick suck, okay?" the prisoner said wearily. "I'll sign the paper."

"'Dick suck'?" Harry asked. He looked at Rose, who shrugged. *Gotta look it up,* he thought.

"Give me the fucking papers," the prisoner demanded.

"Let me examine you and you're out of here."

"I want out now!"

"Jonesy, behave!" the lead guard barked. "You are not in charge! He'll behave, doc, just do what you have to do."

"It'll just take a second."

With that the student carefully approached the man. He circled around to his back and listened to his heart and lungs. What would Dr. Finkel do, he asked himself. Then came his revelation – *I know, I'll make this a focused exam.*

"Lie on your back," Harry suddenly ordered. He quickly looked at Rose, who looked at him with wide eyes.

"Can you take some notes for me?"

She nodded her head. Harry turned back to his patient.

"Lie on your back," he repeated.

"What did you say?" Jones shouted.

"Listen to the fucking doctor!" one of the guards shot back. He looked at his comrades. "Lie him down!"

Three of them forced the huge prisoner down, looks of resentment on their faces.

"Pull down his pants just a little bit, let me just check to make sure he doesn't have any diseases or anything. I just need a quick minute or two."

Shaking their heads almost in unison, the guards complied. Harry stared down at Jones' genitals, wondering what to do. Tentatively he lifted the man's penis, aiming it straight at the ceiling. Then he carefully looked at it from various angles, moving it as one might handle a stick shift. Rose leaned forward, taking notes.

"Genital exam – well developed male genitalia..."

One of the guards snickered. Jones began to tremble slightly.

"And what do we have here? Rose, write down the presence of warts on the penile shaft. Sir, did you know you have genital warts? That carries the risk for cervical cancer if you have sex with a female. Of course, in this case you probably got away with it, considering it was with your boyfriend."

The trembling increased.

Jones tried to sit up, but two guards pushed him back.

Harry moved the penis around, north, south, east and west, looking for lesions. Jones' movements had graduated to shaking.

"Normal range of motion...and what do we have...Rose, write down the presence of vesicular lesions. Mr. Jones, you may have herpes. I do hope you are informing your partners. They do have a right to..."

"I want out of here now!" the prisoner growled, every bit acting like a cornered animal. He was beginning to spasm.

"We're almost done," the student answered reassuringly. "Almost done with the exam. Now we're going to look at your scrotum. We'll start with your right testicle. Ready, Rose?"

Harry lifted the right testicle, gently palpating it and flipping it like a pancake from one side to the other. The patient ceased all movement. Harry took out a short measuring stick.

"Rose, it measures four by three by...two centimeters, is oblong in shape and has no obvious lesions. There is, however, a questionable venous malformation at the distal pole, which is palpable. It is..."

He gave it a slight squeeze.

"...non-tender. This can be worked up in the out-patient setting..."

At that moment Jones detonated. He violently began thrashing and jerking, ripping at his irons with all his might. The veins on his neck looked like bulging pythons. The guards looked on with amusement – no one alive could overcome the chains. Jones' face took on the features of a mighty animal fighting for his life, and he glared at his tormentors with hatred and rage. And then, beyond all belief, his right hand burst free.

The guards shouted in unison and immediately grabbed his hand, but the prisoner was already working his left arm. His body seemed to be a coiled spring that had snapped into unimaginable violence.

"We need help here!" one of the guards screamed.

The door swung open. The guard outside looked at the scene in disbelief.

"We need backup," he cried out. Two state troopers waiting outside the trauma bays started running towards them.

Sarah Kennedy also happened to be walking by.

"I was looking for you, Rose...what the hell!"

"Get Dr. Finkel stat!" Harry cried out.

"He's putting in chest tubes," the instructor shouted back. "Tell me to order a B-52. Now!"

"A what?"

"Fifty of Benadryl, five of Haldol and two of Ativan. Give me the order. Just do it!"

"Okay, okay!"

She broke into a run, headed for the med cart.

The four guards did their all-out best to restrain the struggling man. One of them pulled his taser and pressed the barrel against his forehead.

"I'll pull the trigger, motherfucker!" he warned in a low growl.

With a loud metallic snap, the man's left arm now broke free and grabbed the weapon, which fired, sending two barbs packing a thousand-plus volts into the guard standing two feet away – the man began to violently spasm as he backed away and crashed into the door, crumpling to the ground, effectively blocking the troopers from entering - they began pounding the door and slowly started pushing against his weight to open it. Pandemonium was in the air.

Improbably, the students now sprang into action. Harry grabbed the left wrist and pulled down on it with all his might. Rose jumped on the man's knees to stop them from wildly kicking out at the men. It was all she could do to prevent being launched into the ceiling. For the longest twenty seconds of all time the scene was pure madness. Then finally, the troopers burst in, followed by Sarah Kennedy.

She held a large syringe filled with fluid and armed with a very large needle. She aimed it towards his thigh.

"Do you want me to pull his pants down?" Rose gasped. She was holding on for dear life. Like everyone else in the room she was dripping with sweat.

"Fuck no, I'm going through 'em," the instructor hissed, plunging the needle into the prisoner's thigh, down to the hilt. And then she calmly walked to the head of the stretcher and placed her hand over the man's nose and forehead, putting all her weight into it. It stopped a lot of his struggling.

"Thirty-two years, and I'm still doing this shit," she grumbled, shaking her head. (And glad I snuck in that third milligram of Ativan, she thought, a secret she'd take to the grave.)

Within three minutes the man lay snoring on the stretcher. The guards quickly replaced his shackles with even bigger shackles, all the while shooting Harry looks of pure fury. Compounding everything was that they had been made to look incompetent in front of the troopers. The guard who'd been shocked remained seated on the floor, groggy but slowly coming back to his senses.

"Okay, boys," Sarah said, wiping her face with a towel. "He's a little kitty cat now. We'll sign the damn forms, and when he wakes up, get his ass out of here! Good work, Rose. Now, let's go."

She gently but firmly grabbed her student's forearm and led her away. Rose turned to look at Harry – she mouthed the word *later* to him. Harry, his face flushed, nodded excitedly.

**

When Harry returned about twenty-five minutes later to the nursing station, he found Finkel sipping on coffee, joking with Anderson. Anesthesiologists, surgeons and the OR teams were here now and, as far as the ER was concerned, everything was in wrap-up mode. Practically everyone was taking a well-deserved break. In the background, the med student saw Rose, who was looking at him, radiating pride.

"So, uh, I hear you guys had a most interesting case," Finkel casually said, glancing at Sarah, who smiled and winked at him. The doc chuckled and looked at his protegee. "So, you ain't a virgin anymore. How 'bout that, folks, let's hear it for Harry."

Everyone laughed and broke into brief applause, Rose clapping the hardest. Harry blushed and looked away, thoughts racing.

"And let's not forget our nursing student," the nursing instructor interjected loudly in a friendly voice. "It was your first roll in the hay also, wasn't it, Rosie?"

There was more applause, and it was the nursing student's turn to blush.

"And look at the time, just about five o'clock," Finkel said, looking at the wall. "Shift's over, Harry. Good work, my man, and as the saying goes, get out while the going's good."

"Actually, I was thinking of getting something in the cafeteria first."

Finkel looked at his medical student looking at the nursing student. His hands joined together in namaste, and his head bowed ever so slightly.

"Then, all I can say is, *bon appetit.*"

*****

Part Nine
Space Pearl

Finkel watched Angel hobble in his direction and sighed deeply. The doctor slumped behind a desk. He was assigned to a little-known part of the hospital known as Crawl In, a gloomy area attached to the main ER, designed for lower acuity patients.

Years ago, chief Tannenbaum had quietly snatched up this unused, unmodernized and seemingly forgotten space and filled it with eight exam "rooms," with curtains for walls, old desks, chairs, stretchers, and barebone essentials for equipment. It was a perfect safety valve for stressed out or overworked docs and midlevels who needed a break, and it kept many non-emergencies out of the Emergency Room. A win-win all the way.

The doc was feeling extremely unwell, with an aching body, pounding head, burning chest and electrified skin. Covid and the flu had already ruled out, and Eileen, CMFIC, had - most likely correctly - diagnosed him with 'viral crap'. She told him to go home, but he adamantly declined, much preferring to work in this easy section. It's just what the doctor ordered, Finkel protested. Why waste a sick day on actual sickness. So here he was, slogging through his shift, trying to make the most of things and counting down the hours…and then he saw Angel.

The guy was just here, he whined to himself, shaking his head until he realized that this only made his headache worse. What is it now Angel, backache, toothache, talking to your radio? Please go somewhere else, I'm not in the mood...

"Doc, long time no see," Angel boomed, still more than twenty yards away, strutting in his direction. Minutes before, he had been observed standing with other frequent flyers, staring at the ER's work roster/calendar taped to the front registration desk (done in the hated name of transparency), asking a friend to point out his favorite docs – they all had at least one. And now he was headed straight for his *numero uno*, the poor doctor shivering in a small cubicle.

Angel sidestepped around some sort of fluid, all the while rehearsing his lines. Acting too sick could get you in the Big Room - tell an ER doctor you can't breathe or are having the worst headache of your life, and they'll stick you with needles and put tubes in places you always thought were sacred. Acting too mellow could land you in the resident's clinic, where you just might get tested to death. No, he was glad to be approaching his all-time super doc, the great Doctor Finkel, and he was ready.

Finkel monitored Angel's progress with an air of exhausted resignation. Eileen spoke with the wisdom of the Nile, he thought, I should have gone home. I don't know how I'm going to survive this man.

"Doc, how you been?" his patient asked jovially, sitting down heavily on the chair alongside the doctor's desk.

"I'm fine, Angel. So what brings you in today? Make it fast."

"You look a little off today, Doc, you feeling all right? You getting enough sleep?"

Finkel looked at the small man in front of him with a mixture of annoyance and astonishment. *He's* playing doctor now, he thought incredulously, all the while fighting off waves of icy chills. He clenched his jaw, trying not to let his teeth chatter. When he opened his eyes he saw in the distance a small group of well-dressed people, some making notes on long yellow pads, walking slowly around the area. Someone tapped him on the shoulder. He whirled around and saw Eileen. She put a finger to her lips and motioned for him to leave the exam cubicle.

"Be right back, Angel," he said, getting up stiffly.

"Not a problem, Doc, take your time," his patient answered magnanimously. "We got all day."

Finkel frowned, and then walked over to the head nurse. It was her turn to frown.

"You look like shit," she observed.

"And do you know why I look like shit? I feel like shit. Did you bring me here just to pass along this wisdom?"

"No, I brought you here to say that the hospital CEO and his productivity team are here, and you better behave. And try not to look like you're about to die."

"The CEO? I've never seen him down here. Is he lost?"

"Bob, this is important. Yesterday they went through the surgical ICU, didn't like what they saw, and now John Conway isn't their nurse manager anymore."

"Johnny? He's great. Those fuckers."

Eileen reached out and gently held his arms. To Finkel's great surprise and relief, her touch did not cause pain. If anything, Mr. Happy actually seemed to move a centimeter. Well, at least I'm not completely dead, he thought with some relief.

"Bob, you are to be polite and respectful and, I know this is hard for you, you are to be appropriate."

"Appropriate, hmm. Really? For you, I would do anything. I'll even touch the patients, and I'm great at faking washing my hands…"

"Bob!"

"What's in this for me?"

Eileen shook her head. The group was heading their way.

"I'll get you wonton soup. They're ordering in the ER."

"I was hoping for a blowjob."

"You're near death and still that's all you think about. You really are a pig, aren't you?"

"Eileen, at least I know who I am," the doctor replied solemnly. "And besides, studies prove that if a man ejaculates often enough, he expels dangerous radicals from his prostate, and his chances of getting cancer go down. We're talking cutting edge medicine here."

"Oh goodie, so you shoot that crap into us. Anyway, you help me with my job, then we'll see about yours. And try to stay alive until they leave. Do it for me."

With that, Eileen left to rally her troops, while Finkel returned to his cubicle. Angel was contentedly reading a section of a newspaper he'd fished out of the garbage. The doctor sighed.

"Angel, you're holding it upside down."

Angel shrugged, folded the paper and laid it on the desk between them. Finkel stared at a used tampon nestled between two of its pages. If I weren't so tired, I'd kill him now, he concluded.

"Doc, I'm worried."

"You are worried."

There were shouts in the main ER, followed by the sound of glass shattering, followed by a booming voice intoning the words, "Code Gray, ER, Code Gray, ER," over the ceiling speakers. Finkel paused for a minute, trying to remember who was working the shift next door.

He watched the small, well-dressed group baby-step in sync down the hall towards the ER door, where they stood tippy toe at Crawl-In's portal windows, nervously trying to peek inside the large room.

"Yes, Doc, very worried," Angel said again, looking around carefully.

"Yes, Angel, it's now in the minutes that you are officially 'worried,'" Finkel said flatly. Finally, he turned back to his patient. "Okay, let's have it. Why are you worried?"

"I'm going to show it to you."

"Show 'what' to me?" the doctor asked, distracted by the commotion twenty yards away, in the department's main arena. In a way he wished he was there – it would mean that he wasn't *here*. And the bonus would be that the chaos might even take his mind off this bug of his.

Angel slowly reached into his pocket. Finkel stared at him, fighting off waves of shivers. He slouched under what seemed like a ton of viral particles sitting on top of him. Man, wonton soup sure sounds great, he fantasized, it's so superior to regular chicken soup, it's truly cutting edge...damn, I should have asked Eileen to get an egg roll.

Looking this way and that, Angel carefully placed something on the newspaper. Finkel leaned forward, stared, eyes widening His jaw dropped just a little.

It looked to be a large pearl of some type, the size of a walnut, pinkish pastel in color, smooth and glistening, with wisps of whitish smoke imbued within. Flecks of light green adorned its surface. The doctor couldn't take his eyes off it, and within seconds he had fallen under its spell.

"It's beautiful," the doctor whispered, reaching over to pick it up. "I've never seen anything like this."

As was typical in this big city ER, people were in crisis everywhere, with sights, sounds and smells of pain and disease filling the air. But this magical pearl, so enchanting to behold, so haunting in appearance and so smooth to the touch, seemed to absorb all the madness. The cubicle was filled with calm, and for a moment Finkel forgot that he was ill. He felt like he was enveloped by magic, floating in a gentle breeze.

The weakened doctor was at peace. His eyes closed. He imagined himself hovering over a primordial forest, the sound of ferns whispering, mixing with the sweet whistles of trees rustling in the gentle wind. He felt blessed, almost in love, and everything around him was soft and gentle. Sleep almost came upon him.

"Did you come by this legally?" he finally whispered, not taking his eyes off this object of exquisite beauty. He gently rolled it in his hand.

"Yes, it's very legal," Angel whispered back, looking this way and that.

"Am I allowed to ask where you got it?"

Angel leaned closer.

"It came out of my ass," he quietly replied.

"I beg your pardon?"

"It came out of my ass. Doc, I'm worried."

All neuronal activity ceased within the good doctor. He dimly sensed the pearl starting to stick to his hand. With a monumental effort, requiring the last of his strength, Finkel carefully placed it back on the desk, closed his eyes, and didn't move for several seconds. Angel shifted uneasily in his chair.

"Doc, you having a stroke or something? You need a doctor?"

"I'm okay," the doctor whispered, his eyes shut tightly. "Why are you here?"

"You know, Doc, for the past few weeks I've been having ass pain every time I take a dump, and sometimes all the way up to my dick. I don't know, is there some kind of wire or pipe that connects these places? So, anyway, I been constipated for a whole week. This morning I decided to get tough. So there I am, sitting on the toilet with this nail up my ass, sitting and sitting, and pushing and pushing. Nothing! So I say a prayer, and squeeze and squeeze and squeeze with all my might, until I thought my head would explode, and POW! this thing blasts out of me like a rocket. It hit the water so hard my ass almost drowned…then it floated to the top.

"Now I'm feeling like really strange, like something broke loose on the inside. Doc, is it possible my ass had a heart attack? I tell you, I'm worried."

When I regain the use of my arms, I am going to strangle this humanoid, Finkel decided. First, I'll inject him with monkey shit. Then I'll…

At that moment Eileen walked up. She poked him in the ribs.

"Look sharp, boss man's here," Eileen whispered. "And get this guy out of here."

As she walked away. Finkel finally opened his eyes and looked at his patient.

"Angel, two things. First, your ass is not having a heart attack. Second, how much fucking Norco will it take to get you out of here, like right now."

Angel looked up at the ceiling, making mental calculations.

"Around twenty."

The doctor furiously scribbled something and handed the prescription to Angel.

"Go!" he commanded.

At that moment the CEO and his entourage appeared. They all stared at the patient and his doctor.

"Do you mind if we observe?" the group's leader politely asked. "We didn't mean to interrupt."

"I was just leaving, sir," Angel said, standing up. "This doctor here, he's a miracle worker. He just saved my life. I love this man."

"We always strive to provide the highest level of evidence-based, outcome-oriented, relationship-driven care," a member of the group declared.

"That's good, right?" Angel asked, looking at Finkel. The doctor, struggling to stay alive, nodded.

As Angel walked away, the CEO nodded approvingly to the ER doctor.

"Good work," he said, patting Finkel's shoulder. "Carry on."

"Yes sir."

As the group wheeled around, the CEO caught a glimpse of Angel's pearl, still lying next to the newspaper. His eyes squinted, and he returned to the cubicle. He looked at the object, then at the doctor.

"What have we here?" he asked, approaching the desk. "Do you mind?"

"Sure, why not," Finkel replied wearily.

The CEO picked up Angel's pearl. He stared closely at it, rolled it in his fingers, sniffed it, and even rubbed it against his cheek to determine its texture.

"Is this a gem or something?" he inquired. "Where did you get this?"

"That?"

"Yes, that."

"It, well, it came from, above."

"'Above,' as in space? Is…is this a space rock?" the CEO asked intently.

The doctor paused, his mind starting to race.

"Yes," Finkel finally answered cautiously.

"Absolutely fascinating. May I ask how you came upon this?"

The doctor took a deep breath and decided to plow ahead. What the hell, he thought, no guts, no glory.

"I can't completely reveal my source, but word's out that it's from a large rock first seen tracking from Uranus. It fragmented when it reached our atmosphere and fell into the ocean. The man who retrieved this for me is an expert in his field as well a dear friend - I call him my personal angel. I brought it in today to show everyone."

The CEO smiled and turned to his small group, the space pearl snug in his palm.

"It's fascinating," he said. "You may not know this, but while hospital management is my career, astronomy is my passion."

A chorus of *ooh*s and *ahhs* emanated from the small group.

"The true Renaissance Man," someone cooed approvingly.

With all his might, Finkel kept totally still – he was locked in a three-way battle, fighting off urges to shiver, laugh, or simply continue breathing. A truce finally ensued, and he radiated a Buddha-like calm.

"I probably should tell all of you now that I am one of the few people in the world in possession of a moon rock," the CEO continued, all the while fondling Angel's gift to the world.

Another chorus, this time of *oh my God*s ensued.

"And with that, I guess we break for lunch," the CEO said, reluctantly putting the pearl back on Finkel's desk. "What's everyone in the mood for?"

The group froze.

"Sir, why don't you choose," someone softly spoke up.

"Don't mind if I do," the CEO answered. He rubbed his upper lip, then subconsciously rubbed his hand on his suit jacket. "I have it – Szechuan!"

Yet another chorus, this time of *perfect*s, echoed back.

He turned to Finkel, who stared back politely, and the two men shook hands.

"It's been a pleasure, sir," he said graciously.

"The pleasure's all mine, sir."

The CEO turned to his entourage, which snapped to attention.

"If anyone has any comments or suggestions for this good doctor, just pass them along as we leave."

He strode away, followed by most of his retinue. A few remaining members of his team dutifully and awkwardly approached Doctor Finkel. Someone cleared her throat.

"Good work, doctor. Remember, teamwork makes the dream work."

"The best preparation for tomorrow is doing your best today," another said.

"Change does not have to be perfect; it just has to be a little bit better," a third person chimed in.

"And the only perfect job is a blowjob," Finkel quietly mumbled back at them.

"Excuse me, doctor?" someone in the group asked, somewhat bewildered.

"I said 'the patient always comes first,'" he replied in a slightly louder voice.

They gratefully nodded their agreement and walked away, except for one very well-dressed man. He lingered a bit, looking around the cubicle.

"What a shithole. You do this every day?" he asked in near disbelief.

"Yeah, I do, actually."

"I guess it takes all kinds," he said, shaking his head.

He looked down at the desk.

"That your paper?"

"No, it was here when I arrived..."

"Good, I need something to read on the train."

Finkel watched him scoop the paper up, fold it and stick it in his attaché case. The tampon string seemed to wave bye-bye at him. And then the very well-dressed man left.

Eileen walked up. She seemed relieved.

"They're gone, and the food is here," she said. "I even got you two egg rolls. Ready for chow?"

"Very much so," Finkel gratefully said, slowly getting up from his chair. He stared at the pearl. It lay on the desk, melting a little, not quite as magical as before. "First, I think I'll wash my hands."

"Wash your hands? I thought you only washed them before going to the bathroom. You must be dying."

"Let's just say that a heavenly vision came upon me. And I'll also be humming the first stanza of 'Happy Birthday'". I read it on a poster."

The doctor went to the sink. He snuck a look at the pearl and gave it a wink. Then he turned to Eileen and bowed. She looked at him, shaking her head, smiling in spite of herself. And with that, they departed Crawl In, heading for the break room, where salvation and delicious food awaited.

*****

Part Ten
The Protein Mission

The annual Meet and Greet, a party honoring the residents and med students, was in full swing. The DJ did her best, and at least a few bodies did sort of sway.

The catering was pretty good, and since this event was being held across the street from the hospital, there was even foo foo booze (of course Marten, a first year from Luxembourg, criticized the food and drink constantly, calling it 'pedestrian').

A medical student took a big sip on his whiskey sour and turned to his mentor, who was standing off to the side with Eileen, the seen-it-all ER head nurse.

"Doctor Finkel, can I ask a stupid question?"

"Harry, there is no such thing as a stupid question, only a stupid person who asks it," the doc responded sagely, subconsciously rubbing a dusky bruise under his left eye - a gift from two nights before, when he'd leapt over a counter to subdue an incoherent wild man assaulting an aide. "Do go on."

Harry hesitated, shuffling his feet slightly for balance. It was clear that he was not handling his liquor well. He visibly struggled up some courage, and then leaned forward. Two nearby med students unsteadily leaned forward as well, slightly holding on to each other. Eileen looked at them, then at the floor, shaking her head.

"I'm sure you're aware, sir, that this hospital can get pretty rough, and that we deal with some, well, sub-optimal people..."

"Sub-optimal, huh? Yeah, I was wondering about that."

"Do you ever feel like we're doing the world a disservice by saving them and turning them loose again?" the student asked.

Finkel wearily glanced at Eileen, who shrugged, and he turned back to the students. How did I get stuck with this babysitting assignment, he wondered. He rubbed his bruised face again and cleared his throat.

"Harry, one day you'll realize that everything has a purpose. Nothing is random, and just because we can't see it doesn't mean it's not there. Our patients indeed were put here for a reason, whether we'll ever recognize it or not. That psychopath from a couple of days ago - for all we know, he's going to sire the next President."

"I never thought of that," Harry exclaimed excitedly.

"Me neither!" one of the other students gasped.

"Heavy, man," the third rumbled.

"Hey, you believed it," Finkel murmured, rubbing his chin with satisfaction. "Pretty cool."

Eileen looked at him and rolled her eyes.

"But I digress," the ER doctor continued, seeming to build up steam. "I have discovered the purpose of North Central Medical Center. Listen up."

He looked in every direction, then at them, beckoning with a finger. They huddled around him, conspiracy in the air. Eileen sighed quietly as the doctor began.

"Let me tell you something. This is classified, but I trust you guys. Last week, I had this NSA scientist who overdosed, and he was brought to our ER. After a while I got his vitals back. His sat was decent, his EKG started to behave, and soon I was pretty much out of the woods with him. In and of itself, no big deal. Then he woke up and started talking. He was slurring big time, but he was making sense, and I had time to listen. Boy, did I listen. And I took notes, lots of them. The next morning some guys in dark suits checked him out of the hospital, but I had my notes...

"It sounds crazy, but he told me there's this planet just a few light years away, where the inhabitants have no way to metabolize carbs – they lack the enzymes. They exclusively rely on protein.

"Thousands of years ago they extinguished all other life forms on their planet, they literally ate them into extinction. So, the only way they can survive is to go on these protein missions. They send out teams to survey candidate planets to check out the availability of suitable prey, to determine which are worthy of invasion, to be followed by a harvest. Their MO is to take the place over, send in fleets of container ships, thousands of them, round up the inhabitants, and fly them back for slaughter. Millions and millions of tons of protein would be shipped. And then, eventually, after they'd devoured everything there, they'd move on to another planet.

"Last month they set their sights on Earth. Yeah, our Earth. An elite team of scouts secretly landed, not too far from where we are at this

moment. After a comprehensive review, where they surveyed their subjects literally top to bottom, they returned with their verdict – our species is not fit for consumption! They left and they will never return. We're safe!

"Using their Wang and Blue Gene supercomputers, the NSA was able to intercept and translate the bulk of their report. And this is the gist of what it said: 'We have thoroughly examined these creatures who call themselves 'humans,' using a sample size we believe to be sufficient. Sunspot activity on their star forced a premature closure to the mission, so we did not have time to review other species. Still, we were primarily interested in these bipedal mammals, so we consider this report adequate. And these are our findings:

'By and large humans are in poor health and fall well below intergalactic nutritional standards. They are teeming with various viral, fungal and bacterial particles, many of which emanate from their genitalia. They seem to be in very poor physical condition, with enormous fat to protein ratios, and are riddled with minimally treated diseases. Most eat their food with teeth bought at a place called K Mart, as their original ones seem to melt away quickly. A majority also have various degrees of insanity, and a very high percentage also have lower back problems from vehicular accidents in a land called Texas from years before, and many still carry their CAT scan reports with them.

'Many if not most Earthlings seem to be heavy users of many pain medications, with the exception of Toradol, which they apparently are universally allergic to, and that could complicate our recipes. Also, even more of them routinely carry in their system massive amounts of alcohol, which would pose fire and explosion hazards during space travel.

'We aborted the project at this time. After thorough review of the data, which we confirmed using univalent and bivalent modulation, rigid confidence intervals, and integral co-variant charting, we unanimously conclude that the planet Earth is not a suitable candidate for a protein mission. We must not eat these creatures!

'As a minor aside, we also think they would require an unacceptably large amount of cleaning, not to mentions all the flavorings and spices to render them even remotely palatable.'

"It's a true story, provided by that NSA dude. And do you know where these aliens got all this information? They spent an entire

Saturday night in our ER waiting room, observing and taking samples! So, it could be officially said, if it were not so top-secret: North Central's ER saved planet Earth. Thanks to our patients we're out of the woods. We are forever safe!"

Finkel solemnly looked at his audience. The party sounds swirled around them. The students gaped at him in silence. Eileen looked down again and shook her head.

Finally, one of them spoke.

"Sir, is this for real?" Harry demanded.

Finkel looked intensely at his protégée.

"Yes. Remember, don't tell a soul."

"Oh my God, I think I need some air."

"This is unfucking believable!" the second student gasped.

"Heavy, man," the third medical student rumbled.

With that Harry turned around to leave. The other med students went with him, the stunned group waddling away like frightened penguins, leaving the doctor alone with Eileen. She looked at him with piercing eyes.

"You do know you just fucking ruined my high."

Finkel shrugged.

"It had to be done," he replied calmly.

"I'm getting a drink. Want to come along?"

"But of course, my dear. Let's have some fun. After all, we have all the time in the world."

With that, the two of them strolled arm in arm to the far end of the room, in search of ethanol.

*****

Part Eleven
The Radiology Bash

You were allowed to smoke at this Christmas party – in the bathroom, of course, but at least once there you could smoke what you wanted. After all, it took place *across* the street from the real hospital and lay outside its jurisdiction, or so the rationalization went. The only unofficial rule, maybe more like an advisory – you can't be partying here tonight if you're working the day shift tomorrow.

Bob Finkel and Ronda Tyler, the self-described ER power couple of the century, walked hand in hand into the massive party room, having wrapped up a private, interpersonal, goal-oriented meeting in the adjacent Medical Records Department, the only permanent fixture of the annex. (It even had real walls and its own bathroom!) They couldn't help but smile.

"Look at all this, my dear," Finkel said to her. "See what happens when we cavort? A party breaks out."

And it was a huge, marvelous party, enveloping the entirety of the remaining first floor of this very boring box of a building. Usually, this cavernous space was partitioned into multiple mid-level admin fiefdoms, but the walls-on-wheels, desks and cabinets had been rolled out of sight (despite the annual sniping from the section chiefs who still, somehow, magically, were always the first to arrive - you could always find them by the shrimp, feasting until they were flamingo pink). Tonight, the gently darkened room had magically transformed itself into a giant dance hall, replete with pulsating red and green lights, rimmed with tables laden with amazing food and rivers of drink. And the music was great – the live band knew just what songs to play and when to play them, from down and dirty to let's-go-easy-on-the-chubby guys.

X-Ray's annual Holiday Bash, open to all the hospital (excepting patients) was the first of several parties the hospital would host here. It was also known as easily the best of them all, the best attended, by far the best stocked, and the most, well, extreme – rumors abounded that in the past three years alone, four marriages and two divorces were direct outcomes of this event. Needless to say, the two nearby hotels, as always, were completely booked by the myriad of partygoers who, having discovered the meanings of life, love and lust on the dance floor, would now test them out to their heart's content in warm privacy.

Folklore had it that after a major hospital donor wed the Chief of Radiology's eldest daughter (following a major scandal), he bequeathed an endowment to build North Central an annex, on the condition that the first three weeks of December forever be allotted for hospital-wide festivities, with the first always to be held by Radiology, and he endowed this particular shindig with a very sizeable, dedicated fund. Still another tradition held that because of this robustly colorful past, more leeway was indeed shown toward this annual event; lots more was a lot more acceptable.

This was really one of the very few times when even the shyest, those with the most hang-ups and tightest of butts, felt perfectly natural laughing out loud and acting as if they were kids again. Contrast this to the Executive Committee's private "soiree" a week before at a local restaurant. There, a tipsy VP playfully goosed the CFO, and was loading up her cardboard box the next morning. Try that stuff here and you just may get lucky.

Here they all were, everyone celebrating having survived yet another year of being dedicated, caring and hardworking, albeit slightly overworked, underpaid and very much taken for granted. For most, just making it to this crazy night was an accomplishment in and of itself, one they'd always remember, at least parts of it, just as they'd done for all the others in the past.

Finkel and Ronda surf-danced across the floor, towards the (unofficial) ER turf, very often stopping along the way to chat with all their friends and foes – it was hard remembering who was who after a few drinks. Theirs was a lovely voyage, and it seemed to go on forever. You see, everyone in this giant room knew everyone else - for nearly half of their waking lives they lived with each other, and this huge party was pretty much their huge, extended family at play.

Finally, they reached their port of call, with all the hugs, kisses and high fives you'd expect when coming home. After a bit Ronda gently bit Finkel's cheek and headed off to speak with a friend. Finkel watched her swaying hips, and swore she was putting on a show for him (probably true). Then he looked up and smiled when he saw his best friend walking up.

"Well, well, who do we have here," Finkel said, hugging his fellow partner-in-crime. "It's the one and only Dean Miller, the man, the legend."

They raised their glasses, each filled with gin, clinked and drank, Finkel sloppily, Dean a little less so. Finkel looked at his friend quizzically.

"You on the wagon or something?"

"Just keeping my ammo dry, brother."

Finkel pondered this response. Then his little light went on.

"Ohhh…for Peg Ferguson? I guess yeah, sure, she's a nice girl, great doc, I'd even let her take care of me, but…"

"It ain't for Peggy, I assure you," Dean said, scanning the crowd. "Our junior high romance is over. And I really gave it the ole' college try."

"Well, I can't say that I'm shocked or even surprised…hey, you don't need any consolation or empathy, do you?"

"Nah," Dean answered with a shrug, looking this way and that.

"Okay, good, so, for the record - did you ever play at least a *little* baseball with her? Come on, man, talk to me. I'm not good at this shit but let it all out. I've got big time ADD and I'm pretty high right now, so don't worry about getting too personal. I won't remember much of anything you say."

The building pulsed with hot, thumping music. Dean shook his head.

"Nothing much to say, I barely got to first. It's strange, we worked so many shifts together. I mean, we talked all the time. She really seemed to get me and knows I'm at least halfway normal. I figured it'd be an easy segue from being good friends to, whatever. Boy did that plan crash and burn. I gave it my best. You know, by the fifth date if you're not getting somewhere, something is off, way off. Sex was just some unspoken taboo. God, I swear I would just touch her and she would start holding her breath.

"We spoke a few days ago. She kept saying how sorry she was, and how she would make a much better mother than a wife. It sounds like she plays for the other team. That's cool and all, I guess, but she sure as hell fooled me. Anyway, I wish her well…sorta sad, though.

"So, we're friends, again, maybe even good friends. We had some decent times...great conversations. I'll have no problems working with her or hanging with her, even tonight if she gets out on time. But it must be said, deep down I never felt the heat either. So there, that love boat has officially sailed, and Mr. Happy is now going back into action. Actually, I've been thinking a lot about someone else for quite a while now. So now, my good friend, session's over - so here's to life, and all its complications."

They clinked their glasses and drank, this time Dean giving his an enthusiastic chug. Suddenly he turned towards the far doorway, and all motion ceased. Finkel followed his gaze and smiled approvingly.

Samantha had just walked in, wearing a sparkling blue dress, looking radiant. Dean couldn't stop staring at her (hell, half the room turned to look at her.) The nurse scanned the room, and when their radars locked onto each other they glowed so intensely you could practically see and feel the heat.

Sam watched Dean pat his good friend on the shoulder and walk up to her, forcing herself to breathe when he approached and gently take hold of her arm.

"You're amazing to behold," Dean said, awed at how happy he was to see her. He got the sensation, as ridiculous as it seemed, that on this dance floor the rest of his life might be measured from this moment on.

"Didn't recognize me with my clothes on, did you?" she asked coyly.

Dean leaned forward and kissed her. She put her hands around his back and pulled him closer and they wrapped their arms around each other.

"Wow," was all he could say, when they finally let go and looked at each other.

"Wow, indeed," she quietly said, half to herself.

"Will you dance with me Sam?"

"Dean, I'll always dance with you," she whispered in his ear.

They kissed again, and as luck would have it, the next song happened to be Unchained Melody - a gem for two people who just want to hold onto each other (with the right person, it's enough to make you believe in heaven). They swayed together, each wondering if what they were now feeling was the start of something special.

"Still love me?" he asked, not even sure what he was doing – his father once told him that these were great pickup lines in his day - and he hoped that one day he might try them out. Now seemed to be the time.

"I will say that there's a bit of fire," she replied softly, not missing a beat. "And, what's your name again?"

They looked at each other, laughed out loud, hugged and continued to dance. Dean couldn't help but notice the perfection of her chest against his.

*

Ronda and Bob, hobnobbing with their comrades-in-arms, were all smiles at the sight of their respective best friends enjoying each other. When, finally, their favorite people bowed to the band and began walking back to them, hand in hand, they applauded them. There were some more hugs, some small talk, and then Ronda spoke up.

"Let me borrow her for a while, Dean, we're gonna freshen up."

"Just bring her back, please."

"Not to worry," Ronda said, gently tugging on Sam's elbow. They picked up a few friends along the way and disappeared around a corner.

Finkel and Miller, the duo reunited yet again, surveyed the premises. A great many of the two hundred plus people here in this dance hall were in the midst of having the best night of their year, whether they would admit it or not, and it was joyous to behold.

"Nice party," Dean said finally, contentedly. "Possibly with the potential to turn out to be a great party, if…"

Finkel solemnly nodded his understanding, trying to seem wise and all-knowing.

"You two guys looked pretty damn comfy out there on the dance floor," he finally remarked. "I'm impressed. You know, I was starting to worry that you'd become all work and no play.

"But now, let's get down to the serious stuff, since we've got a few minutes. I preface these remarks with this question: don't you think it's borderline illegal how hot all these women are? Good Lord, look at that one in the green dress. What color is that lipstick anyway, 'come fuck me' red? My friend, this is an all-star crowd. And the pain, oh, the pain. We'd normally peruse the room and make lurid and inappropriate remarks about all these beautiful… but it's a brave new world out there now, isn't it?"

"I sure hope so, man," Dean replied. "I am not rocking this boat; it took me long enough to get on board. But I must say that I totally agree with your assessment. There are some definite OMGs in this place."

"Yeah, Ronda might look askance at the sight of me salivating over anyone but her. Anyhow, it's fun to have survived yet another year of fun and games. To survival!"

They again clinked their glasses.

The good friends then spent a bit of time making (they deemed) non-sexist and constructive critiques about various members of this holiday crowd, still knowing that most of the comments they made, and the stories they told, toned down as much as they were, would still land them in hot water had they been spoken across the street. By this party's standards, however, they were being positively straight laced.

"And who the hell are you two leering at?" Ronda chuckled, approaching them from behind. She did seem, well, different since her brief encounter with Sam, who very carefully followed her. Both were holding drinks.

Dean's eyes locked onto Sam's. She smiled and curtsied.

"Evenin', sir. And how might y'be?" she demurely asked, affecting a crappy cockney accent.

"And aren't you the gorgeous scullery maid (whatever a scullery maid really is)," the doctor cockneyed back, reaching for her hand, feeling so very relieved when she wordlessly took it.

"And might I say you're kind of cute yourself," she said, not breaking eye contact.

Ronda peered in the direction Finkel was now looking at.

"Ohh, are you ogling Tracy from HR? Forget it, my good doctor, she's a *nice* girl, as in *way* too nice for you. Besides, my dearest, aren't you still on refractory time?"

"It was not an 'ogle', but rather, a medical exam," Finkel explained, sipping his gin. "I save all my ogles for you – and if the truth be known, I give really good 'ogle'".

"And you, Doctor Dean," Ronda continued, whispering sort of quietly in his ear. "From what I've heard from a *very* reliable source, tonight you just might want to play the hand you've been dealt…just saying. I'd avoid even the slightest whiff of controversy."

"You're preaching to the choir," Dean said. "Not to worry."

"Did you just say 'whiff,' my dear?" Finkel interrupted in his own crappy English accent.

"Yes, my prince, a *whiff!*" Ronda replied haughtily, seductively sniffing her upper lip. "And remember - all your whiffs, and ogles, they belong to me."

Finkel nodded and grinned at her.

"Girlfriend, that was purely professional," Finkel stated, wrapping his arm around her shoulder. "I shouldn't be betraying patient privacy like this, but okay, I was checking her out to look for problems. Lumps and bumps, know what I mean? I should be sending her a bill."

"Lumps and bumps?" Ronda asked wryly. "Undoubtedly your payment options will be 'card, cash or ass.' No wonder you're divorced…wait, you know something? You never actually told me why you did get divorced."

"I don't consider myself 'divorced,' my beloved, but rather 'pre-owned'," Finkel responded, pulling her closer. "Well, when the physical stuff ran its course, and it wasn't all that great to begin with, the 'betters' were soon outnumbered by the 'worses' by like a thousand to one. Plus, when she drank, she trended towards being a mean drunk – and she was drunk a *lot*.

"Boy, did we fight – each waking day was like playing Russian roulette. If someone made a movie based on that marriage, it would have been called, 'Thirty Million Things I Don't Like About You.' Still I did actually take one thing away from that travesty; it was me realizing how stupid I really am. And as for that 'cash or credit card' stuff, nope, ain't interested. As for the 'ass' part, nah, I got me a girlfriend."

"You just called me 'girlfriend' twice now," Ronda whispered. "Did you mean that?"

Finkel looked at her and smiled.

"If you'll have me."

The two them kissed, oblivious to the nodding heads and many smiles they generated. The rumors were true!

Dean and Samantha just kept smiling at each other.

After a bit Finkel and Ronda came up for air, and they happened to see HR Tracy weaving through the crowd. Dean and Samantha followed their line of vision.

"She looks like she's hunting or something, like a lioness at a watering hole," Samantha said, a little impressed.

"Yup, she is," Ronda agreed. "I know for a fact Tracy's shooting for Watkins, the GI fellow – she told me she's already packed her toothbrush and curling iron in her purse, not to mention those special vials she...holy fuck-a-moley!... she's making her move! You go, girl!!"

"I am shocked and appalled at your unholy imagination," Finkel said, all the while himself gaping at the lanky blonde deliberately/accidentally bump into her target. "One must wonder if she's as good as she looks...medically speaking, of course. Watkins will find out soon enough, I guess. I just hope he's a gentleman and is the one who gets the towel."

"Bob, you are so romantic..."

"People," Samantha said, cutting them off. She peered into a far-off corner of the room and pointed. "That's the morgue doctor, isn't it?"

"You mean Sanders, as in Jeff Sanders the pathologist?" Finkel asked.

His eyes scanned the crowded room, filtering out a kaleidoscopic array of images, until he noticed a small, bespeckled, overdressed man who seemed to radiate inconspicuousness.

"Goodness gracious, weirdo Sanders," he pronounced. "That is he in the flesh, standing at his post, the punch bowl, just like he does year in and year out. Wow, he's alone. Usually he brings a rental, to show everyone how easy it is for him to date a knockout. The one from last year was a real doozy. She looked normal, actually, except for the heavy makeup, and her giving everyone she met the eye.

"When Sanders nodded out, which happened pretty early on, his 'date' and 'ole Doc Miller here might possibly have had a private liaison in Medical Records. Shit, oh shit! Dean, I'm sorry...I didn't..."

"I'm not sure what you're talking about," Dean replied nervously, glancing sideways at Samantha. She looked at him, smiling – and mouthed the words *don't worry about it*.

Ronda was non-plussed. She was grinding away to the pulsing music.

"Yeah, don't worry about it, big guy," she replied, turning to Dean. "You were divorced, unattached and allowed to do whatever you wanted. And by the way, these girls like to party. I heard that after you, that gal punched her timecard and turned quite the profit that night – you really must have primed that pump of hers. Her 'all you can eat special' was quite the rage among several of our male colleagues, not to mention two women."

"Two women," Finkel said to himself.

"I told you not to mention 'two women,' my dear."

"Yup, it was a weird end to a rough year," Dean said carefully, wondering what really was permissible to say at a party, especially with Samantha next to him holding his hand. What the hell, he finally thought, if you can't open up even a little to people you party with, what's the use of going to the party – and I know Sam knows the stories, everyone does.

"And yeah, I took two grams of zithro after that, just to be safe. I guess I just wasn't used to being single. I married on the young side, but it was never much fun. I kept waiting to fall in love with her but it never happened, and I felt sort of lonely during most of it. But being *alone* was for me a whole new level – I never even lived by myself before. You do funny things. I'd like to think that stuff is over, and that I've moved on…you guys think I'm crazy now, don't you."

He anxiously looked at Samantha. She shook her head and kissed his shoulder.

"I'll take care of you, Dean," she whispered.

Sighing with gratitude, he wrapped his arm around her. Then he led her to a nearby table.

"Hey brother, what are you doing?" Finkel called out.

"Re-supply," he answered. "We'll be back with some goodies. For everyone!"

The ER people around them bowed and applauded.

"Hurry up then," Finkel urged. "The peasants are hungry!"

Within seconds the couple was stepping up to a line of amply stocked tables. Dean suddenly turned her around to face him. She allowed herself to be so positioned, and then she looked up at him, smiling, with just a trace of wondering....

"What's up, doc?"

Dean wrapped his arms around her.

"Can I kiss you again?"

"You never have to ask."

Dean soon found himself in some magical place, somewhere he never dreamt he would be or even deserved. He finally pulled away from Sam and stared at her intently.

"I want to start something," he whispered, his face close to hers. "Sam, I am so into you. You in the mood for a beginning?"

"I'm with you all the way, Dean," she said, biting her lower lip. "All the way."

They looked at each other and kissed again. Their embrace could have gone on forever had they not been so rudely interrupted by the sound of fists rhythmically pounding tables.

"Get a room...but first bring us food!" the intonation went. Then the chants began. "We want food! We want food!"

Dean looked at Sam, then smiled.

"I wouldn't mind getting a room myself," he said to her.

"Not to worry, Dean, we'll figure it out. Wow, that's some serious pounding."

"Yeah, nothing's worse than starving peasants. Let's get moving. It's time to feed the masses."

They proceeded to load up several plates with food, and two bottles of top-shelf booze.

Finally, as if walking a tightwire, they juggled their way back to the oohing and aahing group and triumphantly set the intact plates and bottles down all around.

Back at home base they laughed and talked with one and all, reminiscing about all the mayhem, catastrophes and madness of the past year, which now brought many of them to tears, but now of joy. First prize for having survived the year was now being able to laugh at it.

Miller and Sam gently swayed, chuckling at the stories. Suddenly Dean raised his glass, then stopped halfway, mildly befuddled.

"I had some important things to say...shit, I forgot what they were – but I think it had something to with how much I love you all," Dean said. "So, a TOAST - to Sam, and to everyone who's made a difference in my life, my colleagues, friends, and friends to be. When I'm in the ER with you guys, I really feel like I'm home."

There was a solid two second or three seconds of silence, then everyone started to clap.

A bit later Ronda froze as she looked across the dance floor, and her eyes grew wide. The four friends were now standing next to a round table, where they had parked their goodies.

"Oh my god, my god!" she exclaimed. "Dr. Sanders is looking this way."

"Sanders actually moved?" Dean asked, half to himself. His right hand was very discretely rubbing Samantha's bottom. "He's usually like a garden gnome, except he can move an arm up and down in order to sip whiskey. Folks, this is a reportable event."

"What's wrong with Sanders, he got the cooties or something?" Sam asked. She was alternating sips of her gin in one hand and bites of food from the other, whilst subconsciously rolling her hips against Dean's hand.

"Nah, he's just your typical forty-year-old who lives with his mother and is afraid of girls," Finkel said, trying hard not to stare at HR Tracy shyly flirting with her target, closing the trap. He thoughtfully sipped his drink. "Now I'm not saying he's the number one nerd in all the world, but it'd be tough making him number two...and look who just arrived!"

Everyone's gaze suddenly turned to a newly arrived partygoer. She was alone and gyrating to the music, her hands raised in the air as she danced by herself. One could almost hear the *ping* of libidinous glances bouncing off her extremely curvy figure from every direction. *Karlita!*

"Dean, Sam, Princess Ronda, I have a brainstorm," Finkel said excitedly. "It's positively revolutionary, maybe even interesting."

"I think you'd need a brain for that, darling," Ronda replied calmly. "But then again, Bob, you don't have to worry about strokes. See, it averages out. But talk to us and show us the way."

"Listen up," Finkel whispered. Dean and Sam leaned forward, sipping their alcohol in unison, waiting to hear pure wisdom. Ronda was grinning like the Cheshire cat. She knew...

"What say we set Sanders up with Karlita?" Finkel asked mischievously.

"Wow, I'm not really sure," Dean replied, nervously. "Karlita, the *body snatcher*?"

"It's perfect," Ronda practically screamed in agreement. A few nearby partygoers briefly looked at her, then turned away. "The King of the Morgue and the Body Snatcher. If that ain't romantic, what is? Fink, you get a Nobel for this."

"Karlita would eat him for breakfast," Dean replied hesitantly.

"And what is wrong with getting 'eaten for breakfast'?" Ronda serenely replied, looking at Finkel as he whispered something like *that can be arranged...*

"What do you mean, 'body snatcher'?" Samantha asked, her voice just starting to get a trace fuzzy. She was slightly newer to the ER, and still unversed on all its deepest secrets (all ERs have them).

"Karlita's one of our special people," Rhonda explained, looking around. "She likes…well, she's into body parts. It's like a hobby, maybe a religion. If we cut something off, burn it off, squeeze it out, even if it falls off, she discreetly, very discreetly, picks it up and pockets it. Her favorite thing of all time is when a patient arrives with a body part already wrapped up in a towel, like that mangled thumb last week from the girl who was holding the log steady for her mother, who didn't know squat about using an axe. We couldn't possibly re-attach it, and her eyes lit up like it was Christmas. She said, 'I'll take that for you, honey!' I hear she put it in a cigar box she keeps in her locker. From there, who knows.

"Apparently, she's got quite a collection. I mean, fingers, warts, teeth, ears…word has it that she even has some of that penis from the gunshot last month, you know, from that Peeping Tom who zigged when he should have zagged."

"Oh, what a great case - the guy was shot by the husband, and the bullet travelled through his butt straight into his dick," Samantha recalled excitedly. "Body parts, wow. You mean she put his dick in a cigar box? I didn't know that. It's okay…right?"

Ronda looked at her and smiled.

"If they can't stick it back on, I guess it is," she said good-naturedly. "Of course, some of it went to the sheriff and Pathology. We were gonna chuck that pecker anyway, there wasn't much left of it. It's not like she took anything useful, no offense to the poor guy. It was either the bucket or the box, so who cares?

"Eileen follows a strict, 'Don't tell me shit,' policy regarding her. And Karli's discrete, I'll tell you that…plus she happens to be the toughest nurse we have, and that comes in handy on midnights. Night crews are, shall we say, a mixed bag to put it mildly. We need a really good ass kicker with brains in there. She's cool, too, we even party once in a while. You watch, she'll be bumped to charge one day…and there she is, in all her glory!"

"That was a great case," Samantha reminisced, a smile on her face. "It's also what first attracted me to Dean. The guy's lying handcuffed to the stretcher in Two, moaning and groaning. Boy, that bullet lodged in the very tip of his penis – you could see the bulge, like it was a snake that just swallowed something. Anyway, Dean's checking him out, and I ask if we should order a portable chest. He looks up at me and says, 'hell, no, we need a portable dick.' It was then that I realized we were meant to be together."

"God, this is out of the movies," Ronda gushed.

They turned and saw the very curvy woman with long black hair and a short black dress. She was facing them now, her heavily made-up eyes almost closed, rhythmically moving to the music. It wasn't clear whether she even noticed them.

"So, she's here, and Sanders is there," Finkel said with the air of Field Marshall Montgomery ordering troop movements on the North African front. He pointed a finger at an imaginary war map. "We've got to connect point A to point B so we can trigger some really good point C action. Now, l propose we get Sanders here first, sort of soften him up, and then, we bring in Karlita for the kill."

"Yes, commander!" Ronda snapped out, saluting smartly.

"This is cool, right?" Sam asked a little nervously. "No one gets hurt or traumatized for life?"

"Drunken matchmaking is not for the faint of heart," Dean said, looking at her. "And we're gonna make this work. I bet they'll love each other – their tastes seem to be pretty lined up. This might be Jeff's time to shine."

"Well, I for one think Dr. Sanders is sort of cute," Ronda said approvingly as she watched the slight doctor shuffle in their direction. "And so is Karlita. She's a nice girl, sort of. I mean, the piercings, the makeup, the tattoos on her butt, they *may* be a bit over the top, but still...."

"A toast, to Frankenstein and his bride," Finkel said loudly, raising his glass. Ronda, Sam, and a few nearby partygoers who had no idea what they were talking about, all cheerfully clinked their glasses and drank in unison – imbibing when there's a toast going on is a guilt-free experience.

"Jeff, come on over," Miller shouted, trying to make himself heard over the music. With Sam holding onto his arm, he held out a drink, which he'd poured but decided not to touch. Graciously he gave it to the nervous incoming pathologist, who seemed to inhale most of it the minute his hand made contact. Dean smiled at their new guest. In the corner of his eye, he could see Karlita walking over in response to Ronda's gesticulations, concentrating on her own balance.

"It's good to see you, man. How goes it in the path lab?" Miller asked the pathologist, shaking his hand. Sanders seemed grateful for the human contact.

"Oh, no complaints, Dean. We don't get any complaints. We can't, all our patients are dead. Dead. Get it?"

He emitted a high-pitched squeal, presumably a laugh. It did turn a few heads.

"So, you came alone tonight, huh?" Finkel asked.

"Well, yeah, things sort of, fell through."

"That young lady you came with last year, she was nice. Whatever became of her?" Finkel asked innocently, trying not to show any of the pain he was suddenly feeling as Ronda dug her heel into the top of his foot.

"Business trip," Sanders said quickly.

Karlita joined their little group. The pathologist started to visibly gel.

"Aren't you going to make any introductions, Bob?" Ronda sweetly broke in as she looked around. She shot a warning glare to Finkel that could melt steel.

"Oh, silly me. Jeff, this is Karlita – she's one of our best nurses. Really, really interesting person, you're gonna love her. And Karlita, this here is Jeff Sanders, otherwise known as the King of the Morgue."

Karlita stared at each of them with half closed eyes. When she got to Sanders, she gave him a smoky up and down once over.

"So, you're the King of the Morgue," she said, licking her lips. "I've always wanted to meet you."

Sanders stared at her, nearly paralyzed. A drop of spittle glistened on his lower lip. An uneasy silence ensued. Miller put his mouth next to the pathologist's ear.

"Say something, man, say something and be cool," he whispered. After a few seconds he poked the trembling pathologist. "It's your big chance. Say *anything*."

Everyone stared at the trembling doctor, whose face had become shiny with sweat. It was clear that he was not doing well. And then, finally, he spoke.

"Did you know that the average life span of a Siberian nickel miner is fifty-one?"

Everyone exchanged blank stares. Finkel quickly raised his right index finger and then shot it out to his side. Strike one. Finally, Karlita broke the silence.

"I didn't know that," she replied, trying to figure out if that was a joke.

"And did you know a horsefly is more sterile than a man's tongue?" the pathologist continued in his sexiest voice, charging ahead.

"I didn't know that either. Quite interesting, I guess."

All four matchmakers took nervous swallows from their glasses. Finkel made another sign signaling strike two, stoically expecting, then receiving, an elbow from Ronda. Holding his side, he sternly whispered into Sanders' ear.

"Say something else, Romeo, give her your absolute *best* line," Finkel hissed.

"Yeah, please, baby," Karlita asked Sanders, licking her lips again and moving a half step closer – even Ronda and Samantha leaned forward and stared at him. "Give me your absolute best; tell me something important about the universe."

"The *'universe'*?" Dean asked dubiously. "Isn't this overly ambitious?"

The pathologist had turned into a statue.

Finkel gently tapped his girlfriend's shoulder. She looked at him and smiled.

"Come, my deity," he said. "Give the lovebirds their privacy."

He practically dragged her to a nearby table labelled, "Whore's Ovaries." Ronda suggestively stuck out her tongue behind the trembling path doctor's back and made not so subtle licking movements, eliciting shouts of *here, here* from very amused bystanders. Dean and Sam followed, joining them by the table. From there they watched the unfolding events.

Karlita looked suggestively at poor Sanders, who was clearly struggling.

"I'm waiting, baby-cakes," she said.

Sanders took a deep breath. And then he spoke.

"Well – if all of us changed our bathroom habits when we have bowel movements, if we all neatly folded two sheets of toilet paper per swipe, instead of bunching the paper into a ball, in one year we could save enough trees to reforest the state of Massachusetts."

"Really, I'll have to think about that" Karlita commented, after a slight pause. "I'm from Massachusetts. Well, see you later."

She turned and slowly walked away.

Dean and Samantha, who had been straining to hear, cringed. At that moment Linda, the house supervisor, walked over to them. She'd just arrived at the party and was still in her scrubs, although now she was holding a drink in each of her hands.

"Hey everyone, Dr. Peg says she can't make it tonight. Big trauma just rolled in. She said to party on without her."

Dean gave a *so what* shrug and whispered something in Sam's ear. She smiled and nodded. With an air of gallantry, he held out his arm. Samantha graciously, accepted it. They walked back to Sanders, who was hyperventilating, sweaty and shaky.

"Jeff, I gotta go, something came up," he whispered. "You can do this, man. And let it be noted that tonight you gave it your best shot."

"I *can't* do it, Dean, and I don't *have* a best shot," the pathologist replied sadly, sniffling. "We all know I'm a loser."

"Well, this could be your year. At least you didn't come with an escort this time. That alone shows guts and determination..."

"You knew about that?" Sanders asked, visibly aghast. His face contorted with grief and shame.

Dean felt Samantha rubbing her middle finger across his palm. After an awkward pause, he looked at the suffering man, torn between loyalty to a colleague in pain, and his desire. It was a very short battle.

"Who knows, rumors just start. Good luck, Jeff, but you don't really need it. You have it in you, man, remember that. Knock 'em dead... you know what I mean."

With that he turned and walked away, his hand intertwined with Sam's. Sanders followed them with mournful eyes. Finkel and Ronda smiled and waved their goodbyes, as they grazed at the nearby table.

Sanders closed his eyes and bowed his head. So, this is how it feels to be completely broken, he thought to himself....

"Hey, baby-cakes..."

Sanders looked up and stared at Karlita. Her eyes still half closed, she held a sweet looking drink, which she gave to him. He sipped it, too scared to say anything. And then, somehow, he felt a strange calmness. Relax, a voice in his head told him. You have it in you.

Suddenly, memories of countless rehearsals in front of his bathroom mirror surged into him.

"You can say anything you want to me now, I'm very receptive," she said demurely. "Forgive my slurring, that last round might have been a touch too strong – but all the better for your chances."

"Slurring? Au contraire, your enunciation is perfection incarnate," Sanders practically chirped, secretly thrilled at this newfound coolness. Was that me, he thought excitedly, has God given me a second chance? He felt bravery and resolve rushing (well, trickling) throughout his body. If I die, let it be in combat, he thought grimly, so act cool. She's only a woman, nothing more, nothing less. A beautiful, voluptuous woman, who I do not deserve in any way, shape or form. Shit, who am I kidding? God, please…

Trying to sound casual and sexy, he now inhaled deeply and mustered the last, the very last, tattered shred of his courage and spoke in a low voice, realizing he had nothing to lose.

"So, you sweet, sexy thing, tell me, what are you thinking about at this very moment, and what can I do for you to make it right?"

He paused, stunned that these words came out coherently. But he was pretty much out of ammo (bathroom rehearsals don't cover every scenario), and he now closed his eyes and held his breath, waiting to be shot down.

Karlita looked up at him, touched his arm, and spoke.

"I'm thinking how much I would like to slaughter a family while they beg for mercy, chop them up, stir fry them with sesame oil and garlic, and have a delicious meal, maybe with some red wine."

There was a pause of several seconds. Sanders blinked a few times, and finally spoke.

"I just love stir fry. With Malbec, of course."

"And then I would rip the legs off their puppy, bake them at 400 until they were nice and crisp, and dip them in ranch dressing..."

"I love ranch dressing!" Sanders shouted. He suddenly remembered another line from the bathroom. It was now or never.

"Hey, how would you like a cocktail - my cock and your tail. *Get it?*" he squealed loudly, turning heads in his direction.

A pause. The doctor waited. Then Katrina looked deeply into his eyes.

"You're cute, you know that? You sort of remind me of my seventh-grade boyfriend."

"Really?" Sanders whispered excitedly.

Karlita leaned towards him, kissed his face and put her lips to his ear. She whispered something. When she was done, she gently bit his earlobe. Then she looked at him, slightly cocking her head. She smiled at the man, who now appeared to be in extremis.

Sanders was motionless, eyes and mouth half open, the only signs of life being his spittle, now starting to drool down.

"Would you?" she asked in a near whisper, her lips parted.

No response, no movement.

"Would you?" she gently repeated, pursing her lips, looking at him. "What are you waiting for, big boy, would you like to?"

Suddenly Sanders heroically, epically, slowly moved his shoulders up and down, his frozen head moving in such a way to convey that his answer was yes, yes, a thousand times yes...

"Then come on," she said silently, mouthing the words, and took his hand.

Walking across the dance floor, they caught the curious stares of several partygoers, including Finkel and Ronda, who were now at a table labeled "Health Food," loading up on stuffed mushrooms and tiny meatballs. What they saw was Karlita the Body Snatcher steadily guiding the King of The Morgue towards what they both knew was the promised land.

Sanders shuffled faithfully behind, one hand on her shoulder. His face was a mask, wearing either a smile or grimace (it was hard to tell). He distinctly gave the appearance of a half-crazed zombie marching into paradise.

They entered Medical Records. And then, (most of) the lights went out.

And the band played on. Radiology's annual family celebration, from front line to back office, all the services and all the departments, pulsed with joy, laughter and good cheer, celebrating the end of yet another year's worth of memories. Maybe it was worth it after all.

Finkel and Ronda, the founders of this merry band of ER matchmakers, (Samantha lived two blocks away and was most likely turning the key in her lock at this moment, Dean Miller a few inches behind her, most likely caressing her breasts), beamed at each other, looking every bit the proud parents at the wedding. Once again, romance had triumphed. They clinked their meatballs, downed them with champagne and sighed, realizing that after it's all said and done, everybody has a chance, and *all* of us are entitled to a happy ending.

*****

Part Twelve
Night's End

Lars Anderson bolted upright, sweating heavily. The hotel room possessed a cave-like darkness, and for several seconds he didn't know where he was, until the ceiling smoke detector blinked.

Yet another ER nightmare had attacked. He was getting more and more of these, and they all had to do with him forgetting things. This one involved the results of a spinal tap - 60 white cells, all polys, a protein level of 118, and he didn't know what to do. The nurses shouted at him to order antibiotics for the dying patient, and he literally froze. Damn, I can treat this with my eyes closed, he scolded himself. Sure, bigshot, his inner voice snorted, your eyes *were* closed, is that your best excuse?

Earlier he'd dreamt about a patient with a neck injury and bilateral arm weakness – central cord issues, maybe? – and he didn't remember what test to order. After much pacing and handwringing, he finally figured it out – MRI, anyone? – but when he walked to the desk to order it, he'd forgotten his password. While on eternal hold with IT, his patient became hypotensive.

Anderson rubbed his clammy forehead. At least I beat the damn alarm, he thought, grunting at this small victory. Oh well, I'll get into work a tad early and knock off my trillion incomplete charts. Hell, I'd be happy just to make twenty or thirty disappear.

Turning on the nightstand lamp, he looked down at his legs and slapped his thighs. *C'mon guys, let's make some donuts. Two shifts to go and this run is over.*

Carefully shuffling over to the bathroom, he flicked on the overhead light, wincing at the glare. He brushed his teeth and shaved, grumpily taking stock of nausea and a mild headache, and he wondered how drunk he'd gotten the night before – he borderline remembered slumping into bed.

Anderson rarely allowed himself to get toasted. He'd brought in takeout chicken and fries, called home to say his good nights and 'I love you's to his wife and children, then poured himself some vodka and got down to business. For the record, he'd never once worked or driven drunk, had an ironclad eight-hour bottle-to-throttle rule, and never drank alone except when trying to depressurize after a rough shift or to prep for a good sleep. He hardly ever drank in public or even at parties.

He didn't even like the taste of booze. But it let him sleep. Self-medicating like this, he knew, was a slippery slope, but it was now ingrained in his DNA, borne out of a crippling fear of insomnia – for Lars, as with most ER people, there was *nothing* worse than working tired. I don't know how the other people out there do it, he'd wonder to himself. I've *got* to be fully alert and wired at all times – otherwise, things go south.

So, with the alcohol came sleep. He knew he was sober now – he'd become a grandmaster at the math of ethanol metabolism and blood levels. He also knew this hangover was on him. It was odd, though, the bottle still had a decent amount left.

I can't even hold my booze anymore.

Deciding against a shower – *tonight, I'll do it tonight* – he began the early morning ritual, so different than its afternoon counterpart when prepping for a night shift. As always, he felt the tension building inside. And how many times have I done this, he wondered. Hundreds? Thousands? *And after all these years I still get nervous before a shift and worry I'll hurt someone, that this shift will be my ruination, as well as theirs.* For years he assumed he would get used to all this, and that his fears would melt away – but they never did.

Twenty minutes later he was buttoning his lab coat. Making sure his ID badge and stethoscope were present and accounted for, patting the motel room card in his breast pocket, he stepped into his shoes and shuffled to the door. Clicking things off his mental checklist – leftovers and bottle in the small fridge, keys in his lab coat pocket; reading/intubation glasses, puzzles, code gum in his carry bag, etc. – he closed the door and slowly walked down the empty hall, promising to clean the room better when he got back, and to drink a little less. This five-day run will soon be over, he wearily promised himself.

The motel lobby was dead quiet – even the desk person was AWOL.

Anderson carefully made his way down the sidewalk to the parking lot, trying to avoid the occasional patches of late October ice. After a bit he found his car, opened the door and slumped behind the wheel. His engine roared to life, and he turned on the defroster, opting to shiver for a few minutes rather than scrape.

Minutes later he was one of a handful of lonely cars on the cold highway, the eastern horizon now a dark, resentful purple, on the sixteen-mile trek to the hospital – after all these years the doctor swore he knew every rock, every tree, every deer and, yes, every cop along the way. Shoving two cubes of gum in his mouth, he computed this to be a fifteen-minute trip.

Fucking dreams, he angrily thought, *fuck 'em, fuck 'em all! I'm as good as I've ever been.*

Still, he realized that as hard as he tried, he still was having problems. The initial treatment for meningitis – he knew it was vancomycin and, and something…and he was awake now.

Damn, he was mad. The car self-cruised at seventy. Anderson shook his head defiantly, slightly wincing from the headache that motion had just aggravated. To prove he still had a functioning brain he started testing himself. He did this a lot early on in his career, when he would get panic attacks driving to work. *What's the Parkland Burn Formula? Hmmm. What are the families of non-steroidal anti-inflammatories? At what age can you use steroid cream on a baby? What's the sequence for floating a pacemaker…*

Nothing clicked.

God, he was furious at his memory's egregious betrayal. I didn't drink that fucking much, he argued out loud with himself. Twenty years in and I can't even remember the basics. *I forgot the fucking basics,* he screeched inside the car, pounding the steering wheel. *I didn't drink that fucking much!*

His head throbbed and his mouth was dry. He moved his hand over to the center cupholder – of course it was empty.

Damn, this has the makings of being a crap-tastic day.

As his car sped south, past the darkened shapes of the end-of-nighttime landscape, he willed himself to unravel these ER problems one after another, saving the burn problem for last (that always gave him trouble, but there were posters in the trauma rooms, so it was never really that big of a deal). It was grueling but he finally started making progress, though he was concerned at how hard it was getting back on track. Finally, with his exit a mere three miles away, he went after the Parkland Formula.

Okay, motherfucker, you belong to me. Now what is it, percentage of body surface burned times patient weight in kilograms times...

He was staring down the empty road, not really looking at anything, his index finger writing in the air to solve a simple computation, when he saw the deer – it just suddenly appeared in front of him. Anderson knew he'd made a mistake by swerving, but he'd been distracted, and it happened so fast. Instinctively, he cried out in vain protest as his car shot off the road. He could feel the outraged rumble strip attacking his tires. He felt the crumble of pebbles, managed to spit out his gum… and then he sensed the car flipping over…

*

Early dawn was glowing through the windshield when Lars woke up. Amazingly, his car had righted itself, it's engine still running. What happened, he briefly wondered; and then a few things came back. He looked around - no cabin damage, no air bag deployment. Quickly, he did a self-exam – pulse strong and steady; movements of neck, back and extremities normal; no problems breathing, and no new pain, just his hangover – basically everything checked out. Tentatively, holding his breath, he got out of the car and carefully walked around, holding on, half expecting to keel over at any minute – but he didn't. Very luckily, the car was drivable. Alternately cursing his fates and blessing his luck, he stared at the surrounding cornfield he'd plowed into. About twenty yards or so away the outline of the highway, still relatively empty, was visible. Apparently, there were no human witnesses to this mishap. A few grazing deer looked up at him, their small tails swishing in protest.

As he began easing the car back towards the road, albeit considerably much more slowly, he thought he saw the deer that almost killed him. The doctor knew it was crazy, but he swore the deer was staring at him, taunting him. As irrational as it was, he flew into a terrible rage. He started driving after it, trying to run it over (actually driving back into the field), but quickly reconsidered and returned to the highway.

"I wish I had killed you!" he screamed out the window.

As he pulled into the right lane Lars imagined (no, he swore he heard) the deer talking to him.

"So sorry, I was hoping you would die."

Anderson cursed under his breath. A few miles down the road he saw the hospital, a black behemoth silhouetted amid the multi-colored sky. As he exited the highway, he realized that well before it even began, he wanted this day to be over.

**

Parking near the ambulance bay, he tentatively stepped out into the receding darkness, black clouds still pockmarking the sky. All was still. The parking lot had early morning written all over it - just two cars in the doctors' parking lot, and just a smattering more in the ER patient section. They must have had a good night, he thought to himself, maybe I'll get lucky. I wouldn't mind a little luck, at least the good variety. He carefully walked up to the staff entrance, still reviewing clinical pathways.

A few stray snowflakes touched his face. He swiped his ID badge on the outer keyboard and the ambulance door dutifully beeped open. He was in the alcove; to the right was the decontamination room, to the left, an EMS office, and a few feet in front of him, the main ER. Anderson approached it and felt…fear. Way more than two thousand shifts under his belt and still he felt afraid. Very much so.

You are such a wimp, he scolded himself. Just fake it if you have to. You've done it before, you can do it again. It'll come back to you; it always does. And tonight, you celebrate in style…maybe a little less booze, though.

His head throbbed and he rubbed his temples.

He walked into the ER. It seemed garishly brilliant compared with the somber early dawn outside. Anderson looked around, blinking in confusion.

There were several nurses clustered around the front counter, swaying back and forth, laughing very loudly – to Anderson it sounded like crowing. They seemed to be dancing. It didn't make any sense. The room looked so strange, almost unrecognizable.

"Well, look who the early bird drug in," one of them squealed. "You shouldn't be here…"

They all turned to look at him. Their faces were contorted, their eyes bulging. Lars had the sensation he had just interrupted a coven of witches sitting around a campfire.

"What's going on," one of them hissed. "What are you doing here?"

For a few moments there was a thick, unholy silence; nobody moved. And then, several of them started to walk to him, their steps slow and steady, their eyes squinting. The demons were coming for him.

"What, what's the matter?" Anderson blurted out, recoiling in fear, backing up until he hit the wall behind him. He slid down until he bumped onto the ground, and fearfully raised his shaking arms in self-defense. The demons grew closer. They were standing over him now.

"What's the matter?" the doctor cried, his bone-dry throat scratching his words. "What did I do? I didn't do anything! Please!"

A familiar voice boomed out from behind them.

"What the hell?"

Anderson lowered one of his forearms and saw Dean Miller, the night doc, glaring at him with flaming eyes. Miller too began walking towards him.

Within seconds they had him surrounded. They reached out and grabbed his arms and pulled him up. Anderson closed his eyes in terror.

"Please, please…" he begged, his voice parched and cracking, thinking he would faint.

"Put him on a stretcher!" Miller barked out. "Start a line and we'll give him something."

"Don't hurt me, please! Dean, what's going on? Dean!"

Within minutes, two nurses were transporting the sobbing doctor to CAT scan.

***

About an hour later Peggy Ferguson came in to relieve Miller. The two went into the code room for privacy. Miller sat on the stretcher and rubbed his face. His eyes were red.

"So, what happened?" she asked, reaching for his hand.

"Lars came in really early, incoherent and butt naked except for his shoes and lab coat," Miller answered numbly. "He was, like…crazed. It was freaky. CT showed a big tumor with mass effect. Probably a glioblastoma. I had to give him Mannitol and Decadron. They're loading him up for transfer as we speak. Oh yeah, I had to tube him."

"Fuck. Was he in pain?"

"More scared than anything – I gave him lots of Ativan. You know, it was the strangest thing - he had a pretty high temp, but I couldn't tap him because of the mass. Just as I was setting up for the intubation, contemplating this, right before we pushed the propofol, he looks at me with this very weird smile, like he just remembered something. He seemed lucid for a moment. He said, 'I'd cover myself with vanc and Rocephin.' And you know, he was right on – I actually gave him a round. Couldn't hurt, there easily could have been a confounding touch of infection. It's weird, *he* was his very last case."

"Damn it. He's on the young side, isn't he?"

"Forty something. Married, three kids. The kindest, gentlest man I've ever met. You know, he loved his patients so much. I've never seen him get angry…I've never even heard him curse."

"And he was one of our best…"

"He was our best. He was my standard. You know, Peg…that scan was ugly. He ain't gonna win this ball game."

"Yeah, he was dealt a really bad hand," she softly agreed. "Hey, let me get you out of here, and I'll see you tonight. Take an extra hour. We'll have plenty more info by then. But we both know…"

Dean closed his eyes and lowered his head. He rocked slowly, trembling just a little.

Peggy sat down next to him, put her arms around him, and drew the doctor close, just as he began to cry.

"It'll be okay, baby," she whispered. "Give it to God."

****

A few minutes later Dean walked out of the Code Room, flashing back to the scene about an hour ago, his good friend in that very same room, lying on that stretcher, confused, terrified and dying. He walked over to the outgoing and incoming crews, who were grouped by the ambulance entrance, several of them openly sobbing.

"See you guys tonight," he said, reaching out his arms.

They all shared a long group hug, no one wanting to let go. Finally, Miller walked out.

Wow, and to think a few months ago it was Marcus Allen – hard to believe we're all human...

He walked by Anderson's car, stunned at all the mud and scratch marks that now seemed to cover it. *What the...*

At that moment a huge helicopter, with Lars Anderson in it, lifted off. It slowly climbed up the peach-colored sky, headed for a Level One center, where a neurosurgical/oncologic team awaited. Miller watched until it disappeared from sight.

"I'm not good at this, Lars, not good at all," Dean said haltingly, staring overhead at the slowly fading stars. "You know, that's a big reason why I went into emergency medicine - feeling pain is optional. I know it's a flaw, a bad one, but I'm not the good man you are, and sad to say, I never will be.

"You were the greatest…you are the greatest. You taught me many things along the way, and I don't mean just medical stuff – although, I must thank you for that consult about the antibiotics. See? Even when you're dying, you leave me in the dust. And for what it's worth, you are very, very much loved, and that includes me. God bless."

*****

Part Thirteen
The Comeback Kid

"Marcus, pace yourself," Jerry Amoroso, MD, pleaded. "You've got five hours to go. They'll kill me if something happens to you. Besides, you're making the rest of us look bad and... what's in your hand? Four charts? Jesus, hand two of them over."

Marcus Allen had been caught red-handed. "Batching," or the practice of grabbing several new charts at a time, is a no-no in any ER. Reluctantly, he handed two of them over to his temporary boss.

"The rooms are next to each other," he explained cheerfully. "As in less walking all over the department, less cardiac demand, comprende?"

"'Comprende,' my ass," the Summerton ER chief replied wearily. "How'd I ever get roped into babysitting you? The only difference between you and the Road Runner is that you don't go *beep beep*. Marcus, please take it easy. Phil Tannenbaum will fucking have me castrated if you die on my watch."

"Can't you just feel the love," a nurse said quietly as she passed between the two of them, pushing an EKG cart.

"Hey, if you think you can control him, you got him," the director retorted. "My pressure's high enough already."

Amoroso looked the older doctor over. He had (very) reluctantly agreed to supervise Marcus Allen, who'd suffered a massive MI requiring emergency CABG five months' before, on his provisional return to emergency medicine. You could possibly make the case he'd been strongarmed by Tannenbaum, who called in a few favors. (The Big Boss was famous for his great memory.)

Allen had a rep for doing things his way, and ignoring doctors' advice was pretty much a given. He almost exploded into action the moment he'd returned, despite Cardio's strongest recommendations that he ease himself back in. (ER doctors, who deep down enjoy lecturing patients on any and all of their bad habits and questionable life choices, are notoriously terrible patients; in fact, the only ones worse are the nurses.)

"Marcus, you're like a wild man – you're even going into the waiting room to start your exam and get your orders taken care of. Really? We don't have to do that here. Just look around, do you see the world coming to an end?"

Allen had to concede the point. This was indeed a slow ER, almost worthy of the Q-word itself. Not one patient was unstable, not one was tension-provoking. Several of them probably could have been treated with a bowl of chicken soup (though some studies suggest wonton is superior).

"Well, I just thought I'd move things along, that's all. I like it here."

"Yeah, sure you do," Amoroso said dryly. "Tell me, how are you feeling?"

"Never better."

"Would you tell me the truth?"

"Probably not. But this time I am telling the truth."

"Marcus, I babysit you for another week. Humor me and take it easy."

"Okay, okay, I'll keep you alive…hey, remember the lady in Four, you know the one with the headache? I sent her for a CT venogram. I figured she looked suspicious enough to go straight for it…"

"We were going to start with a non-contrast head. We agreed to go slow. Wasn't that the understanding?"

"Please, I meant nothing disrespectful, you were upstairs bailing out the house doc before I finished her full history," Allen explained. "Get this - thirty-seven-year-old female, a smoker on birth control, with a three-day history of worsening headache. It's worse when she's lying down, and it reached killer level when she was squatting to look for something in her closet – sounds like she was performing her own Valsalva maneuver. No migraine history, and she never once asked for narcs. Jerry, I had to go with my gut and rule out CVT."

"CVT, as in cerebral venothrombosis? Marcus, isn't this a bit early into this case to start going after zebras? God, what's the use – okay, what did the venogram show?"

"CVT."

The ER director stared at his colleague impassively.

"Of course it did," he finally said. "I thought that stuff was just on board exams."

Amoroso pondered this – he'd never seen a case. Most likely I have, he now gloomily thought, but I missed it. He shook his head and smiled. So too did the nurse Eric, who was accidentally listening to every word, as he began to wheel the patient out of the ER, bound for the unit.

Finkel and his buddies were wont to call these places "foo foo ERs," but Marcus found a warm endearment to this place. Here he felt almost…nestled. Being a big fish in this charming little pond had its advantages. He also had to admit it was a pleasure to diagnose and treat conditions that did not all originate in Sodom and Gomorrah.

"The intensivist said to bring the patient right up to the ICU," Eric said over his shoulder. She'll write the orders and begin thinners, said she wants to think about it…she also told me to tell you, 'Nice work, doc.'"

"Nice work, indeed," Amoroso finally said. "I honestly don't know why I'm doing this; you should be supervising me. How'd you get so frigging smart? Hey, let's wrap these patients up, and then hit the cafeteria for some lunch. And don't worry, they know how to reach us."

Allen looked around. This ER was almost embarrassingly calm, with only nine – make that eight, now that the lady with the brain clot had gone upstairs – of its fifteen beds filled.

North Central by now would be full, and then there was that ever-present waiting room, bursting with unhappiness - it was typical to have fifteen to-be-seens in there when your shift began, and fifteen new ones in there when your shift wrapped up, despite you having worked your ass off. In *this* ER you are in a state of continuously being caught up. He kept waiting for the ax to fall; for the fateful call (or calls) from EMS, or the ambulance bay drop-offs; they could be ugly. But it never happened. I could learn to like this place, he admitted to himself. I haven't had jaw pain from clenching once – who'd have thought?

"Lunch sounds good," Marcus finally said. "Let me see my two cases, and how about we meet up in twenty or so minutes."

"See you then," the other doctor agreed, and they split up.

Allen had already seen the four cardiograms – almost all ERs, regardless of size or level of insanity, follow a strict ten-minute rule (some even use five) for obtaining EKGs on all chest pains – and these tracings were picture perfect. Combined with their very normal vital signs, lack of any medical history and relative youth, Allen knew these were creampuff cases, possibly cases of worknote-emia, which he often privately diagnosed. He entered the first room.

Inside was a powerfully built man, aged forty-two, lying calmly on the stretcher, an attractive woman standing by his side. A wall monitor displayed a rock-solid heart rhythm.

"Hello, I'm Doctor Allen," he said pleasantly, secretly amused at how readily he'd introduced himself - at North Central you often shunned both congeniality and introductions - at this rate, I might even shake someone's hand one day, he thought. "So, what brings you in today?"

The man took a paper from out his shirt's breast pocket.

"Sorry, Doc, I'm a little nervous and don't want to leave anything out," he said cautiously, and he started to read out loud.

"I have left-sided chest pain going down my arm, with nausea, ff…foresis and shortness of breath. It began in the gym."

Allen very slightly shook his head. This guy's been hitting the Internet big time, he thought.

"Sir, did you mean to say 'diaphoresis,' as in 'sweating'?"

The man hesitated. The woman leaned towards him and whispered something.

"Yeah, what you said," he finally answered.

Allen sighed and began the exam, all four minutes of it. He could have done it in half that time – hell, he didn't even have to do any exam but knew that this kind of ER expected the staff to put on a good show for all cases. So, he indeed *performed* a nice one. He'd managed thousands of cardiac cases and this one was just one more, not worth complaining about, not worth remembering.

His second case was almost a cookie cutter copy of the first. He wrapped it up quickly, departed, and went searching for Amoroso. On the way he bumped into Eric, who'd returned from the ICU.

"I told you we get good cases in this place, Doc," he quietly said, with just a hint of conspiracy. "You know, you might want to think about staying here – I know it'd make Doctor A happy. You know, we both came over from Charter around the same time, and that ER was wild. I was bored silly when I first got here. Of course, these goons with the chest pain sound pretty boring too – I bet you see some decent cardiacs at your other place."

"Yeah, but the chest pains there are usually caused by either a knife or a bullet."

The two shared a quick laugh. Then Marcus heard Amoroso's voice and followed the sound. He found the director on the HERN talking to EMS, frowning. He waited until the call was completed.

"Is it cool to go?" he cautiously asked the director. Going to the cafeteria was always a risky endeavor at North Central, so much so that almost always the docs and mid-levels much preferred the nearby doctor's lounge, where hard boiled eggs, bananas and a great coffee machine awaited. A sit-down cafeteria meal? Now *that* was the stuff of legends.

"I just wish they'd keep their crap to a minimum when they're giving report, these airways are public domain," Amoroso said quietly. "Anyway, let's eat, and it's on me – I'm signing. And don't worry, we're in the real world now, Marcus, they can live without us for a few minutes."

*

As they walked down a pastel blue hallway, signed watercolor prints on the walls, it was hard to miss the glorious smell of grilling burgers. Amoroso turned to his so-called charge.

"I'll say this, man, you're living up to your hype. Nurses, docs, admin, they love you. There hasn't been one complaint, not even a peep. I can see why North Central wants to tune you up and get you back in the game. The question is, you really want back in that game?"

"Yeah, maybe. You know what they say, old habits die hard."

They walked into the cafeteria, got in line and each grabbed a tray. Marcus grappled with his conscience and finally ordered a kale salad with fat free dressing, all the while sadly watching Amoroso get two double cheeseburgers and a large order of well-done fries, which they made especially for him. Then they settled in at a nearby table.

Marcus dispassionately poked at his salad, then watched in disbelief as the director silently pushed the fries between them and one of the burgers right in front of him.

"This burger's yours and we split the fries," he said with a conspiratorial smile. "Go ahead, have at it. I won't bust you."

"Very, very much obliged," Allen said, helping himself, saying you-know-what to the guilt.

God, it all tastes so good, he thought, his eyes half closing as he ate. Is it possible to fall in love with a french fry, he wondered, holding one up, marveling at its beauty. This is what you eat in heaven, he decided.

"So tell me, Marcus, how'd you get this smart?"

The older doctor continued chewing as he pondered the question.

"Jerry, I'm not that smart. I just have two things going for me – I love what I do, and I know what I don't know. There are lots of people who can run rings around me. I guess if I were really sharp, I wouldn't be working in a place where so many of the patients would kill me if they had half a chance."

The director hesitated a moment, then cleared his throat. Marcus paused his feast for a moment, realizing that words were forthcoming.

"You may not know this, but before I came here, I spent lots of time with the more-toes-than-teeth crowd myself - my first ER was downright insane. We could have gone head-to-head with you North Central guys, any day of the week. I was assaulted twice (knocked-out teeth, skull fracture), contracted meningitis, and I converted to PPD positive. And that's just for starters. Ask your buddy Finkel, we worked there for years. We even left at around the same time. Fink switched to your shop – I love that guy, but he sure is one fucking adrenaline junkie, ain't he? And guess where I went?

"You know, sometimes I really hated that job, and a good chunk of those patients. Not all, mind you, it was a privilege taking care of most of them... but there were so many others. Marcus, I swear I took care of hundreds, hundreds, of people who I just knew would go do some bad shit the minute I turned 'em loose. That never sat right with me, ever. I was becoming so cynical, so negative. It wasn't what I signed up for.

"I'm a nice guy, I swear I am. I'm not a cowboy or a hero, and I can live with that. For me, going to work there each day and trying to convince myself that all the violence and crap was somehow *acceptable,* it was sucking the life out of me. I'd wake up each morning and ask myself, what the hell am I doing. I loved my wife and our two beautiful kids – I still do, by the way - and just wanted a pleasant life with them. I never once harbored any illusions or fantasies about saving those people... or the world, for that matter.

"Let the other guys save it, let them rationalize that they're making it a better place. I came here and never looked back. I took with me plenty of memories, three false teeth and chronic headaches, and that's enough. I'd like to think it's worked out nicely. I render good emergency care to good people who need it and who are grateful, and I've never once had to invoke that 'it's not my job to judge' bullshit."

"I know where you're coming from," Marcus said, admittedly with mixed emotions.

"Plus, I'm famous," the director genially added. "You see this ugly face of mine? It's the official face of Summerton Medical Center – their ad campaign put me on billboards, for God sakes. I'm even on the sides of city buses!

"Now brace yourself for my real confession - during my first few weeks here I was afraid I'd fall asleep in front of the patients, it being so slow. But I didn't, and there was just enough bad stuff to keep me in the game. It turns out, shock of shocks, people get sick or injured everywhere – but here they don't split your head open when they're angry."

Amoroso leaned forward.

"You'd be welcome here, Marcus," he confided to the older man.

"What came in on the HERN?" Marcus asked, trying to steer the conversation elsewhere. "Frankly, Jerry, I don't know if I even want to come back, to anywhere. Let's talk later."

"Sure, later. Anyway, that call was about someone coming from the jail, some gangster bigshot on the receiving end of a lock-in-the-sock, with LOC and all that crap. Not to worry, though, he'll arrive with lots of company, plenty of boys in blue, some even in the parking lot. See? We also get some fun stuff, but here it's just a nice change of pace, not what you do 24/7. Marcus, we paid our dues, how much more do you think we owe?"

The director paused when he heard the sirens in the distance. Then he spoke up.

"All right, our friend's almost here. Sorry I talked your head off, and I'll soon shut up, but I'd never forgive myself if I didn't inappropriately offer you my personal opinion about you coming back, *anywhere.*

"Marcus, you're a total success. I mean, look at your career, your family, your accomplishments. You did it, man, you pushed every button, checked off every box. There's nothing more to prove. You can do anything you want now – travel, write the Great American Novel, hang out on a beach, be a bum, you can do *whatever* you want. Man, you've earned your fucking bum-ness, make the most of it! Don't kill yourself, or someone else for that matter, by going back to the well one too many times. And what would *that* prove - simply that you didn't know what to do besides being a doctor.

"I heard you came damn close to checking out that night – let's be honest, man, you *did* check out. You're lucky there was a good crew working. Brother, you really want to empty your gas tank in an ER? I look at you and see myself in fifteen years – so I will respectfully ask, what the hell are you doing? God gave you a second chance, man, use it. You know you're not going to cure the world. Wouldn't you like to enjoy it?

"Okay, torture's over, and thanks for putting up with me. Finish up and enjoy your lunch."

Marcus smiled and bit into his burger, chewing thoughtfully. Of course, he's right, he thought.

They sirens in the distance grew steadily louder, more urgent.

"The heart attack was pretty weird," he finally admitted, forcing himself to reminisce. "I never once believed, ever, that I could die. It only happened to other people. Crazy, right?"

"Okay, so what was it like? You remember anything? White lights, floating? I sorry to pry. I've brought my share of people back, but you're the first person I've ever really had a chance to speak with about…you know."

"Here's the big thing, Jerry, and it's hard to admit - part of me wishes Dean hadn't gotten me back. My biggest memory was just that it was so peaceful."

The sirens suddenly stopped. Marcus put his burger down and looked around. He felt a cold familiarity in the air… *tension.*

"And that would be our bad guy," Amoroso said, wiping his hands on a napkin. "I'll head on back. Take your time. Maybe we can finish our talk later."

"Jerry, you ply me with burgers and fries, and I'll tell you anything."

The director laughed.

"I'll also check the labs on your chest pains. I'm telling you this lab is amazingly fast."

"Boring cases, but a bit odd, if I must say so," Marcus said, relieved at the change of subject. "Those big guys had the most normal EKGs I've ever seen. They even had the same symptoms, come to think of it, like word for word. One guy was reading off a piece of paper, and the other had to close his eyes when speaking, like he was trying to remember his lines..."

He stopped, realizing how strange his words sounded.

"So did my guys," Amoroso said quizzically.

They looked at each other. Having spent their careers constantly scrolling for the worst-case scenarios, their minds rolled through multiple explanations, as if they were playing the ER version of one-armed bandit and were waiting for the answer to present itself.

Suddenly each saw the same thing, and it wasn't three lemons or cherries. Allen was the first to shoot to his feet, followed by his companion. There was a slight commotion emanating from the ER.

"Breakout?" they asked each other simultaneously.

"Doctor Amoroso, return to the ER stat!" the overhead blared. "Code Grey!"

"That's a violent patient. What the..." the director blurted out, just as the overhead began to scream.

"CODE SILVER, EMERGENCY ROOM...CODE SILVER, CODE SILVER, EMERGENCY ROOM...!"

Loud popping noises erupted from that direction. They heard shouts, and screams.

"Shooter!" they yelled, sounds of bedlam starting to pour into the dining hall, filling it with terror.

Amoroso ran to the cafeteria entrance, and suddenly whirled around.

"I'll handle this! Get out as fast as you can. If we need you, I promise we'll call. Now run to safety! That's an order."

The tall doctor stared at his charge for a second or two, a haunted look in his eyes. "This may a be bad day, Marcus. You do know that, don't you?"

"I do. Jerry...be careful, brother!"

Amoroso smiled tightly and then he bounded out of the cafeteria, headed for the ER, vanishing almost instantly.

Marcus looked around. Personnel and visitors alike were running out the other exits away from the commotion, some screaming.

No, no way I'm leaving him, Marcus realized, starting to stand up. *I belong there.*

At that moment there was a massive explosion emanating from the ER.

Marcus first noticed the odd scent of burning air, and then the blast wave smacking him violently, knocking him back onto his chair, which toppled over. His head smacked on the ground with a thud, and a roaring noise and dark smoke seemed to smother him. Instinctively, he curled into the fetal position, coughing. He seemed to drift off for a second.

There was a thick silence, and then he heard someone faintly crying for help. Soon there were other voices.

Get up, his mind screamed. They need you in the ER!

He shakily pulled himself up, fighting off nausea, using an overturned table for support. He felt hot air pulsing against his face. He had the sensation of standing in a rushing stream, but this time the ripples and vibrating waves were eerily hitting his upper body, not his legs.

The doctor had a bad headache and some trouble with his balance - he diagnosed mild concussion - but there was no neck pain, and no visual or obvious neuro deficits. He felt grateful that he was recently taken off big-time thinners – otherwise he'd have a lot more than just a headache; he'd be the owner of a full-fledged head bleed.

Marcus staggered through the smoke, breathing bitter air, his balance wobbly, until he touched a wall. Lights flickered erratically in the adjacent hallway, and he stutter stepped down it, hands on the wall, inching his way into the ER. There were fewer shouts but there were still those gunshots (the popping they had heard) and metallic crashes everywhere. The noise was steadily growing louder, and he started to cough. He finally touched the door leading into the department and paused.

So what the hell you gonna do inside, his inner voice warned. You're unarmed. You're also short of breath.

Stop thinking about it then, he shouted to the cautionary voices, we'll figure something out. Pain before shame. I have to go in!

He swung the door open and looked around.

There was smoke everywhere, with shadows moving in every direction, including his. There were bright yellow bursts of gunfire. People were shouting, some were screaming. Marcus started yelling for Amoroso, for Eric, for anyone. He started to run in the direction of the least smoke, and then he tripped, over something.

He landed heavily on the body of Doctor Jerry Amoroso. Breathing heavily now, he peered closer, trying to get a better look, and then realized that most of the director's face was gone. He began to retch.

With fading strength, his lungs now on fire, he crawled through the all-consuming whiteness, cries for help still present, but now much less frequent. He couldn't stop coughing and began clutching his chest, which was now hurting. Shadows roamed ominously through the smoke, as if searching. Some weren't that far away. Everyone's dead or damn close to it, Marcus grimly thought. The fight's over, now get the hell out.

He moved commando style, bumped into and crawled over Eric's body, headed for what he perceived to be the ambulance entrance. He had to crawl faster; the shadows were now very near. He felt a sharp jab in his back and two powerful hands grabbed his feet and began pulling him back into the smoke. His fingernails scraped the floor as he tried to claw away from them to no avail. Then he heard a hoarse voice speak to him.

"Remember me, I was your patient. So, what brings *you* in today?"

The man burst into laughter, and the doctor had the sensation of being sucked into thick, blinding smoke.

The last thing Marcus Allen remembered was screaming, "NOOOOOO!!!"

*

"Marcus, wake up!"

The doctor lay gasping on the floor, his eyes bulging in the dimly lit bedroom. He was drenched and shivering.

Beth Allen held her terrified husband, trying to mask her own fear. Soon, she too was wet with his perspiration. Slowly the man calmed. Beth helped him back into bed. She motioned for him to stay put, turned on the bedroom light and went to the dresser, returning with a dry set of pajamas, which he slowly changed into.

"Another ER dream, huh?" she finally asked, already knowing the answer.

"What else, they've been coming since I was cleared to return," he said wearily. "What time is it?"

"Almost ten. Good morning, officially."

"Good morning, back."

"What was this one about?"

"I don't remember much, except that there were explosions, smoke, screams…and there was a hero."

"Hero? As in *you*?"

"I don't think so. The whole thing is fading away as I speak."

"Great dream. I'm a little glad you didn't remember more."

"I was so scared. Is this God's way of telling me not to go back?"

"You tell me."

"Beth, it's time to make the call. I told them I'd give them an update…and my final decision. It's time to speak to Tannenbaum."

"Do you know what you'll say?"

"I've been thinking about it non-stop, and we've been talking about it for way too long."

"Could you really stand being with just me from now on?" Beth asked cautiously.

Marcus looked at her. *She looks the same as she did forty years ago.*

"I was more worried if you could stand being with just me from now on."

"I think I'll manage."

They shared a laugh, and he watched her walk away to get his phone, which she kept in another room while he slept. She'd always been his cheerleader, partner, and best friend. I'm the luckiest guy in the world, he thought, I'm still married to my girlfriend.

He looked at her walking back to him, holding the phone, enamored by the way she moved.

"Here we go," she said, handing it over. "I entered the number to his office. All you have to do is hit the call button, and whatever you do, you do. I'll be in the other room, calling the kids – they want to come over for your birthday."

"Fantastic. So, exactly what do I say to Tannenbaum?"

"Just open your mouth and start talking. The right words will come out. And I will support whatever you decide. But…stay alive for me, please? That's the only favor I ask of you. We still have a future."

"And you're okay with me just being… me?"

"I'll manage. You've always been Marcus to me, not Marcus W. Allen MD, the world's greatest physician. Ready to just be *you*?"

"I would hope so. And what's the 'W' thing? My middle name is Dennis."

"Oh, that stands for 'Welby.' I threw it in for special effect."

She turned to leave. Marcus reached for her hand, smiling, and they stared deeply into each other's eyes. The magic's still there, he thought, so amazed.

"After the call, how about some lunch?" he asked, his index finger on the call button.

"Sure, what did you have in mind?"

"Burgers, and some well-done fries?"

"That can be arranged," she answered coyly.

"And then, we can come back here, and maybe have a date?"

"That can be arranged, too. Remember, though, I'm a virgin. Go, make your call. I'll give you privacy."

He watched her walk out of the bedroom, smiling. His fingers subconsciously traced his ribbon-like chest scar, a reminder of his glorious, painful and all-too brief humanity. Then he pushed the button.

Give me one more plateau, he begged. I promise to make it count.

"Phil Tannenbaum here."

The sound of the director's voice startled him, and he almost hung up. But he didn't.

*****

Part Fourteen
The Magic Bathroom

"I just can't take it anymore," Peter Moore confessed to the ants below him.

Dr. Peter Moore, hired shortly after Marcus Allen's sudden cardiac event, slumped on the toilet seat, staring at the tiny brown ants casually crisscrossing in front of his shoes, oblivious to his existence. But Peter was more than aware of them. As his life had veered out of control, he'd become quite attached to them, and he now sought out their company. They were so calm, so very Zen, and led simple, nicely ordered lives (granted, he recognized that he knew nothing about them, or anything about Zen for that matter).

Still, he considered them his friends, confidantes, soulmates...

For the past few weeks, Peter had been paying lots of visits to the staff's secret hallway bathroom (privately known only to them as the Magic Bathroom), way more than normal, and way more than enough to start the whispering. He didn't care. At first, when he felt the panic within starting to boil his mind, he'd run to his car and sneak a few cigarettes. After he was ordered to stop, he switched over to bathroom breaks; he'd sit down and shut the lights - the quiet blackness let the heat inside his brain cool off a bit. He could spend fifteen or twenty minutes in total peace – apart from the other ER people, no one seemed to even know about this place. And then he'd be able to work for a few more hours.

As for the ants, one day he just looked down and noticed them. They just went about their business, serenely ignoring him. But he didn't mind, they were the natives here, he was just a strange visitor from a parallel universe. They were always there, always doing the same thing (whatever that was). He loved this predictability, this eternally stable continuity, however alien it was to him. Give me some of your time, he whispered to them on one of his visits, and I'll give you my story...

And so it began. When things would get out of control, at least once or twice per shift, when he started trembling, Peter would head for the Magic Bathroom, and pour his guts out to his little friends. Tonight, he needed them more than ever before.

"Peter, time to go. We need you in the ER. Come on, guy."

Dean Miller rapped gently on the door. To his consternation, there was no sound from within, although he knew for a fact that Peter was inside. An aide walked past, disgustingly shaking his head and mumbling something about 'crazy doctors'.

"Peter, I know you're in there. Open the door."

"Leave me the hell alone," was the reply.

"This has been a really rough week for me guys," Peter was telling his friends in a confidential hush. "I'm broke. It seems that my soon to be ex-wife maxed out the credit cards and emptied the checking account. And guess what – a car was picking her up after she told me she was leaving. A guy was driving. A fucking guy!"

"Peter, I'm having trouble covering for you," Miller's muffled voice plaintively registered through the metal door. "You're taking care of eight patients, including a crashing asthmatic. You just ran out of the ER. That was uncool, man. Things may be difficult, but this is not going to help."

Moore ignored his colleague. He resented the fact that instead of receiving empathy from the ER, he'd only gotten all sorts of 'we've got problems, too' stares. He looked at his little friends and resumed his desperate whisper.

"Sorry for the interruption, guys. So, I chase her out of the building when she left, confront this guy, and we get into a fight. It was broken up, but he got the better of it. He was going to fucking beat me up, in front of my soon to be ex-wife who's been sucking his dick. How's *that* for total humiliation?"

Dean shook his head. His go-gentle approach clearly was not working.

"Peter, don't make me call Security."

"Security, here's where I have security," Moore sneered back. This small, quiet room seemed to be the most peaceful spot in the world, the small brown patrol of insects on the tile floor its happiest, most peaceful residents.

"How do you do it, guys," he whispered, turning back to the ants. "I mean, you got it made in the shade. You didn't go to school for a million years, you don't pay bills, you don't get sued, or divorced for that matter. As far as I can tell, you don't even go through mid-life crisis. Someone just steps on you or mops you up, and pow! that's it. That ain't bad."

Miller beckoned to a passing security guard.

"Is there a key to this thing?" he asked. "I think one of the doctors inside isn't feeling too good."

"There's a master in the office," the guard replied. "Be back in two minutes."

The heavyset guard turned and rumbled down the hall.

"Did you hear that, Peter? You've got two minutes to open the door and make this go away. You'll be fine...listen, you're not the only one with personal problems. *I've* got personal problems. There are ways to deal with them, and you know as well as me that *this* is not the way."

Peter listened carefully to his friend. During happier days, they had worked together at another hospital, and their wives were friends, and sometimes they'd even socialize on the outside. He took a sip of the coffee he'd brought into the bathroom, thinking of the times he and Dean had shared together. *Shit, we're both single now*, he thought.

"Dean, I can't come out," he finally said.

"What? Why, for God sakes?"

"There's nothing for me out there. I just can't take the pressure anymore. I'm tired, I'm burnt out, I'm empty. And I'm not leaving."

The thought of an ER doctor spending the rest of his life in a small hospital bathroom almost made Dean laugh out loud, but the potential severity of this situation gave him pause.

"Peter, *out there?* You just can't stay *in here.* You're in a fucking bathroom! Come on, man, do you hear what you're saying?"

Jim Prescott, the third doctor working this brutal night shift, stomped over, wild with anger. He shot Dean a hostile glance, then started banging on the door.

"Get out, dickhead!" he snapped, paying no attention to the small cluster of curious observers a few feet away. "I'm sick of covering your shit."

The furious doc was met by dead silence.

"I've had it with this guy!" he raged at Miller. "Dean, it's fucking Halloween night, and there's a full moon. Now, I'm not superstitious, but really? Halloween? Full moon? It doesn't get worse, except for the fact that your asshole med student Harry just said the 'Q' word. Haven't you taught him anything? I tell you, this place is going to hell in a hand basket. And now this, this nutcase is bailing on us! You do know that his asthmatic is starting to crash."

Prescott slammed the door with his fist. And he turned to Dean.

"Get him out of the crapper, Miller. Let him finish his shift, then go home, get some counseling or jump off the fucking roof. I really don't care."

With that he turned and stormed back to the ER. Suddenly he whirled around.

"This won't look too good for you either, Dean. Remember, you brought this guy on board."

When Prescott was out of sight, Dean sighed and turned back to the door in near desperation. His friend inside could easily get his medical license suspended, or even revoked, for doing something like this. Forget about his job here, most likely it was already toast.

Dean's own anxiety level was rising at having been away from the turbulent ER for so long. He started thinking about that asthmatic. There were only a few minutes to make things right.

"Did you hear that, Peter? Listen, take a vacation, get help, but now go back to work. There's more to life than this stupid bathroom."

Peter snorted. 'Stupid bathroom' indeed.

"Did you hear what he just said about our center of the universe?" he whispered to the ants. "By the way, we mortals call this place the Magic Bathroom. It's very special, and very secret. There's even toilet paper here, and no graffiti."

"You have about one minute. I think I see the security guard. You can still make this all look completely understandable."

"Hey, Dean, you know the last thing she said to me?" Peter rasped; he was starting to feel…funny. "She said, 'You are nothing to me. I hardly know you, and what I do know about you I don't like. As far as I can tell, you come home for just three things - to shit, fuck and change your socks.' And then she walked out."

"There will be better times, I promise."

"Don't make promises you can't keep."

"Peter, what's going on?" Dean asked sadly. "We go way back, talk to me. I know things have been rough for you, but what triggered this?"

"Well, let's see. For starters, in the past few days alone my cat ran away, my houseplants died, and my dog was hit by a car. Times ain't any getting better, Dean."

Miller felt more than a little guilty – for weeks he had noticed Peter to be more subdued, more weary, more disheveled. And all that overtime? Lately, Peter was signing up for every available open shift. Everyone assumed it was to save up for a car, a vacation, a lawyer, or something. And it turns out they were warning signs, he now figured, maybe even cries for help.

"Here comes the guard!" a bystander eagerly shouted.

"Peter, out now!" Miller bellowed, pounding the doors in desperation. "If you can't do it for me, or yourself, do it for that asthmatic!"

Peter Moore looked down at the ants. They seemed to be entranced by the rhythmic thunder of Miller's fists, swaying, dancing, to the sound.

"Amazing, in the midst of all this you somehow seem to be enjoying yourselves," he said to them. "I wish I had an eighth of your coolness. Hey, I bet you guys even know the secret of life. It's probably something insanely simple, like finding a chocolate bar." He started to chuckle.

"We're coming in," Miller said, hitting the door again and again, the guard noisily jangling a huge key ring.

"I can't make you understand what is happening inside me, Dean," Peter said sadly. "I am so sorry."

"They're coming to take me away," he said, looking urgently at the ants dancing below him. "I don't want to leave, I can't leave. I can't take the pain, the emptiness. You guys have the right idea. Please! Don't let them take me, I beg you...help me. Please!"

He sat there, rocking back and forth on the toilet seat, whispering over and over, I want to stay here, I want to stay here, I want to stay *here*. Suddenly there was the sharp sound of a key shooting into a cylinder. Peter looked around, desperate for a way to escape – then he noticed this one ant sitting on the top of his shoe, head cocked, as if looking at him. Peter returned the gaze and cocked *his* head.

The door burst open. There were some excited oohs and aahs from the bystander section. Then everything became silent.

When Dean and the security guard burst in, they looked around, stunned. The room was empty.

"I thought you said there was a sick doctor in here," the guard said with annoyance. He was still panting from his fast walk down the hallway.

"There was," Dean protested, his eyes wide with confusion. There were murmurs of agreement from the bystander gallery.

"Well, no one's here right now, and I very much doubt he flushed himself away. I would go so far as to say that this bathroom is quite empty."

Miller looked around, very much stunned. The small room indeed was quite empty. Except for some ants on the floor, there was no sign of life.

The guard shook his head and smiled.

"I'll give it to you this time, doc, because you helped me out with that sick note and all, but please, let's just call this a drill and get on with our lives. Okay?"

Dean nodded uneasily. Did I just hallucinate all this, he asked himself. He turned to leave. Looks like the Magic Bathroom just played a full moon Halloween trick on me, he thought, feeling a touch queasy. Maybe it's time to stop working nights. And maybe, just maybe, when I get back into the ER, Dr. Peter Moore will be there like nothing happened, taking care of his patients. And life will go on. I sure hope so.

"Ain't that right, fellas," he asked the ants, who were scurrying into assorted cracks and crevices in the tiles. One stopped at the sound, and it seemed to look at him, cocking its head, making Dean reflexively blink. Then peacefully, quietly, serenely, it continued on its way and disappeared into the wall.

***

Part Fifteen
The Barbarians of Maryland

Margo Meyers stared helplessly at the phone.

"I wish there was something I could do, baby," she half shouted, her voice tinged with sadness. Their small home seemed empty without Charley, her all-time favorite ER doctor (who just so happened to be her loving husband).

"Can someone tell me again why I'm here?"

"To interview for that job, I guess. And I'm sorry for it all going south. And I'm really sorry I'm not with you."

"It seemed so easy on paper – roll the dice, go for the interview, and return the same day," Charley Myers said. "I'm just a little beat up. I did learn two important things today. First, it is officially stupid to work a twelve-hour shift and then take a long train ride; and second – apparently, I'm not capable of sleeping on a train."

Their connection was terrible. His car had broken down yesterday and going to Maryland by rail seemed to be a viable option. Ugh. He was now calling from a noisy station in Baltimore, two hours behind schedule, and was walking from one spot to another, vainly searching for a quiet place to talk. The clattering trains in every direction had other plans.

"We both figured, what's to lose, give it a shot and see what happens," he said, cupping his ear. "Now, I just feel foolish. That trip went on forever, and the longer I sat through it the more I realized this is not simply a 'shot' – it was the longest of shots. Even the car was telling me to stay home."

"This interview was a set-up anyway," Margo reluctantly agreed, pained at his dejection. "You even said it. Those people want to give the illusion of following *'due process'*, but we both know they're giving the job to that Ehler creep, the guy everyone hates. All he's got going for him is connections. What a sham."

What can I do to help him, she thought. I encouraged this.

"Yeah. Damn, I want this directorship big time. Margo, I wanted it for the two of us. That's why I'm here. I figured I had nothing to lose."

"I know. I wanted it too and feel sort of guilty I encouraged you," she half-shouted, wondering how much he heard. "Part of this is on me."

"…hard to admit, but I may need this job. I still have plenty left in the tank – I do – but the writing on my wall is starting to spell out *Father Time*.

"I've always dreamed about running a department. I'd put my thirty years' experience to good use. I'd teach what I know so that no one repeats my mistakes, and I'd offer up whatever pearls I picked up along the way. This is where my future is, and that's what I would have said to these people – that's why I'm here."

"You're preaching to the choir, my love."

I've got to help him, she thought.

hmmm, the back of my throat is tickling…

"Margo, this could have worked, too. I've got so much left in me. I just don't want to work another million shifts. Plus, we'd have been closer to your family. This was win-win all the way, that's why it…"

His words drowned yet again. Margo waited a few seconds, trying so very hard not to be sad. Try to be tough for him, she thought, although in truth she was fighting off tears.

Suddenly, a fragment of an idea started percolating within her. Not yet sure what it was, she filed it away for future reference.

"I know, you're perfect for this job," she finally said. "But deserving it and getting it are two different animals. And yeah, it sounds like they'll play the game, go through some motions, and coronate that pompous jerk. Do you know he has zero respect at his place?"

"Yup. So, after a 'thorough' two-month search, if you'll excuse the expression, it's down to the two of us. It's weird, they might even ask me to be his assistant."

"Would you really work for that creep?"

"Not even at gunpoint."

They both laughed.

it feels a little raw, too…

"Yeah, maybe I should come home and take the next train back – there's a trillion of them, and one's gotta be headed back to our neck of the woods. Screw it, this thing's a joke. I don't want to be the strawman. And to think, I've got the creds…"

"You've got great creds and you're a great doctor! Everyone knows you make Tannenbaum look good, he gives you his dirty work, and you clean it up. You may be his assistant, but they sure treat *you* like the chief. And you still see patients, just the opposite of that Ehler creep. Everyone knows his residents do all the work, all he does is co-sign charts and go to meetings - why would a lazy, make-believe doctor want to give that up in the first place…"

More station noises.

"…catching up to him, too many enemies," she heard her husband say.

I have to rescue this man, she decided. After all, he rescued me. What can I possibly do…

Suddenly, that little idea in her brain seemed to say, 'hello, look at me'. She nodded and smiled. We'll talk, she promised. And welcome aboard.

"Wait a minute," she heard herself saying. "Go for the interview. I'll drive down tomorrow and meet you. We'll make a mini vacation out of it. Worst-case scenario, we'll have steak and champagne, and take advantage of each other for three days. Babe, something tells me we may remember this weekend. Let's go for it. Please?"

"Well…okay, I'm with you all the way. I'm here anyway, what's to lose? You sure you want to do all that driving?"

"To have some alone time with you, I'd walk barefoot."

Another wave of noise. After a few moments Charley's voice re-emerged.

"… come on down, we can make some magic, and Sunday we hang with your family. Tell your mom to make that chocolate cream pie I like so much. Monday or Tuesday, I do the return drive. Sound like a plan?"

"A great plan. We'll make some lemonade yet. Anyway, I'll leave early tomorrow and meet you at the hospital. One-ish, right? Think you'll be done by then?"

"Easy. I'm interviewing second, and this may be the world's fastest interview. You know, I just wish I had one eighth of Ehler's self-confidence. He's already trying to recruit some new docs, he even offered Keller a job. You believe that?"

"Keller called me and said that Ehler's been bragging about not leaving until tomorrow himself and that he might even arrive a bit late for the interview. He said stuff like, 'we'll get there when we get there, I ain't kissing anybody's ass,' and 'I don't want to waste any more time down there than I have to.' He actually said that. Then he starts going on and on about real estate values... ahhh, what can you do."

"Don't worry about anything, babe. I love you, I love you, I love you. And remember, you're penciled in for a one-on-one meeting, win, lose or draw. I'll take you on, and you'll love my perks."

"I'm already planning a comprehensive agenda. Oh, and for the record, I'm driving rentals from now on. Travelling by train is now officially off the table. When is that stupid car ready, by the way, did they call?"

"The part came in. We can pick it up Tuesday."

"Great. Well, I'll grab a cab and check in at the hotel."

"Hey, boyfriend husband, you'll save all your dances for me?"

"For the rest of my life and for all my lives thereafter. I'll call you from the room."

oops, I feel a little cough coming on...

Margo got off the phone, and realized, shock of shocks, that she was coming down with a bad case of impending bronchitis. Ooh, better call in now, she thought, I wouldn't want to give this bug to anybody. She then pushed the speed dial to call the hospital.

*

Margo sat in her living room, angry and frustrated. *He's worked so hard, he's so qualified, and he's not going to get the job. He's being penalized for making it look easy, while that overrated, pompous creep...he actually came on to me last week at the fundraiser, though of course he came on to everyone, except his wife... oh, this just kills me.*

She began packing for the trip, praying for...what? Guidance, acceptance, dropping a bomb on Ehler's house, all came to mind...she just couldn't decide. And then there was that idea, or whatever it was, she had while on the phone. Maybe it was about more than just having a sexy rendezvous, maybe it was sprouting some roots.

Her conversation with Charley kept replaying in her head. He was always so cheerful, so hopeful, and this air of exhaustion, resignation and defeat that seemed to envelope him burned her brain like acid. So unfair, she thought sadly. There's got to be something I can do, right?

She found herself lying alone in bed, thinking about Charley. What a difference a day makes – twenty-four hours ago, he was lying next to her, and they rolled onto their sides to face each other, and shared a good night kiss. And then they kissed again and hugged each other tighter. Then they kissed again, and again…and twenty minutes later they were both in a restful, very satisfied sleep.

Sleep tonight was a lot slower in coming, so she decided to fight it off instead. She set sail for her dream-cation, her private (enchanted) space between thoughts and dreams. It was a game she'd played since she was a girl. There she'd be immersed amongst the most beautiful things, and sometimes had the most amazing adventures. Perhaps here an answer awaited. Let's do it she, thought, closing her eyes…please let me in.

*…and yes, soon she was floating, pastel lights popping all about her - she took them to be shooting stars up close, and felt perfectly comfortable making a wish…what can I do for the man I love, she asked them…time is short and there are no do-overs…please help…*and she sensed that her idea was starting to take shape and formally enter her mind, making itself right at home…well, okay then, she cautiously welcomed it, wondering what it looked like. As sleep rushed upon her, she was smiling, and just before it drifted her away, she felt, rather than heard, the words *rest up, keep your mind open, and soon all will be revealed.*

*

Something must have downloaded into her while she slept, because two a.m. found her on the highway, driving to Close Quarters, open twenty-four-seven. A short while later, having avoided and/or deflected the many curious/suspicious glances aimed at her, she was back at home, content and hopeful. And she slept again. *Phase One, check. Many thanks, to whom it may concern.*

**

A few hours later, after having gotten an address from her friend HR Tracy, she loaded her car up and drove off. Fuming, determined, still unclear as to exactly how her plan would unfold, she cautiously drove to her target's house, and waited at a respectable distance, her small grey car blending quite nicely into the early dawn air. After a while she saw Dr. and Mrs. Conrad Ehler pull out of their garage (almost the size of her first house), and carefully...*carefully*...she began tailing her victims-to-be.

She'd seen plenty of spy movies and knew how to do this. Their shockingly red Mercedes – you could practically see this car from space - gave her an almost unfair advantage. She never took her eyes off the prize, her thoughts fueled by fantasies of justice at any price. They never had a clue – they were arguing too much to notice anything else.

***

The gods of traffic conditions must have been smiling upon her, because Margo found it surprisingly easy to tail them. She made every green light they did, and the highway traffic was on the slow side. The few times she was cut off she still was able to just look for that gaudy splash of red down the road, and she'd get back on target.

When the red car finally pulled into a service station, in southern Jersey, she just couldn't find a way to secretly approach their car from the rear, with them in it, and she had to let them go. This is harder than I thought, Margo frowned, wondering if she would ever get her chance – *it's been almost four hours, don't these people ever eat or go to the bathroom?* And then, a plague of stomach rumbles descended upon the bickering couple when they crossed into Maryland, and they entered a small shopping mall featuring a reasonably upscale convenience store selling high-end munchies and booze. A sign read "Bathroom Only For Customers". Thank you, she thought sheepishly, sorry I doubted.

Keeping her distance, she watched them park fairly close to the store and walk inside. Now what, she thought. They'll easily see me walk over to their car. I'd be found out in a second.

If you can't hide, don't. Go straight to them and do what you set out to do. Be quick and choose your actions carefully.

She made a point of parking directly behind their big car. With considerable speed she jumped out holding two bags, one large and stuffed with food, and a much smaller one. She walked around to the front of her car, about-faced and patted the rear of the big red car, a bit more than one foot away. Dropping to one knee she reached into her small bag for a few things and got to work. Within ninety seconds, the sabotage was complete.

Phase Two – check! Now, cover your tracks. And they must NOT look at the back of their car. Look around, you'll figure this one out.

She stuffed the empty bag into the larger one and scurried to the line of stores. She saw the Ehlers through a window, intently studying a row of wine bottles. She kept walking, looking around, looking for…and then...yes!

She raced over to a small, nearby group of what seemed to be college students. They were gregarious, energetic, and apparently quite broke. They'll do nicely, she thought after watching them carefully pooling their money. She opened her purse, removed ten fifty-dollar bills, and ran over to them. They all stared at her, but their initial suspicion melted away as she animatedly told them about her plight, and they all nodded yes! Eagerly they all huddled, spoke intensely, placed hands over hands, and then shot them skyward with a one-two-three GO! If an outsider had been watching, he'd also have seen Margo hand them five of the fifties, and to one, a small object.

Wait for my two signals, she had told them. Then she walked back to her car, looked at them and winked. They all waved back, shared a laugh, then got serious, and walked to their designated spot. Margo closed her eyes for several seconds, very aware that the next few minutes might well shape her future life.

Sure enough, going into her tenth minute of carefully and very visibly adjusting her groceries into the back seat, looking quite unobtrusive and extremely average, she heard voices behind her. She whirled around and found herself staring at the Ehlers, who were walking up to their car, locked in debate yet again. Lynette Ehler dutifully juggled two large bags of goodies.

Margo straightened up and beamed with delight at this apparent "what a small world" coincidence, and she vigorously waved to them. They each did a mild double take when they saw her, then vigorously waved back, wearing so-so smiles, recognizing but not remembering her in the least. After a few seconds she walked up to say hello, moving laterally to align their field of vision away from their car, while tugging on her ear.

"I'm Charley Meyers's wife, we met at the fundraiser last week."

Ehler tightly nodded with satisfaction. He knew she looked familiar.

"Of course, we knew that honey. How are you?" Lynette said sweetly. "Wow, talk about coincidences! We seem to like shopping for our junk food at the same strip mall."

"I wouldn't call aged Roquefort and forty-dollar wine junk food," Conrad said to her tersely. "Talk about coincidences. Who would have thought, here in the middle of Shitsville. It's Margie, right? So, what the hell brings you here?"

"Probably the same as you, getting some stuff for tonight. I'm meeting Charley down there after his interview."

Ehler nodded, then lowered his voice as he leaned a bit closer.

"Been stalking me, haven't you?" he slyly winked. When Ehler saw his wife leaning in, straining to listen, he straightened up and put on an air of innocence.

"So, how is that good looking husband of yours, he okay?" Linette asked, shooting a glare at her husband. "Please tell me he's taking this interview seriously."

"He took an early train, he's down there already. And yes, he's quite okay, and he's very serious. Thanks for your concern."

"Down there already?" Ehler blurted out, stifling a laugh. "What the hell's he doing, rehearsing questions in a motel room? That's precious. Well, whatever – Margie, I think it's great. I like to hear stuff like that; it shows drive, initiative. Charley's a good kid."

Margo struggled not to appear furious, which she was. *He's ten years your senior, has twice your experience and, unlike you, has never been in a courtroom unless it's as an expert witness in cases that involve jerks like you.*

"Yeah, Charley's all right," she finally got out.

"I bet he's a lot more than all right," Mrs. Ehler said graciously. "I'd be proud of him if I were you. He's come a long way."

And a great big 'fuck you a million times,' trophy bitch.

"Sure, I'll be proud of him," she finally managed to say. *Boy are they asking for it.*

"Atta girl, you hold on to that attitude," Ehler said with a professorial air.

That having been the longest social conversation they'd ever had, they'd officially run out of things to say. They shuffled in place uneasily. Margo couldn't help but notice how elegantly dressed the Ehler's were. Looks more like they're expecting to get sworn in on the spot, she thought. Wow, yet another reason to wish them very, very bad luck. They're making it so easy.

"Are you returning to the city today?" she asked.

"God no," Ehler chortled. "We're dining tonight with the lieutenant governor at the mansion, blah blah, blah and maybe get back late tomorrow. We'll play it by ear."

The doctor lovingly patted his bagful of wine.

"Only half of this wine is for the formal dinner. The truth is my hot wife here is getting me drunk tonight."

"He's such a wild man," Linette scandalously whispered.

They shared a phony round of forced cackles.

"Well, it's time to go, dearest," Conrad said.

They turned towards their car. Margo scratched her nose. Suddenly, screams broke out about ten yards away. Everyone turned to the commotion.

A man lay face down on the pavement, shaking with seizure-like activity. A nearby woman clutched her abdomen and fell to her knees, dribble and green vomitus bubbling out of her mouth. Three bystanders were in a frenzied panic.

"We need a doctor! Is anyone here a doctor?" one of the women screamed. "I think there's blood coming out of his ear!"

"Doctor Ehler, what should we do?" Margo asked anxiously.

"Call a fucking ambulance. Let's go, Linette!"

"But they need us, Conrad."

"No, they need EMS."

With that the ER doctor grabbed the bags out of his wife's arms and tossed them in the back seat. He hopped in the driver's seat and motioned to his wife.

"Get in, Linette, now!"

"But..."

"IN! NOW!"

Dutifully, she scurried around the front of the car and got into the passenger seat. The red Mercedes left rubber as it shot out of the parking lot. Margo watched it until it re-entered the highway and disappeared. Then she turned to the victims and walked over, scratching her nose again. The commotion suddenly melted away.

"Nice work, guys," she said, clapping her hands.

The group collectively smiled at her. Two were dusting themselves off, one wiping mashed avocado from her face. Everyone was laughing.

That sure chased them away, Margo thought. All it took was asking him to be a real doctor.

After everyone high-fived each other, she reached into her pocket, and gave them the remaining fifty-dollar bills.

"Many, many thanks for a job well-done. You guys should be in the movies."

"As a matter of fact, you are speaking to none other than the Livingston Drama Club," one of them said gleefully said.

"I can believe that. Well, you were all great. I'll watch for your plays down the road."

After a group hug and warm round of goodbyes, Margo drove off, her commando mission alive and well.

nice move…

What can I tell you, no guts, no glory. And, uh, thank you once again.

not to worry…you and Charley were meant for good things…drive safely.

First, I think I'll check out that store myself, and maybe pick up some wine and cheese…and use the bathroom. She looked in the direction the Ehlers had taken, and waved goodbye to them.

****

The critical part of her plot would soon begin – and she wouldn't even be there to see it. She didn't have to. Margo had to dab away tears of joy that were running down her face.

Oooh, I am so evil. Charley, love of my life, if you somehow find about this tiny little sin of mine…who am I kidding, I can't wait to tell you… please know I did it for you…and for me, of course. Now, step on it, and get me to the hospital stat.

The rest was up to Maryland.

*****

Conrad Ehler cursed the dense stop and go traffic, which if seen from space no doubt would appear to be a gigantic Slinky pulling a bright red car behind it. He snarled and honked at every driver he cut off. He weaved in and out of lanes, growing more and more impatient.

Linette frowned at the scenery as they sputtered their way down the turnpike, shaking her head.

"What a boring drive," she finally said. "Do you think we should have helped those people back there?"

"What people?"

"The ones at the strip mall. The ones on the ground, they looked bad."

"I didn't see anyone – what are you talking about? And don't worry about this boring drive, it's almost over. There will be plenty of time for excitement when I get that job. Vacation, conference time and personal days alone add up to ten weeks. And that's for starters. Yeah, it's gonna be fun. The key is to kick some butt in the beginning. Then they know they can't give you any shit.

"God, where did these people learn to drive!" he hissed at a tailgating car – in his rear-view mirror he could see the man giving him the middle finger – he lowered his window, shot out his arm and gave it back. "The back of a tampon box?"

"You know, back there you were doing eighty in a fifty-five zone," Linette pleaded. "Can you just slow down a little, you know how I get carsick. What's the rush anyway, you got the job. They already promised. This whole thing's a game, right?"

"Number one, the speed limit is really for losers who don't know how to drive. Number two, we have connections in this fucking state and don't get tickets, and number three, I want to get this over with ASAP, because it *is* a game. What a waste of my precious time."

Traffic suddenly congealed again for no obvious reason. Accident? Construction?

"That's another thing," Ehler snapped, sticking his left hand out of the driver's window and giving yet another car behind him the finger. "Why am I even going to this fucking interview? All they needed to do was to interview that Meyers creep, thank him for coming, and call me up to congratulate me. All done. Case closed. This is an insult. I'm gonna get that bastard Conrey for doing this. I'm getting his ass fired! He'll be mopping floors by next month…hey!!!"

He swerved to avoid a car merging into his lane.

"Son of a bitch," he grumbled, leaning on his horn. "These Maryland drivers really do suck! Have you noticed that everyone seems to be looking at us? What gives?"

"I think they're jealous of our car, they drive American crap down here."

"Anyway, so when I take over, the first thing I do is kick that dirtbag Conrey to the street. Then, I'm gonna clean house. You know, the trouble with the world today is that there are too many vice presidents in it. That'll be fun, when I kick 'em all to the curb and I fill their spots with my people. You know, I might even bring in that Meyers kid. I've worked with him. He gets along with everyone, has a clean record and doesn't make waves. It will make me look magnanimous…look at that, another tailgater! That's all they do down here. Must be a state religion. I tell you, I'm gonna kick some butt if this doesn't stop."

"Oh Conrad, as the kids say these days, you're so binary," Linette gushed.

"It comes down to this, babe, a man's gotta do what a man's gotta do. Hey, you…"

A large Cadillac that had been tailgating them suddenly shot into an opening in the left lane and pulled alongside them. Traffic again slinked to a crawl. The couple peered into the car and saw four elderly men. They seemed oddly menacing.

"Looks like they recognize us or something," Conrad muttered. "Or maybe they're all senile, and don't recognize anything."

He was still snickering at his joke when the Cadillac's rear window opened and a man with an ancient, leathery face stuck his head as far out he could, to within several inches away.

"What's with him?" Conrad asked himself, opening his window as well. "Okay, here goes, be nice to the geezer."

"Top of the morning, sir, can I help you?" he asked, turning on the charm.

He leaned toward the man, smiled, and stared. The man stared back. Suddenly the old man's head reared back a bit and he spat a massive wad of phlegm directly into the middle of Conrad's face, coating it like a duvet. The doctor recoiled violently as if shot, and he grimaced in disgust, his body spasming. Linette had to grab the wheel.

"Go back from where you came, dogmeat!" the man rasped. "You're going to die."

And then he sat back and raised the window. Traffic eased a bit and the Caddy pulled away.

"He got me, he got me good!" Conrad shrieked. Linette fearfully started inching the car off the road.

"Oh my God! It's in my nose, my mouth," Conrad sputtered, turning to his wife.

Linette stared at him in horror.

"Your face is disgusting, let me wipe it. Here, let me wipe it."

She grabbed a tissue from her purse and began rubbing his dripping face.

"God, I'm getting so sick," she whispered, instinctively letting go of the wheel to cover her mouth. Conrad grabbed it frantically, but not before the Mercedes and the barrier wall scraped one another, making an awful noise.

"Stop that, now you're smearing it into my eyes!" Conrad yelled, grabbing the tissue. "Shit, and there's no rest stop between here and the exit. Damn, shit, fuck!"

Angrily, he began wiping his face on his sleeve, as he got his car back into the middle lane, cutting off two cars in the process.

"This can't be happening!" he shouted, pounding the steering wheel. He looked down at his sleeve. "I can't believe it; this is a thousand-dollar suit!"

Suddenly, another car pulled alongside them. Inside was a middle-aged couple, with three teens in the back seat. The front passenger window opened.

The car honked. What now, Ehler thought. He leaned out of the car.

"And what the fuck do you want?" he snapped, his face dripping.

"What I want is for you to get your filthy ass out of Maryland," the driver snarled. "Go crawl back to your New York cesspool. How dare you drive into this state! Pull over and I'll explain it to you in person."

His car crossed over in front of Ehler, and then onto the shoulder. The hazard lights started blinking, and a large, angry man got out, waiting.

Ehler did a double take when he saw him, then shot past the stopped car.

"Good thing I'm wearing my best suit, asshole, or I'd kick your hillbilly ass!" he screamed.

"What's this all about?" he asked anxiously, looking into his rear-view mirror.

"I've flown down here for a couple of family visits, but I've never really driven through Maryland before," Linette said with a shaky voice. "Maybe that's how all Maryland low class people are. Maybe it's all the crab they eat. Maybe we should try to understand them."

"You do realize I just had someone spit in my face, and another person just threatened my life. Ahh…is another guy following us?"

Traffic lightened again and they sped up for a few more minutes, looking this way and that. Before long, it happened again.

A souped-up Chevy now pulled alongside them, filled with staring teenagers. The passenger side window lowered.

What now, Conrad dismally thought, lowering his window just a smidgeon. What now.

A barrage of insults erupted.

"Get out of Maryland, scumbag!"

"Haul your ass back to New York!"

"I see you again, I'm cutting your balls off! I'll cripple you, man! Hear me?"

One of the passengers reached into a bag and threw two raw eggs against Ehrler's drivers side window. They smashed and splattered, and then the car roared off. The trembling couple looked at each other.

"I'm getting scared," Conrad said. "Call 911."

"Maybe we're in a funeral procession of psychopaths and their leader just died," Linette said helpfully. "Here comes another car. Oh, they're just women, they can explain. Let me handle this, you know, girl to girl."

A Toyota, windows open, crept alongside them. Two well-dressed, matronly women looked at them, their faces blank. Linette sighed gratefully and leaned out to them, beaming her very best smile. They looked like grandmothers out of a Rockwell painting. In the back seat a young Tom Sawyer-ish boy stared at her curiously, the window down.

"Can I help you, dearie?" Linette asked graciously. "Your boy is so cute."

"Bitch, why don't you just get out of here. Your kind ain't welcome in Maryland."

Linette's mouth dropped open. Then her eyes turned steely.

"How dare you say that to me! Who do you think you are, you lowly peasant! We go wherever we want. My husband will have you both arrested, get it? He knows people!"

"Oh, so you're a big shot? Let 'er rip, Earl."

With that young Earl moved his left arm outside the window and curled up his hand. Linette's eyes widened, her jaw starting to drop. Suddenly the boy flicked his wrist and launched the uneaten half of a ketchup-laden cheeseburger directly at her. It shot out like a kamikaze drone and splatted into her open mouth, right on (in) target.

"Just a warning, you piece of crap," the other woman said, before her car crept off.

For about a minute they sat in numbed silence. Conrad drove slowly, looking around fearfully. Linette was the first to speak, after she had coughed, gagged and retched out most of the gooey burger chunk. Ketchup dripped from her nose.

"I want to go home," she said in a quavering voice. "Conrad, I really don't feel well."

"I don't know what's going on. I do not know what is going on."

"I don't want to know what is going on, I just want to go home. Now."

"This road is full of maniacs. These are the craziest, least friendly people I have ever seen. This state is one giant insane asylum. Look at this."

A veritable procession of cars now passed them, nearly all filled with threatening people. Some cursed at them, some spat, some threw food and garbage, some gave them the finger, some just glared, some did all the above. Conrad and Linette hunkered down in their seats, low-rider style, not making any eye contact, praying for this journey to end.

"Thank God we're almost there," the doctor said, looking at the upcoming exit sign. "I'm speaking with the governor about this. If I have to, I'll have the National Guard called up, I'll have this fucking highway closed…"

He was interrupted by the flashing blue lights of a state police cruiser behind him.

"Yay, the good guys are here!" Linette shouted with relief.

"What took these jerks so long?" Ehler said, pulling off to the side of the road. He tried to collect himself, rehearsing what he would say. "I'm gonna order these assholes to start kicking some butt!"

In his rearview mirror he saw a giant state trooper finally get out and walk to the rear of the car, taking notes. He then walked alongside their car and rapped on the driver's window, signaling for Ehler to lower it. His boots almost came up to the window.

"It's about time, officer," Ehler snapped, his outrage starting to rekindle. "Start taking notes."

"License, registration, and make it quick!"

"What's the matter with you?" Ehler asked, exasperated and annoyed. "Just do your job! I want to report these assholes."

"Shut your filthy mouth!" the giant officer commanded. "May I see your license and registration, *please*! Next time I won't ask, and you will regret it. Consider that a threat and a promise."

"He doesn't sound like a good guy to me," Linette said fearfully. "Conrad, I think I'm gonna puke."

Ehler looked at her, and shook his head *no*. He took out his wallet, pulled a special card inside it into a prominent position, and with trembling hands passed it to the trooper, who watched his every move, his right hand resting on his holster. The officer then walked to his car. The doctor sat there, his face glistening with thick, sticky spit, watching from his rear-view mirror as the man spoke into his radio.

"I know I wasn't speeding," he murmured. "Maybe, just maybe, I did cut someone off."

They sat in uneasy silence for several minutes. Finally, the trooper exited his car and walked up to them. He handed over the license, registration and several tickets.

"They have to be answered in person," he said sternly. "Personally, I'd toss you in jail and throw the key away."

"For cutting someone off?" Ehler asked incredulously, looking at the papers. "This is a lot of money!"

"And lots of points, cupcake, lots of points."

Ehler grumpily stuck the papers in the center console.

"This guy is so fucking obtuse," he mumbled.

Suddenly he was grabbed by his collar and his head was pulled out the window. His face was inches from the trooper's, who looked at him, violence in his eyes. The doctor held his breath.

"Don't fuck with me or I'll haul your New York ass out of this car so fast you will truly learn the meaning of the word pain," the trooper hissed. "But of course, you might like that. So, *sir,* two things. One, get off my highway right now – I don't want you polluting it. And I don't, repeat DON'T, ever want to see your pervert face again, or I'll rip it off. I don't know who your bigshot friends are but consider this your final gift. And you tell them they wasted the last of their get-out-of-jail chips on your pathetic ass. Get off this highway now, and I'm going to follow you. Move it and don't come back!"

Ehler nodded fearfully, his eyes bulging.

The officer turned and walked back to his car, but not before taking one final glance at the rear bumper, which prominently displayed three stickers, reading: GET ON YOUR KNEES AND LICK ME,

DOG SLAVE; PROUD TO BE A NEW YORK ATHEIST; and IF YOU BEAT ME, YOU CAN EAT ME.

As the trooper walked away, shaking his head, Ehler and his wife exchanged looks of total horror. Carefully, he eased his car back onto the highway, the flashing lights of the patrol car behind them. When they got off at the very next exit, the cruiser honked angrily and sped on.

Driving down side streets, almost at their destination, the pair relaxed (just a little).

"This is the worst day of my life!" Linette said, suppressing a retch. "I'll die before I live here."

"I'm speaking to the governor…oh no, not another one. Wait, this one looks like a priest…he is a priest. He's signaling us and pulling up."

"Don't, it's a trap!"

"Gimme a break, he's a fucking priest. God owes me a break."

Ehler rolled his window down one more time and found himself looking into a kindly face. The priest was just on the other side of elderly, a little portly, with twinkling eyes and a neatly trimmed white beard. He was drinking a shake. He leaned to his right and lowered the passenger side window.

The doctor looked at his cowering wife, who was covering her mouth with a hand, and thinly smiled.

"I told you, it's okay," he said, lowering his own window. "Hey, he reminds me of Kris Kringle."

"It's a trap," Linette warned again. "You know those Catholics."

"Oh, stop. Top of the morning, Father, can I help you?"

"Has it ever occurred to you that you deeply offend decent people? Please, go back home, wherever that is, and ask God for forgiveness."

Ehler flared with anger. *That's it, I've had it with these people!*

"Let me tell you something!" he shouted. "I sick of you, I'm sick of all of you! We're moving down here and we're taking over! We're gonna keep doing exactly what we've been doing, and we're gonna do even more of it! And then we're gonna force all of *you* to do it. And I don't care who it offends! What do you think of them apples, Sanny Claus?"

The kindly man stared at the doctor and winked. Ehler squinted with apprehension. And with a lightning quick motion the priest splashed his chocolate milkshake directly into Ehler's face. He nodded his head, waved goodbye and drove off smiling, seemingly mouthing the words *nice shot* to himself.

The doctor howled with disbelief and rage. He rubbed his face off once more with the one remaining clean spot of his sleeve and sped away.

"I can't believe he did that!" he roared. "I feel like I'm driving through Hell!"

"Look, there's the hospital," his wife *gurgled.* "I, I don't feel so good."

The very next moment she lost her battle and heaved. A foul-smelling, chunky green puddle bubbled gently on her husband's lap. She began to cry. Conrad began to whimper.

******

Margo was sitting in the hospital's parking lot, working on her puzzle, when she saw the no-longer shiny Mercedes haltingly inch into a nearby slot. Slinking down, she watched Ehler and Linette shakily get out. Almost unrecognizable, the two staggered towards the hospital entrance, her hands covering her face, and him giving everyone he passed the middle finger. Doctors, staff and passersby hurriedly moved out of their way, as the two snarled at anyone even remotely near them. The moment they entered the building, several people reached for their cellphones.

Oh, my goodness, Margo thought, quietly nodding her approval upon seeing their appearance. *Phase Three, ding, ding, ding, big time!*

She opened her door and got out, holding another small bag. She walked over to their car, noting with amusement the keyed gashes on the driver's side, and splattered eggs and garbage on most of the windows. Carefully and quickly, she covered the three bumper stickers with three new ones: SUPPORT OUR TROOPS, THIS CAR CLIMBED MOUNT WASHINGTON, and HONK IF YOU LIKE GIRL SCOUT COOKIES. She silently thanked the novelty section of Close Quarters, and saluted the six bumper stickers – *bye, bye, guys, you all did great!* Then she turned, calmly went back to her car, and got back to her puzzle, innocent to the world and all its passers-by.

Who knows, we may have a shot after all, she thought. Babe, the rest is up to you. This commando superspy is taking a break. She reached her left hand across her right shoulder and patted it.

Phase four, YES!!

****

John Conrey, vice president and chief medical officer, sat behind his large, richly burnished desk, reviewing a stack of papers. To his side Clark Stacker, the hospital's president, checked his cell phone.

"There's some ruckus down in the parking lot," he said, looking up. "A couple of wackos. Security's on it and we called the police. No big deal, they don't seem to be armed and not particularly dangerous, just, well, strange. We'll monitor the situation. Anyway, John, are we set for this meeting?"

"Clark, everything seems to be in order for Dr. Ehler," Conrey said with satisfaction. "It's a solid package. If he decides to play some last-minute hardball, we're willing to give a little on the vestment period. But I don't think that'll even be an issue. He's got a sweetheart deal here, and he knows it. So, we give him the job, make sure we're nice and grateful to that uh, Doctor Meyers, and wrap this thing up. It's long overdue."

"Amen to that, it's very long overdue," Stacker agreed. "And with this guy's wife a niece of the governor, I've been assured of getting, shall we say, 'good news,' about our application for that proposed specialty center. Not a bad day's work, wouldn't you say?"

They were both chuckling when the intercom rang.

"Sir, there's a man here who claims to be Dr. Ehler."

"Well then, send him in."

"Are you sure?" his receptionist asked quietly. "He seems to be…"

Her whisper was cut off by the impatient VP.

"Just send him in," Conrey said impatiently.

"As you wish."

The door opened and both Conrey and Stacker rose to greet their guest. Their smiles froze when Conrad Ehler entered.

The man before them was disheveled, wild-looking and appeared to be splattered top to bottom with a variety of substances. His inflamed eyes, smeared with alien mucous, glowed a dull red. He also stank.

It took a few moments for the hospital chiefs to recover.

"Who are you?" Stacker blurted out.

"I'm Doctor Ehler, you got a problem with that?"

The hospital executives exchanged worried looks. Then Conrey cautiously extended a hand to greet the candidate.

"Uh, welcome to Maryland, Doctor."

Ehler ignored it and slumped into a chair, ominously staring at them as would a wild beast. Conrey and Stacker also sat down, not taking their eyes off this man, and trying not to breathe through their noses. Both subconsciously patted their well-concealed sidearms neatly packed inside their jackets.

They sat in silence, until Conrey cleared his throat.

"How was your trip down here?" he cautiously inquired.

Ehler made no move and remained silent. Conrey shifted uneasily. This was not what he expected. He quietly opened up Ehler's folder to compare photographs. They seemed to match.

"Well, then, shall we talk about this position?" he asked. "The directorship?"

"The people of Maryland don't need another director. They need a zookeeper."

Conrey and Stacker paused, trying to digest the words.

"What was that sir?" Stacker asked. "I didn't follow."

"All people from Maryland need to be de-wormed and then left to rot in Hell."

"I'm sorry, I'm just not getting any of this," Conrey said nervously. "Let's start over, from the beginning. You are Dr. Ehler, correct?"

Ehler just glared at him.

The phone rang and Stacker picked it up.

"Just be on standby," he whispered. "We're okay for now. Oh, and we also need some air freshener. John, please continue."

"Fine, let's keep going. Dr. Ehler, we're here today to discuss this position and your future place in this organization...uh, what was that you said about Maryland, just before?"

Ehler leaned forward. The other two men involuntarily leaned back.

"I said that all people in Maryland suck big dick. I hate every one of them!"

Conrey was flabbergasted.

"Are you really Dr. Ehler? You are, right?"

"In the flesh. One of your Nazi pig state troopers just checked my ID. Wanna call him?"

"Hey, watch it," Stacker said sternly. "My brother is assistant chief."

"Then that makes him assistant chief Nazi pig."

Both men sat there is shock.

"I can't believe you just said that," Stacker said, his hand now quite close to his gun. "You do want this job, don't you?"

"As long as I don't have to touch anyone from this state. I don't think I could wash the stench from my hands."

"That's a horrible thing to say," Conrey said angrily. "I resent that."

"Are you from Maryland?"

"What's that got to do with anything?"

"I thought so. It means I'd wipe my hand with toilet paper after shaking hands with *you.*"

"Dr. Ehler, I'm beginning to wonder if you really are the right man for this job," Stacker said with a tinge of disgust. "Do you want it or not?"

"I'd rather shovel shit in Shangri-La."

Conrey and Stacker looked at each other in disbelief. Finally, Conrey turned to the now former candidate.

"Well, you're getting your wish. I'm not going to offer it to you."

"Be still my heart. Let me tell you something, I wouldn't let my dog take this job. All people from Maryland are psychopaths and I don't have the slightest desire to help them in the least. What I'd like to do to them, frankly, is flush them away!"

Conrey and Stacker exchanged looks of disbelief. What had just transpired was so beyond the collective range of their experience that each, for a moment, thought this was all some sort of hallucination.

Conrey was the first to speak.

"I guess, I guess, that wraps up this interview," he said numbly.

"Gee, how 'bout that," Ehler said, spitting a chocolate sprinkle onto the rug. With that he rose and stormed out of the office, leaving the door open behind him. Conrey and Stacker helplessly stared at the sprinkle, both speechless.

Suddenly the intercom rang, startling them.

"What is it?" Conrey asked nervously.

"Sir, there is a Doctor Charles Meyers here for his interview."

"Send him in, I guess."

They braced themselves. Oh crap, another New York doctor, they glumly thought.

"This is the last time we go outside the organization, you hear me?" Stacker snapped.

Charley walked in brightly. He sniffed the air, and involuntarily looked around.

Carefully, both administrators extended their hands, half expecting a violent response. To their deep relief Charley shook theirs warmly. Conrey stared a moment at his hand, motioned cautiously, and they all sat down.

"It's nice to be here," Charley said. "Thanks for considering me."

"Do you like Maryland?" Conrey asked tentatively.

"Maryland? I love Maryland. The people are lovely, the state is beautiful. The whole thing is great. Oh, and my wife's family lives about twenty minutes away."

"Do you really mean that?" Stacker asked sternly. "Are you telling the truth?"

"Of course," Meyers said, puzzled at this most curious query. "A resounding 'yes' to all the above."

"Pardon us a second," Clark Stacker said. He motioned to Conrey, and they converged at the far corner of the office. Charley watched them, wondering what the hell was going on.

Suddenly Stacker whirled around.

"Are you related to, or friends with, this Ehler guy?" he asked curtly.

"Not at all," Charley replied, making a slight face. "I've met him at a few meetings. That's all."

Stacker grunted and turned back to Conrey.

"John, he looks good on paper, seems to be sane, and he looks presentable," the president whispered. "Give him the fucking job, get this done with. The board's already all over my ass for dragging this on so long."

"Agreed. And yeah, he does look pretty strong. What terms do you propose?"

"Fuck the terms! Cross that lunatic's name off the contract and give it to him. Wrap this shitshow up! I'm out of here. And now, what the hell am I going to say to Project Development?"

The president brusquely left the office, shaking his head in disbelief. Conrey walked to his desk. He sat down and pretended to examine Charley's application and CV, his hands mildly trembling.

"Dr. Meyers, I've been reviewing your credentials and must say I'm impressed. Do you really want this job? And, once again, do you *really* like our state?"

"Yes, and yes."
"Then, sir, let's get down to business."
"Sure, let's."

****

That night in Annapolis, Charley and Margo celebrated his new position with a steamed blue crab and champagne dinner, all courtesy of his new hospital. After they finished, Margo looked into his eyes.

"Fantastic dinner, fantastic day, my director husband," she said. "And for the record, fantastic fireworks upstairs, wow…are you trying to kill me?"

"Just doin' my job, ma'am. Darling, you have no idea how glad I am that this all worked out – in so many ways. You know, this is a real game changer for us."

His wife looked at the beautiful night sky and turned to her one true love, joy and happiness pulsing through her veins.

"You're preaching to the choir," she finally said.

"I wonder what happened?" Charley asked. "It was almost like *my* interview was the one for show. They practically just checked me for a pulse and then hired me. They upgraded us to a suite, gave me a signing bonus, and now they're paying for travel and moving expenses, the works. And I thought it was a given that the job would go to Ehler."

"Maybe 'givens' aren't what they used to be," Margo said, blinking back a tear. "Life's funny sometimes, isn't it?"

"To put it mildly. You know, for a moment I thought both those guys were nuts. They seemed almost traumatized, like they had seen a ghost or something."

"My theory is that those people took one look at you and fell in love," Margo said gently. "I know I did, years ago. So what is North Central going to do without you?"

"Oh, they'll manage. I was just about to tell you - do you know who called me this morning to wish me luck on the interview? Phil Tannenbaum. How the hell did he find out?"

"Don't ask me. What did he say?"

"He called to wish me success and said he'd be happy if I got the job, or happy if I didn't. He'd support me whatever I do. I tell you, this guy's got eyes and ears everywhere."

"I bet that knowing your boss, he's already thought about having to replace you," Margo said. "Who do you think's on his short list to be the next Number Two?"

"He mentioned Dean Miller - can't say I disagree."

She raised her glass, as did Charley, and they clinked.

"To you, to Dean, and to all the good guys," she said. *Not to mention to a really cute, well-meaning commando.*

She leaned across the table and kissed her husband. Then they sipped their champagne.

"Want to go up to the room after dessert?" the new director asked. "I have this total need to be close to you…"

"Dessert?" Margo asked softly. She stared at him and thanked her lucky stars so much she could feel tears trickling down her face. "That's where you come in, sugar. I want this night to go on for ten years. Let's go."

Mission accomplished.

****

Part Sixteen
Applause

Lydia Anderson sat alongside her husband. The dimly lit downstairs bedroom was silent. Lars lay very still, the slow rising and falling of the chest his only movements. He was dying.

There was a soft, respectful, knock on the door, and she let two of his best friends, Dean Miller and Bob Finkel, come in to pay their last respects. Lydia and her children quietly moved to the fringe of the room as they approached the bed. They watched the two men simultaneously, spontaneously, walk to each side, and then get down on one knee before Lars, bow their heads and place their hands on him. Lydia couldn't shake the illusion of knights from a grey past bidding their fellow warrior, comrade and friend, farewell.

Lars could sense them, but not feel their touch. He was weakened and unable to respond, but he could sense them. When Dean leaned forward and whispered, 'I love you, Lars, you've always been my hero,' the stricken doctor tried to smile, but couldn't. Finkel leaned forward, shaking, trying to whisper something but couldn't; somehow Lars sensed a tear fall onto his face.

Finkel, the Ice God, crying. Who would have thought…
who would have thought, indeed…

Then the two men straightened up, walked over to Lydia and hugged her and the children. They gently said something to her, and they all hugged again. Seconds later, Lydia Anderson and the children were again alone with her husband, their dad.

Lars felt no pain; he seemed to be hovering, looking down on the scene from above – he saw himself lying in bed, his wife crying into a towel. He dimly wondered if this image was the hospice meds working, or his disease. Most likely both, he vaguely concluded.

perhaps it's something else, something else…ever think of that…

He heard a sound, or thought he did. Low, steady, humming and crackling, odd but not unpleasant. It took too much effort to analyze;

he just lay still, listening to its steady approach. The room's darkness gave way to just a glint of light.

What's happening? How come this doesn't feel that bad…

shhh…

What's happening to me? Am I dying?

your body is…but you can't die…

Tell that to my cancer…and now, what's that sound? Something like a stream running over smooth stones. Like the times Lydia and I went camping.

interesting…

Where is Lydia?

she's here, sitting next to you, holding your hand…

And Lars felt Lydia's hands, caressing his. He, he felt them.

Thank you, thank you.

it's okay…

Summoning his rapidly evaporating strength, he actually smiled.

The hands stopped moving, then picked his up, and she kissed them; they became wet with her tears.

I forgot how soft her lips were.

"It's okay to go, my darling, it's okay…"

Lars wanted to tell her he never wanted to leave, to say he was sorry, but realized it was not meant to be. The remaining scientist in him knew that – he had nothing left. 'Meet me on the other side,' he'd wanted his last words to be, 'I'm not afraid of death, I'm just afraid to be without you.'

That sound grew louder - what is it, he wondered vaguely.

soon, soon you will know…

Should I be afraid?

you will know only peace…

I can't be without Lydia. I can't be without the children.

"Lars, I love you so much, but it's okay to let go, I swear it is." Lydia implored. She started tenderly kissing his face. "Stop the suffering."

The rushing noise grew louder. Lars started listening intently. He sensed humming. Are those… voices…are they singing?

"Lars, it's okay to let go, it's okay."

Though his eyes remained shut tightly, Lars could swear he was becoming immersed in a faint light, which seemed to slowly grow ever brighter. The vague sounds grew steadily stronger. Somehow, the doctor had no fear. His sensation was that something, some thing, inside him was completing some task, wrapping things up, tying up the loose ends of his life - but what about Lydia and the kids.

no fear…

The sound grew louder; it was not one but, rather, many smaller sounds combining into one. The dim light intensified. Lars swore he could now make out shapes. Faces?

"Lars, I love you, I love you so much."

He could feel her lips on his forehead. He tried as hard as he could to smile but wasn't sure if he did. The light grew whiter, the sound started to envelope him. There were shapes in the light. Are they people?

you could say that…

Am I really going to die? While I'm at it, big shot, why don't you tell me the secret of life…

your life will cease, all lives do, but your soul is eternal – it can't die…Lars, the secret is living a life worthy of your soul…and Lars, you did it…good going, good going…

The glowing light illuminated shapes that were now around him, many of them. A symphony of notes and sounds seemed to fill the room.

Lars could hear his pulse beating in his ears. It seemed to be slowing, as was his breathing. He got the sensation he was gasping the cool air, but felt no fear, only tranquility. He felt Lydia's lips on his face. It's okay, she was whispering, over and over.

"I love you, Lars. It's okay. Let go, my darling."

The shapes were now all around him. He could make out faces – no one seemed familiar, but somehow…

The doctor sensed his heart skipping beats. Lydia's kisses seemed to be becoming more urgent. The noise seemed to be morphing into applause and shouts of support.

Who, who are they?

just some of the people you've brought joy and love to, friends, family, those you have helped, those you've cured, those you've saved…there are many more, but they're not here yet…

What about Lydia and the…?

yes…you will see them again…

Lars knew he was about to stop. Not yet please, not yet. Not yet! he silently begged. Now, my final request - give me the strength to…

Granted the last shreds of his worldly energy, the last iota of his life force, Lars Anderson opened his eyes and looked at Lydia. She gasped and smiled at him, tearful, her eyes wild with joy. Their young children approached, holding hands, wide eyed.

"Goodbye, my darling," she managed.

"I love you, all of you," he whispered. "And I will see you…"

"And we will see you," she gently replied, her eyes shining. "And, may these be the last words you hear – Lars Anderson, I love you."

Okay then, he thought.

Lars almost imperceptibly nodded and looked at his family. His faint smile came easily. He closed his eyes and started to float, the deepest compartments of his minds bursting open and making peace, each releasing their darkest secrets, regrets and hatreds, which swirled upward, upward, before disappearing with a gentle *poof*. His last breath of air was his sweetest.

Yeah, let's go.

Okay then. Welcome home.

***

Glossary of Terms

Absorbable sutures: stitches that don't need to be taken out – they dissolve on their own. Used for delicate tissue such as intra-oral, for deeper than usual lacerations which need double layer closures, and for many surgeries.
ACLS: advanced cardiac life support. The big brother of CPR.
Admit: used as a noun, it means a patient who's been accepted for admission.
Agency people: temps, hired by outside organizations to fill immediate needs of an organization. These include rent-a-doc, rent-a-nurse and rent-a-tech positions. They are well paid for their efforts as a rule. Many are great, but some just don't give 100%, which can cause friction and resentment with the staff, who are usually paid less than the temps.
A-fib: an often-serious abnormality of the heart's atrial contraction. This rhythm, if left untreated, can lead to a stroke.
Airway – any part of the respiratory tract, but in the ER it usually means the mouth, throat and the neck areas. Usually, small mouths, large tongues and short, fat necks are warning signs of a potentially difficult intubation.
Alligator forceps: a small hand-held, scissor-shaped device with a movable end that looks like an alligator opening and closing its mouth. It's used to grab hard to reach objects, usually in the ears or nose.
Albuterol: a medication used in aerosolized form to treat asthma, COPD and other breathing problems.
AMA: against medical advice.
Anesthesia: a medication used to induce loss of consciousness, or the common nickname for Anesthesiology, a major medical specialty.
Anterior wall: the front of the heart. Critically important to survival; an anterior wall MI is particularly serious.
Aorta: the largest artery in the body, emerging from the left side of the heart. Sometimes nicknamed Big Red. If a weakness develops in the vessel's wall, it bubbles out and is called an aortic aneurysm (AA). A common area for an aortic aneurysm is in its part furthest from the heart, the abdominal section, and is called an abdominal aortic aneurysm (AAA). A leaking AAA often presents as abdominal pain also felt in the

back, and often requires immediate surgery. If the bubble bursts – ruptures - the outcome is usually fatal.
Arrest: the sudden loss of cardiac and/or respiratory function.
Artery: a blood vessel carrying blood away from the heart. It has a pulse.
Aspirin: protective when given to cardiac patients, and sometimes non-hemorrhagic stroke patients.
Ativan: trade name for lorazepam, a sedative and anti-seizure med. Often used in the injectable form.
ATP: adenosine triphosphate, the molecule that provides energy to the cells.
Attending: any physician who has completed his/her fellowship or residency program. Can also refer to the patient's family doctor, a consultant, or any physician taking care of them while in the hospital.
Bagged/being bagged: the act of breathing for a patient. It's performed by placing a bag/valve hand-held mask (often referred to as an "ambu bag," a popular brand) over a patient's mouth, and squeezing it rhythmically, sending air into the lungs. Referred to as "ambu-ing."
Benadryl: trade name for an antihistamine that can be given orally or by injection. Utilized for allergic reactions, adverse medication reactions, and for its side effect of sedation. It's given in its generic form – diphenhydramine – but still always called Benadryl (sort of like Jello).
Betadine: a commonly used skin disinfectant.
BFL: bad fucking luck.
BiPap: a breathing system designed to force air into a patient's lungs, thus aiding someone struggling to breathe. It consists of a mask that covers the mouth and nose, attached to a respirator. It is very similar to C-Pap, the system used at home by sleep apnea patients. Sort of a last resort on a "diff breather" - if BiPap fails the patient is usually intubated and placed on a ventilator.
Big Red: slang for the aorta, the largest artery in the body.
Blue translation phone: special telephones, often blue, used to call up translators. They've been known not to work just when needed most (a running joke).
Bolus: an amount of IV fluid infused rapidly.
Breech presentation: refers to an abnormal fetal position in late pregnancy, which should be head down in the womb. Any variant of a normal position could conceivably be referred to as breech.
Brugada Syndrome: A hereditary condition associated with sudden cardiac death, often striking young adults, and sometimes during sex. It is associated with a classically abnormal EKG (which is often enough to

make the diagnosis). ER docs often have to float a temporary pacemaker (pacer) for stabilization, but the definitive treatment is a permanent pacemaker placed in the OR.

Bus: Slang for a bunch of patients that arrive at once, as if they just got off a bus that pulled up. Commonly seen a few minutes after church lets out, or when a football game ends, or if the gods simply don't like you.

Carwash CT: slang term referring to (usually) trauma patients. The patient is CAT scanned from head to pelvis looking for injury, as if they were on a conveyor belt in a car wash. Not spoken in mixed company.

Cath lab/team: patients who are having a heart attack usually have a cardiac catheterization done as soon as possible. This test determines if stents can be placed in the arteries of the heart, or if the patient needs to undergo bypass surgery. The members of the cath team include its pre-designated doctor(s), cardio/cardiothoracic nurses and techs and x-ray personnel, just to name a few.

CAT (CT) scan: stands for computerized axial tomography, which is a highly detailed series of computer-driven X-rays. A major ER tool.

CC: a measuring unit, standing for a cubic centimeter, synonymous with a milliliter, or ml. It is basically a small amount of fluid. Five ccs, or 5 mls, are equal to one teaspoon. Only the letter abbreviations of either term are spoken in ER conversation.

Central cord syndrome: a potentially serious neck injury involving the upper spinal cord, usually heralded by bilateral arm weakness.

Central line: an IV placed in a major vein, such as the internal jugular (neck) or subclavian (chest). Usually reserved for serious or potentially serious cases. Central line insertion etiquette now entails covering the patient with a sterile field, head to toe, with only a small opening over the insertion site It's come a long way from the 'wipe their chest with a betadine soaked gauze pad and stick a needle in their chest' days.

Cerebral Venous Thrombosis (CVT): the presence of a blood clot (thrombosis) in the venous blood pockets of the brain. Symptoms range from headache to seizure and stroke and death. Luckily, it's rare.

Cervix – the part of the uterus that faces the outside world, hence it's proclivity of getting infected from sex.

Champagne tap: perfectly performed spinal tap, with no red blood cells in the cerebral spinal fluid. Their presence is sometimes an important finding, but usually they're just due to the trauma involved with the tap.

Check the x-ray for tube placement: After an endotracheal tube is placed into the trachea, an x-ray is quickly obtained to be sure the tube is in the correct position, that is, not in the esophagus (the food pipe).

Cherry picking: a frowned upon activity of selectively choosing less-complicated patients from among those waiting to be seen. Often used to inflate one's numbers of patients cared for, or for monetary gain, or simply to make one's work easier (at the expense of your colleagues).

Chest tubes: plastic drainage tubes inserted between the ribs into the pleural spaces surrounding the lungs, which can fill with air, blood, pus, sterile, inflammatory or cancerous fluid.

Circle: as in "circle the drain" (as in "dying"). Enough said.

Cirrhosis: severe scarring of the liver, often caused by drinking or disease. Associated with severe fluid buildup in the belly, mental status changes – from confusion all the way to coma - blood clotting problems, and severe GI bleeding.

Clotting pathways: chemical actions employed in the blood stream to combat bleeding.

Code: a code is a cardiac or respiratory arrest, caused by heart or lung dysfunction, trauma, infection, etc. Can also be used as a verb, as in "the patient is coding," or "coding" the patient to provide care and resuscitation. (ER) codes are often run in a specially designed and equipped room, known as the Code Room, also referred to as a Trauma Bay, but most are actually performed elsewhere, whether off hospital grounds (thank you, EMS), or non-ER areas of the hospital such as the ICU or the regular med-surg floors.

Code gum: some ER personnel pop chewing gum in their mouths prior to arrests, traumas or other major events, for both good luck and good breath.

Code team: a pre-designated team, culled from different specialties and subspecialties, to run to the site of codes.

Codes: a hospital's call to action, usually broadcast via the overhead speakers.

Code etiquette: The ER is an ADHD friendly environment, and it is almost assumed that everyone has multiple screens playing in their head at any one time. Talking about dinner, dates, other patients, etc. is common, except during the worst of times (or if family is present.)

Color codes: Blue, the most common, is for cardiac and/or pulmonary failure. Red is for fire; Pink is for newborn or baby abduction; Grey is for a potentially violent individual, and in smaller hospitals often signals a need for able-bodied staff to respond. Silver means an active shooter.

Compressions: the act of using the heels of the hands to press downward on the sternum (breastbone) to squeeze blood out of the heart during CPR (cardio-pulmonary resuscitation).

Contrast/Non-contrast: If a medical dye is injected intravenously or swallowed for a radiologic procedure, such as a CAT scan, it's a contrast study. When a patient does not receive any dye, it's a non-contrast.

Cover the house: in some hospitals, especially the smaller ones, and more so at night, the ER doctor may be the only physician in the hospital capable of handling serious situations that might arise. Many hospitals use hospitalists, who may not be adept at intubating or delivering babies.

CPR: cardiopulmonary resuscitation.

Crash: severe, usually rapid, deterioration of a patient.

C-spine: the seven cervical bones of the neck.

COPD: chronic, severe lung disease, usually but not always linked to smoking. Many COPDers often require supplemental oxygen.

Crash cart: a wheeled metal cart with several drawers that contain supplies and meds used in life-threatening emergencies. On top of the cart is usually the cardiac defibrillator.

Crowning: the moment the head of a baby being born is visible at the entrance of the vaginal opening.

CTA: short for computerized tomographic angiography, words used only in textbooks, court or in dictated cases. Known mostly as a CT Angiogram, or CTA, it's a CAT scan of the arterial blood vessels.

Cynicism: the most commonly practiced religion of the emergency medicine world.

Decadron: a potent steroid; frequently used to treat brain swelling or inflammation, such as seen in croup, which affects the larynx (voice box) and upper trachea (the "pipe" connecting the upper airway to the lungs).

Defibrillator: a machine that generates electrical shocks to the heart, designed to restore normal cardiac rhythm. Used for dangerous rhythms such as ventricular tachycardia or ventricular fibrillation.

Diff breather: someone short of breath.

Dilaudid: a powerful pain killer, in the opiate family.

DOA: dead on arrival.

Double-x: a female, whose sex genes are *xx*, versus a male, who sports an *xy*, on the 23rd chromosomal pair.

Doorway Doc: pejorative slang for doctors who have minimal physical contact with their patients, sometimes not even entering the room.

Doxy: short for doxycycline, an antibiotic often used for STDs.

ED: Emergency Department. More "appropriate" than ER, this term is usually reserved for outsiders or for formal situations – in other words, ER people almost never utter it. (If someone describes themselves as an "ED doc," they may likely be a sex therapist.)

EKG: electrocardiogram. An image of cardiac activity.
EMR: Electronic Medical Record. EMRs have largely replaced paper charts in the ER. There are many EMRs in use, which range from very easy/intuitive to terrible. Non-computer savvy physicians have been known to retire rather than tackle a new system.
EMS – Emergency Medical Service, which responds to 911 calls. They are the unsung heroes of emergency medical care.
ER: Emergency Room. Most emergency personnel use this term.
Endotracheal tube: written as ETT – a tube, usually plastic and available in different sizes and diameters, used to take control of breathing during emergencies. Referred to as a "tube" by ER personnel, who never use the full name or the initials. The word tube may also be used a verb, as in "the patient was tubed."
Epiglottitis: an infection or inflammation of the rim of the glottis, a flap at the entrance to the airway. It can cause severe, often lethal, airway problems. Epiglottitis can be terrifying. Much less common since the vaccine against the main culprit came into widespread use.
Extrapyramidal dystonia: abnormal, involuntary movements of the face and body, often spasmodic and twitchy; often caused by meds.
FACEP: Fellow of the American College of Emergency Physicians.
Face catching fire: Oxygen is a major fire hazard, and patients receiving oxygen via face mask or nasal prongs should never, ever, smoke. Of course, there are those who try to smoke "around" the oxygen tube. With a little bit of bad luck they just may find themselves up that famous waterway without a paddle. (This is the 'duh' part of the glossary.)
Flaring nostrils: abnormal widening of the nostrils when breathing, often associated with respiratory difficulties.
Floating a pacer: inserting a cardiac pacemaker. Often performed at the bedside by ER or ICU personnel, but preferably in the OR by a cardiologist or cardiothoracic surgeon.
Four-point restraints: securing both arms and both legs.
Fournier's gangrene: a serious infection of the male scrotum/penis or female vulva, with extensive tissue destruction. As serious as it sounds.
Free air: Air found outside the Respiratory and GI systems, where it belongs. Potentially dangerous. Usually picked up by X-ray or CAT scan.
Frequent flyer: a patient with multiple ER visits. Sometimes it's legit, most of the time it's not. Usually a negative term.
Full moon: Working in the ER on full moon nights is bad luck.
Glide Scope: a tiny camera mounted on the end of a flexible tube used to facilitate intubations of the trachea. This technique is steadily

replacing the traditional method of relying on sight alone (which is a lot more fun – when successful).

Glio: short for glioblastoma, a deadly form of brain cancer.

Gluing eyes: Liquid tissue adhesive, also known as glue, is used for minor lacerations that don't need stitches. Whatever it touches it sticks to, and that includes eyelids. This is extremely annoying and often very frightening to the patient, but it's temporary and usually harmless.

Goombah: very off-color slang for a significant mass, usually cancerous, seen on X-ray or CT.

Guarding: involuntarily tensing one's abdominal muscles when it is gently pressed, to avoid feeling pain. Often found in the setting of significant infections, inflammation and other intra-abdominal issues.

Gurney: a stretcher.

H: an abnormally high level.

Hard board: a small, surfboard shaped board placed under the patient's back. It enables more efficient cardiac compression during CPR.

Haz mat: Short for hazardous material. Every ER has a haz mat room where patients and EMS personnel can be detoxified, before entering the hospital.

Head nurse: a traditional term, now going out of vogue. Now referred to as nurse managers. For all the bluster and bravado of the docs, head nurses pretty much run the show.

Hemoptysis: coughing up blood. Causes include cancer, trauma, clots.

Heparin: a blood thinner used to prevent or treat blood clots.

Hep lock: small tubes placed in a vein and taped into place, so that meds and fluids can be given as needed, rather than leaving an IV setup in place.

HERN: Hospital Emergency Radio Network.

Hospitalist (house doc): a doctor who works full time in the hospital, taking care of admitted patients. A rising specialty in the medical world.

Hot potato voice: a muffled sound to the voice, as if there was a hot piece of food in the mouth, such as, well, a hot potato. Often associated with swelling of the tonsils or back of the throat. A serious finding.

House Supervisor: usually someone from the nursing department who is charged with overseeing the nursing staff and ensuring quality patient care. Serves as liaison between the hospital's various sections and often acts as a trouble shooter. Plays a very important role at night.

HR: abbreviation for (the Department of) Human Resources, the new catchword for Personnel, Staffing, Employee Relations, etc.

Humeral neck fracture: a fracture of the upper part of the arm bone, the humerus. Usually affect older patients.

Impending bronchitis: the most common cause of sick calls in the world of medicine, possibly the whole world. Treatments include sleeping in, eating out and taking day trips.

Internal jugular (or IJ): a large vein on either side of the neck, often used for IV access, usually in critical situations. A favorite of vampires.

In extremis: near death, often visually apparent.

Intubation: placing a plastic tube through the mouth (sometimes the nose or neck) into the trachea, the "pipe" that connects the mouth to the lungs. Used in emergencies or pre-emptively in the OR, when control of a patient's breathing is critically needed.

Intubation box: a small storage unit, the shape and size of a toolbox. It contains tubes and lighting equipment required for intubation.

IT: Information Technology. Staffed 24/7 in every hospital to bail out murderous docs and nurses trapped in computer hell.

IV: Intravenous. A common method of administering meds. Can also be used as a noun, as in "I started the IV."

J wire: a metallic guidewire, curved at one end giving it a J shape, used for the placement of central vessel lines.

Jaw pain/ache: a symptom that sometimes can (but not always) indicate cardiac problems, even without actual chest pain.

Joules: a unit of energy passed through the defibrillator machines during cardiac emergencies. A common amount used is three hundred sixty joules, but this can vary, depending on patient size and situation.

KCl: Potassium chloride. Normally beneficial, dangerous in excess.

Kissing tonsils: When tonsils become inflamed or infected, they may swell, sometimes a great deal. When both the left and right swell they may actually touch each other, hence the name "kissing." This is potentially dangerous, as there is a risk for breathing and eating difficulties.

Knife and gun club: Two guesses.

L: an abnormally low number on a lab test.

Lac: abbreviation for a laceration.

Lactic: referring to lactic acid levels which, if elevated, can signify serious, potentially fatal levels of disease. Normal is under 2.

Large bore: tubes that are wider to allow for more rapid and easy passage of air or fluids in and out of the body.

Laryngoscope: an instrument for examining the larynx, usually with the purpose of illuminating it so a breathing tube may be placed through it.

Lateral neck X-ray: a side view X-ray of the neck, where the cervical bones are, aka C-spine.

Levels of ER patient acuity:

I – Life threatening.
II – Emergent, with potential to become life threatening.
III – Urgent.
IV – Less Urgent.
V – Non-Urgent.

Lithotomy position: the patient lying on her/his back on a stretcher, usually with knees bent, in preparation for an exam or procedure.

Little mouth, little neck, fat tongue: physical characteristics that often preclude a good view of the upper airway, creating a difficult, sometimes very, very difficult, intubation. It should be noted that while nurses judge people by their veins, ER people judge them by their necks and mouths (they won't admit this to outsiders, but when intubating, they also really appreciate toothless patients).

LP: a lumbar puncture, also referred to as a spinal tap.

LP kit: a complete, sterile kit with the instruments needed to perform a spinal tap.

Loaner: someone pulled from upstairs to fill a staffing need in the ER, usually a tech or nurse. Mostly from the ICU, OR and Recovery Room, but many nurses from the med-surg floors have also been used (and more than one has chosen to switch over to the ER for keeps).

LOC: an abbreviation for loss of consciousness. Can also refer to level of consciousness.

Lock in the sock: a common makeshift jailhouse weapon. Can cause some real damage.

Lytic: as used in the medical world, a chemical that dissolves blood clots, which are a leading cause of strokes and heart attacks. They are usually very helpful, but sometimes cause major, sometimes fatal, bleeding complications.

Mac: a type of intubation blade, curved in shape. Some docs prefer straight blades, especially in pediatric emergencies.

Magnesium: a common element useful in several emergencies, notably obstetrical and cardiac; overdoses, and severe, refractory asthma (the latter is controversial and something of a Hail Mary option).

Mannitol: a diuretic often used to shrink a swollen brain.

Mass effect: potential brain damage caused by abnormal pressure on the brain. Causes include infection, abnormal collections of fluids such as blood, or a tumor. Can be fatal.

Meningitis: inflammation or infection of the meninges, which cover and protect the brain.
Meta analysis: combining several large studies, involving a great many patients. As a rule, the more patients in a study, the more accurate and reliable are its results. It's useless to infer that if two patients received drug A and both improved, Drug A must be good - this is in the realm of anecdotal medicine, so popular on the Internet.
Mid-level: a nurse practitioner or physician's assistant, assigned to work with physicians. They range from pretty good to amazing and are indispensable in emergency medicine. On paper or at meetings they are both referred to as APPs, or advanced practice providers. This author's prediction is that the term "mid-level" will disappear as soon as there is found a better word than APP. This author has worked with mid-levels for over thirty years, and has never once heard the phrase "who's the APP on for today?" uttered.
MI: myocardial infarction, more commonly known as heart attack.
Mono test: a blood test for mononucleosis, caused by a virus.
MRI: magnetic resonance imaging. A very advanced, zero radiation, form of X-ray, often preferred over CAT scan.
MVA: motor vehicle accident. Sometimes called MVC, as in collision.
Narc: Short for narcotic pain medication.
Narcan: an opiate reversal agent. May be given by injection or intra-nasally.
Night shift: usually from either 7pm or 11pm to 7am the following day.
Nipple pinching: a frowned upon but still somewhat popular technique to test levels of responsiveness or revive lethargic or somnolent patients. Few actually admit to doing this.
O2: oxygen. ER people almost always say O2, reserving 'oxygen' for more formal settings or presentations.
Nurse Practitioner (NP): a mid-level, who often works with a physician but who can sometimes work on his or her own. All NPs are nurses who then take at least two years of advanced training. Used interchangeably with PAs, there's no inherent difference regarding their knowledge base or clinical skills.
OD: overdose, either voluntary or accidental.
On-call: a medical person, not actually at the initial point of care, who is the pre-designated go-to person for admissions, consults or backup.
Oxygen dependent: requiring supplemental oxygen to survive. Many people with severe lung disease have this problem.
Oxygen saturation: oxygen levels in the blood. Never actually spoken by ER people, who use the terms "O2 sat" or "pulse ox" instead.

Considered by many to be the fifth vital sign, the other four being pulse, blood pressure, respiratory rate and temperature.

Pacer Pads: Sticky pads placed on the chest and back and attached to the defibrillator or an external pacer.

Parkland Formula: used in serious burn cases, it determines how much and how quickly fluid is given in the resuscitation process. It's posted in every trauma bay.

PE: short for pulmonary embolism, a blood clot in the lungs. Often presents as coughing up blood (hemoptysis).

Per os: Latin term, meaning 'by way of mouth.'

Perf: short for perforation, it is an abnormal hole, usually in the GI system (as in "perforated ulcer") but also occurring in other situations, such as trauma.

Physician's Assistant (PA): a highly trained medical professional who works with physicians. Along with Nurse Practitioners, who essentially perform the same tasks, they are nicknamed "midlevels," a term slowly giving way to "APP"s, or advanced practice practitioners.

Placebo: a harmless pill, procedure or activity designed to bring mental relief to an individual who believes it to be real. Often quite effective, thus the term "placebo effect." It even works on many people who know it's not the "real thing".

Poly: short for a polymorphonuclear white blood cell, which specializes in fighting bacterial infections.

Pons: part of the brainstem, between the midbrain and medulla oblongata, critical for survival. Administering 3% sodium too fast can cause a catastrophic stroke, causing the "locked in syndrome" - near total paralysis sparing only the eyes and the eyelids.

Popcorn: probably the number one food staple in the ER, although cookies and room temperature pizza are also contenders. No night shift is considered complete without the smell of burnt microwave popcorn.

PPD: a skin test that diagnoses silent TB infection. Tested often on health care workers. If positive, then several months of oral meds are administered to prevent full blown tuberculosis.

Propofol: a rapid acting injectable med that provides profound sedation. It is usually used for quick procedures like intubation or putting a dislocated bone back in place. Nicknamed 'milk of amnesia' for its resemblance to milk.

Pumper: a blood vessel, usually an artery, that, when injured, pumps blood with each heartbeat outside of the body. (Injured veins tend to ooze blood.) They can be quite dramatic, depending on the size of the vessel and the strength of the pulse.

Q: Latin for "quaque," means "every." Indicates times or frequencies of dosage. Q2H means every 2 hours; Q4H, every four, etc.)

Q sign: very off-color slang for a patient who is extremely lethargic or outright unconscious, with a wide-open mouth and the tongue stuck out at a downward angle. A similar, equally off-color, term is the 'O sign,' when the tongue does not stick out. Never uttered outside the ER or ICU.

QA: Quality assurance, a system designed to optimize clinical care provided to the patient population. Also known as QC (quality control), QI (quality improvement), QM (quality management), etc.

QTc: part of the EKG that shows the speed of certain electrical impulses in the heart. Prolonged QTc is associated with dangerous rhythms.

Q word: a five-letter word beginning with "q" and ending with "iet," meaning calm and silent. When spoken in an ER, a devastating, calamitous hell will descend on that ER. Saying it is the only absolute taboo in all of emergency medicine. One is only permitted to use its first letter, if at all, and many ER people will not even utter the word outside the hospital.

Rad: short for radiologist (one who reads X-Rays, CAT scans, etc.

Radio: Each ER has a VHF radio that EMS uses to communicate with the hospitals. They are also called "the HERN" (Hospital Emergency Radio Network) or HEMS (Health Emergency Services).

Rapid a-fib: atrial fibrillation that, when rapid, can trigger rapid ventricular response, producing an abnormally fast pulse. Not good.

Resident: a physician who has completed his/her first year of post med-school training, this being 'internship.' Residents' training, known as residency, is tailored to their particular specialty, and can last for up to five years. Post-residency training is called a 'fellowship.'

Reverse/reversal: giving the antidote for a dangerous substance, usually opiate overdoses. Reversal agents for other poisons and drugs are also available. Reversing opiate ODs rapidly wakes the patient up, and they have been known to become angry and/or violent when they do.

Rocephin: brand name for ceftriaxone, an antibiotic.

Sat: short for oxygen saturation, indicating it's amount in the blood. Normal is 95% or above, acceptable is usually over 90%.

Satisfaction scores: questionnaires given to patients. Taken very seriously by Administration, but generally resented by the rank and file.

Sepsis: a serious condition caused by invading pathogens, usually but not always bacterial. Can deteriorate into septic shock, which is often fatal.

Shotgunning: A frowned-upon practice of ordering buttloads of often unnecessary tests, in the hopes something will turn up. Also done as a stalling tactic towards the end of a shift, effectively dumping the case on the incoming clinician.
Signing out: at the end of each shift, the outgoing doctors and nurses give their incoming relief a report on each patient they are caring for.
Sinus rhythm: normal cardiac rhythm.
Size eight: a common size (width) of an intubation tube used on men.
Sling and swath: a common technique to immobilize a joint, almost always the arm and/or shoulder.
Sodium: one of the body's major electrolytes (chemicals), and critical for survival. Patients with levels below 120 often are admitted. Sodium levels that are too high or too low can be fatal. Typically given via 0.9% physiologic saline infusions, although severe cases may need a burst of 3%, risky in and of itself. (Sodium mixed with chloride is table salt.)
Stat: it means immediately, from the Latin word 'statim.'
Stridor: a squeaking noise heard in the neck during inhalation or exhalation. Usually indicates upper airway compromise and is often very serious.
Submandibular: the areas of the neck beneath the angles of the jaw.
Sutures: sutures are basically thread, and they come in various thicknesses and materials, such as nylon, silk, etc. They are affixed to various sizes and shapes of needles, such as straight or curved. Ironically, the larger the suture size, the thinner the thread is. Thin sutures are good for delicate closures, such as on the face; thick sutures are better for just about anywhere else.
Suture kit: a pre-packaged laceration repair kit containing hemostats, needle holders, scissors, forceps (tweezers)...in fact, anything but sutures.
Swabs: elongated Q-tips used to get samples from the cervix, throat, etc. also used as a verb, as in, "swabbing the throat."
Swan-Ganz: a plastic tube inserted into and through the right side of the heart and into the arteries leading to the lungs. Usually placed in the OR or ICU, it is used to study heart and lung function. It is being supplanted by other studies, and its use is declining.
Systolic: one of the two components of blood pressure, or the top number. The other component, the bottom number, is the diastolic. A systolic over 90 is considered (barely) acceptable in adults.

Thinners: slang for anti-coagulants, used to treat or prevent clots. They range from mild (aspirin is a type of thinner) to big time, which can cause serious bleeds.
Tombstones: tombstone-shaped tracings seen on EKGs. Often seen in devastating heart attacks and can be predictors of a very bad outcome.
Toradol: a non-narcotic pain reliever, similar to ibuprofen. It is in the NSAID class (*n*on-*s*teroidal *a*nti-*i*nflammatory *d*rugs). This med is very effective when given intravenously for colicky type pain, such as that caused by kidney stones. Patients seeking opiates will often claim to be allergic to NSAIDs, particularly Toradol, hoping they'll get an opiate instead. This is a source of amusement throughout much of the ER world.
TPA: A clot dissolving drug, often used in the settings of heart attack or stroke. Fatal bleeds can occur, and deep down many ER docs are a little concerned about using it in a stroke patient.
Trachea: the airway, or windpipe, in the chest. It begins below the voice box and forks left and right in the lower chest, these forks now referred to as the right and left bronchi.
Train wreck: complicated, unstable, unpleasant, be it a shift or a particular case.
Trauma team – similar to code team, but also usually containing one or more surgeons, plus their residents. They are activated for traumas.
Tricyclics: a category of antidepressants, widely used. Dangerous if too many are ingested.
Triple A: An aortic abdominal aneurysm. Can be lethal when they rupture.
Tripoding: a physical position assumed by some people in serious respiratory distress. In the ER it usually presents as a patient sitting upright on the stretcher, leaning forward and supporting the upper body with outstretched hands that rest on the mattress. Can also be seen in patients with a heart inflammation known as pericarditis.
Troponin: a protein released by damaged or dying cardiac cells. Measured via a blood test, elevated levels would be seen in the presence of a heart attack (MI). Slangily called "trope."
Tube: a conduit – a tube - that connects the body to the outside world. Breathing tubes placed in the airway (trachea) permit mechanical ventilation. Can be a verb, as in "tubing" the patient. Other tubes are used to drain organs such as the stomach or bladder, or cavities/spaces, such as the pleural space in the chest, or in the peritoneal cavity in the abdomen.
Tube placement: ET tubes must be properly inserted into the trachea, before it forks into the left and right bronchi. Pushing it in too deeply will

send it into only one lung. Placement is checked with a stethoscope – hearing breath sounds only on one side requires that the tube be pulled back a little to get it above the fork. Hearing no breath sounds at all usually means the tube was mistakenly placed in the esophagus (food pipe) and the lifegiving oxygen is actually going into in the stomach– this is very dangerous, and the attempt must be repeated until it is successful.

Ultrasound skills: The use of ultrasound probes to examine patients is becoming widespread in emergency medicine. Conditions such as collapsed lungs, internal bleeding from trauma, and aortic problems are just a few conditions that can be diagnosed this way. The technique is fairly new, and the skills needed to master it are daunting and almost age-dependent – like a television controller, the younger you are, the better you are using it. It's being taught to students now, meaning that the further out of training you are, the less proficient you probably are.

URI: Upper respiratory tract infection. Usually meant to imply the common cold and bronchitis.

UTI: Urinary tract infection.

Vanc: vancomycin, an antibiotic.

V-fib: short for ventricular fibrillation, the most dangerous of all heart rhythms, aside from asystole, which is technically not a rhythm (zero cardiac activity). Best treated with electrical shock (defibrillation).

Vag (pronounced vaj) bleed: abnormal bleeding from the vagina.

Vehicular accidents, often in Texas: some patients who are looking for pain meds will blame their pain from old accidents and carry copies of their CT results with them as proof they're legit. Sort of a running joke in many ERs.

Vein: a blood vessel carrying blood to the heart. They do not generate a pulse.

Ventricles: the two chambers of the heart that send blood away from the heart. The right ventricle sends blood to the lungs for oxygen, and the left ventricle sends this oxygen-rich blood to the body.

Ventricular tachycardia: aka **V-tach**, it's an abnormal, rapid beating of the ventricles. A genuine emergency.

Vitals: traditionally the pulse (heart beats per minute); blood pressure; respiratory rate (breaths per minute); and temperature (this is going out of vogue, except in the very young, the very old and in the immunocompromised; ERs, ICUs and ORs would also include oxygen saturation (explained above) as the fifth vital sign.

Vocal cords: located in the larynx (voice box), these two vertical cords, actually fibrous bands of tissue, are great landmarks for sticking a breathing tube into the lungs. See 'em, stick the tube between 'em, and you're pretty much home free. Beware when you can't "find" them.

Water intoxication: drinking massive amounts of water can dangerously dilute the blood, with harmful cardiac and neurologic consequences.

Worknote-emia: Visiting the ER in order to get a worknote for a few days off. Symptoms include appearing astonishingly healthy and having a piece of luggage by the bedside.

WBC: stands for white blood cell count. WBCs kill germs and help produce antibodies. Counts under 1,000 or over 20,000 are not good.

Xanax: trade name for alprazolam, a commonly used oral sedative. Related to Valium and Ativan.

Zebra: An uncommon disease or condition, disproportionately chased by ER clinicians, who are trained to consider any reasonable cause of their patient's problem, largely because they get no second chances. This is maybe the greatest divide between the ER and the rest of the medical world, whose mantra is 'when you hear the thunder of beating hooves, don't think of zebras.' If an ER doc were to exclusively employ this "if it walks like a duck and quacks like a duck…" rule, disaster would be not too far away.

Zoo – a slang term, not spoken in mixed company, for an extremely busy, high acuity ER. It often, but by no means always, involves a roughneck patient population. Some ERs are almost always like this, but any ER can become a zoo, as in, "this place is a fucking zoo today!" By the way, ER docs love bragging about their days there, and often assume a "my zoo can beat up your zoo" posture.

About the Author

Mitch Goldman recently wrapped up a 36-year career in the ER, both as a working director and clinical physician. He currently lives in Michigan with his wife, Laura. In past lives he's been an ad writer and NYC cab driver, and is the author of the novel *Apocalypse Blue*.

www.ingramcontent.com/pod-product-compliance
Lightning Source LLC
Chambersburg PA
CBHW060843240125

20711CB00002B/185